In[illegible]

The carriage cam[illegible] seat and peered out the window, wondering if someone had caught them. Maybe someone saw them sneak off the estate and followed them into the forest. Her heartbeat accelerated in dread. She closed her eyes and took a deep breath. With a hard swallow, she told herself that whatever happened, she would tell them this was her idea, that she forced Appleton to help her.

The carriage door opened. Her eyes flew open, and she saw Appleton's shocked expression. "What is it?" she asked him, tentatively peering out of the carriage to see if someone else was in the area.

"There's a gentleman in the middle of the road, Your Grace," he told her. He held his hand out to help her down. "I can't tell for sure, but he looks a lot like your husband."

Her eyebrows furrowed, she followed him to where the horses stood. He lifted the lantern from the carriage and knelt by the gentleman lying on his back in the middle of the road. She quickly examined their surroundings and saw no one else in the area.

Taking a tentative step toward Appleton, she whispered, "You said he looks like my husband?"

"He's been beaten, but there's no denying the resemblance."

The gentleman groaned but didn't move.

Curious, she approached him. His eyes were closed and his mouth was open as he struggled for breath. It was alarming to see him covered in blood, a cut on his forehead and bruises lining the side of his face. His clothes spoke of a commoner, but his face was horribly reminiscent of the husband she'd just buried.

She glanced at Appleton before she proceeded forward. While Appleton held the lantern for her to get a better look at the stranger, she bent over him. "Sir?"

He gave no response. Uncertain, she looked back at Appleton.

"He might be the answer to our prayers, Your Grace," Appleton softly told her.

Could he be?

***

Her Counterfeit Husband

Her Counterfeit Husband

Ruth Ann Nordin

This is a work of fiction. The events and characters described herein are imaginary and are not intended to refer to specific places or living persons. The opinions expressed in this manuscript are solely the opinions of the author and also represent the opinions or thoughts of the publisher.

Ruth Ann Nordin Books
http://www.ruthannnordin.com

Dedication: To Lauralynn Elliott whose kindness and love for writing is an inspiration to remember that books are more than words on paper: they are an emotional experience to be cherished.

<u>List of Books by Ruth Ann Nordin</u>

<u>Regency Collection</u>
The Earl's Inconvenient Wife
Her Counterfeit Husband

<u>Nebraska Historical Romance Collection</u>
Her Heart's Desire
A Bride for Tom
A Husband for Margaret
Eye of the Beholder
The Wrong Husband
Shotgun Groom
To Have and To Hold
His Redeeming Bride
Isaac's Decision

<u>South Dakota Historical Romances</u>
Loving Eliza
Bid for a Bride
Bride of Second Chances

<u>Native American Romance Series</u> (historical)
Restoring Hope
Brave Beginnings
Bound by Honor, Bound by Love (coming soon)
A Chance In Time (novella) – main characters show up in Restoring Hope and Bound by Honor, Bound by Love)

<u>Virginia Brides Series</u> (historical)
An Unlikely Place for Love
The Cold Wife
An Inconvenient Marriage
Romancing Adrienne

<u>Other Historical Western Romances</u>
Falling In Love With Her Husband
Meant To Be

<u>Contemporary Romances</u>
With This Ring, I Thee Dread
What Nathan Wants
Suddenly a Bride

<u>Christian Sci-Fi Thriller</u>
Return of the Aliens

Chapter One

October 1814

"I came to see my ailing brother," Lord Mason said as he entered the drawing room.

Anna, the Duchess of Watkins, turned from the window and inwardly shuddered, not caring for the way he scanned her body. She glanced at Appleton, her butler, and said a silent prayer of thanks for his calming presence. If there was one ally she had, it was him.

Turning her attention back to Lord Mason, she cleared her throat. "I don't know if my husband is up to seeing visitors. His health has taken a turn for the worse."

Lord Mason gave a slight frown and clucked his tongue. "I hope he gets better soon. I'd hate to see you become a widow." His gaze lingered on her breasts. "However, if he did die, you'll always have a place here at Camden. Never doubt that. I believe in taking care of family."

She crossed her arms in a protective measure, feeling as if she was naked before him even though she was fully dressed. She forced a polite smile but darted a silent pleading look at Appleton who stepped forward.

"Lord Mason," Appleton began, "perhaps it might be better if you'd return at a later time. The doctor will be here in an hour to tend to him."

"Oh, that's not necessary. Jason's my brother," Lord Mason replied, turning to face him. "Seeing me will lift his spirits. And in any case, he might have some last words to pass along to me, should I need to take over the estate."

She averted her gaze.

"Your Grace?" Appleton asked her.

She nodded her consent, and Appleton led Lord Mason out of the drawing room. There was little she could do to stop her brother-in-law. When he decided to do something, he did it, regardless of what she wanted. The only person who was able to stop him was her husband.

She released her breath and glanced at the piano. Many times, she'd used music as a way to escape the harsher realities of life, but there was no escaping Lord Mason or the threat he posed if he became the Duke of Watkins.

She walked over to the window and pulled aside the curtain so she could see if Lord Mason left his carriage by the front door. He did that if he planned to make it a quick visit, and thankfully, on this day he wouldn't stay long. She breathed a sigh of relief and closed her eyes.

"Your Grace?"

She opened her eyes and let the curtain fall back in place as she turned to face Appleton. "Lord Mason won't be here for long. There's no need to bring tea."

He nodded and came closer to her so that no one else could overhear them. "I'm afraid your husband looks worse than he did this morning. I didn't say anything to Lord Mason, but…"

He didn't have to say it. She knew what he was thinking. "Is my husband able to talk to Lord Mason?"

"Yes. He's still well enough to speak."

"I wonder what they're talking about."

"I'm sure whatever they're discussing, it can't be of any consequence."

"Probably not." And she doubted Lord Mason cared about what her husband had to say. Most likely, he had come to judge how close he was to becoming the next duke. "He's like a vulture circling a dying prey."

"Not unlike His Grace was when their father died," Appleton softly replied, not hiding the displeasure in his voice.

"I wish I'd known their father. It sounds like he was a good man."

"He was. It was a privilege to be under his employ."

And their mother had been a fortunate lady to have been married to him. What she wouldn't give for a noble husband who would have treated her well.

"Your Grace?" Appleton whispered, bringing her attention back to him.

Wiping a tear from her eye, she swallowed the lump in her throat and let out a weary sigh. With a humorless chuckle, she made eye contact with him. "How I envy you, Appleton. Your lot isn't fixed upon what men decide to do with you. I'm afraid things will only be worse once my husband dies."

He opened his mouth to speak, but Lord Mason strode into the room with a wide smile on his face. "My brother looks good today. Perhaps he'll cheat Death," he said with a smirk.

He didn't believe that any more than she or Appleton did. She took a deep breath to steady her nerves. "In case he doesn't, then I will move to a cottage so you may bring the woman you'll marry here."

"Oh, I wouldn't dream of doing that to you, Your Grace," Lord Mason objected as he approached her.

Without thinking, she shifted closer to Appleton who made it a point to step in front of her.

Lord Mason's eyes drifted from her to the butler, and a low chuckle rose up in his throat. "I assume there's nothing of a more personal nature going on between you two."

"Most certainly not!" Her cheeks warmed at his insinuation. "I have been faithful to your brother."

"It matters not to me how you conduct your private affairs, Your Grace," he commented, a trace of amusement in his voice. "But I wouldn't dare send you away to a cottage. You are my brother's wife, and as such, I will provide for you here. You needn't worry about your future."

A knot tightened in her stomach, and she averted her gaze from his so she wouldn't give away her apprehension.

"I must be going," Lord Mason said. "Until we see each other again, Your Grace."

She curtsied as he bowed, and when he turned to leave, she breathed an audible sigh of relief. Once Appleton led him out of the room, her shoulders relaxed. She went to the chair by her writing desk and collapsed into it. Thankfully, it was over. She hated it when he came to visit. Though he never came out and asked for a more intimate relationship with her, she saw the intent in his eyes. Once her husband died, there was nothing to stop him from taking what he wanted. She shuddered and closed her eyes, focusing on her deep breathing in order to calm her nerves.

After the knot in her stomach loosened, she opened her eyes and stared at the wall, not seeing the portrait of her husband's grandmother. The sound of footsteps brought her attention to the doorway where Appleton came in with a tray. Usually, she'd welcome the tea and biscuits, but today, she had no appetite.

"I can't eat or drink anything right now," she softly told him before he could place the tray on the desk.

"Your Grace, far be it from me to pry, but you've hardly had anything to eat or drink in two days. Please at least take a sip of the tea?"

Though her throat constricted at the idea, she nodded. "I'll try."

As he poured the hot liquid into her cup, he said, "I have unpleasant news for you."

She cringed. "Lord Mason plans to return tomorrow?"

"No, but His Grace wishes to have a word with you."

Her stomach grew queasy. She took a deep breath and stood up. The sooner she got this over with, the better.

"Won't you have some tea first?" he asked.

"I can't."

"Then I'll go with you."

"There's no need. He can't do anything to me on his deathbed."

Without waiting for his reply, she strode out of the room. Perhaps her husband would be exhausted after his brother's visit and fall asleep while talking to her. She hurried up the stairs, knowing if she delayed, things would be worse. When she reached the door of his bedchamber, she stopped and waited for a moment, hoping the pounding of her heart wouldn't give away her anxiety. Clearing her throat, she quietly turned the knob.

She nudged the door open and peeked into the room. The curtains were drawn, blocking out the sunlight. A few candles were lit around his bed. He had the covers pulled up to his neck, and his hands were folded on his chest. She saw his eyes were closed and swallowed the lump in her throat. She stood still, unsure of whether she should whisper his name or take her chances and leave. Her grip tightened on the doorknob.

"There's no need to stand there like a statue, Anna," he rasped, his eyes still closed. "I know you're here."

Disappointed, she stepped into the room and shut the door behind her. She approached him, her slippers quiet as she crossed the large room. It would be over soon.

She sat in the chair next to his bed and got ready to ask him if he'd been able to keep any liquids down when he opened his eyes and shot her a critical glance. "Did it occur to you that I might want some water?"

"Oh, I'm sorry, Your Grace," she mumbled and went to the table by his bed.

She picked up the pitcher and poured the water into the glass. She turned slightly away from him so he wouldn't see how badly her hands were shaking. As much as she kept telling herself a sick gentleman didn't have enough strength to do her any harm, she couldn't so easily forget how powerful he'd once been. She managed to perform the task without spilling any water and set the pitcher down with relief.

Turning back to him, she held out the glass to him. "Here it is, Your Grace."

He closed his eyes and shook his head. "Dimwitted woman. I need to sit up to drink it."

"Right. Yes. Of course."

She quickly set the glass on the table and gathered the pillows behind him and helped him sit up. Slightly out of breath from the task, she grabbed the glass and held it out to him.

He examined the glass and grunted. "I'm parched and you give me a mere drop's worth?"

She ignored his snickers as she poured more water into his glass. When she presented it to him, she feared he would demand she bring it to his lips, but fortunately, he took it and drank the water. All she needed was to spill water on him. When he was done, he handed the glass to her, and she set it back on the table.

He managed to keep the contents down for a minute before he threw up into a bowl. She looked away from him and pressed her hands over her ears so she wouldn't gag. Her only reprieve was knowing she didn't have to dispose of his vomit. Thank God the servants did that. She waited until he stopped retching before she dared a look in his direction.

Gulping the swell of nausea in her throat, she retrieved a handkerchief from the table and gave it to him. He wiped his mouth with it and flung it in her direction. He laughed as she yelped and jerked away from it.

"If nothing else, you were always amusing," he remarked. "Pick it up and dispose of it."

She knelt down and picked it up by the hem so she wouldn't touch anything wet and threw it into the bucket by his bed.

"Sit and listen to me!" he barked.

She sat in the chair, praying he'd grow tired from sitting up. "What is it you'd like to say, Your Grace?" she managed to ask, resisting the urge to look at the door which wasn't too far from her.

"Go," he sharply told her.

Startled, her eyes grew wide. "Your Grace?"

"I know you can't wait to get away from me."

She opened her mouth to protest his statement, but the words wouldn't come. He was on the verge of death, after all. He'd been unable to keep any foods or liquids down for over two weeks and grew weaker every day. She'd done her part in playing the docile wife. Never arguing, turning a blind eye to all his indiscretions, silencing her complaints. The years of suppressed bitterness for the way he'd treated her during their marriage struggled to make its way to the surface. She'd spent so much time in dread of him, but as she studied him, she saw how close to death he was. Why did she continue to let him have any power over her?

"Oh, don't bother holding it in," he snapped before he coughed. "You're pathetic and spineless. I told my brother to do whatever he wanted with you once I'm gone. I told him you're as barren as a desert so he has no reason to worry people will talk."

Something in her snapped, and she reached for the glass and threw it at him. She gasped, pressing her hand to her mouth. How could she have acted out in such a way? To her surprise, he laughed. She was about to demand he explain why he found it humorous, but he began to vomit into his bowl. He motioned for her to hand him another handkerchief, and she made a motion to obey him when she recalled the way he handed her over to his brother.

"I hope you die," she hissed. "You're as disgusting as your vomit."

Then she hurried out of the room. He couldn't follow her, and he couldn't call after her to stop. With any luck, there would be no repercussions to saying those words. If he didn't recover, there wouldn't be. But if he did... She forced the possibility aside. Either way, she was doomed. Whether it was her husband or his brother, she was still doomed.

Chapter Two

He's dead. Anna stared at her husband, hardly believing it. Though death was, in itself, an ugly thing, she studied him, noting the way his vacant eyes remained open. Even as she experienced overwhelming relief, she knew she had a much bigger problem ahead of her.

She glanced at the pocket watch on the table beside his bed. It was just after midnight. The doctor wouldn't come by to check on him until after ten. Her husband's valet had walked out, and considering how many valets her husband had been through, she hadn't been surprised when the last one quit. So there was no one who would check in on him for at least ten hours.

She bit her lower lip and walked to the window so she could lift the curtain and look outside. It was so dark. There wasn't even a sliver of moonlight out tonight. Anyone could be out there, and there was no way she'd see them. She gripped the curtains. Did she dare? Could she get away with it? She couldn't do it alone. Her husband was too heavy. Even if he had lost considerable weight, she couldn't carry him out of the house and dispose of his body.

What she needed was help from someone she could trust, someone who would keep her secret to his grave. Appleton. If there was anyone who'd understand her plight and could help her, it was him. She dropped the curtain back in place and turned from the window. No. She couldn't ask him to do such a devious thing. Not when he was the only good thing in her life, the one person who'd helped her keep going when all she'd wanted to do was give up. Her gaze went to the scars on her wrists. If he hadn't found her when he did, she wouldn't be here now. And he'd saved her for what? So her lot would get worse?

Her attention went back to her husband. The Duke of Watkins. She never did feel comfortable enough around him to call him by his Christian name. Six years. For six years, she'd been under his thumb. And as his last act of imprisoning her, he thought to hand her over to his disgusting brother. Taking a deep breath, she walked over to him, each step slow and calculated as she thought of all the misery he'd caused her. Even now in death, he had a slight smile on his lips, as if laughing that he had gained one more victory over her.

"You won't win this one," she hissed. "If it's the last thing I do, I'll make sure your brother never inherits your title."

Feeling a new sense of determination, she crossed the room and slipped through the door leading to her bedchamber. She hurried over to the cord on her wall that would ring the bell in Appleton's room. If she was going to act, she had to be quick. The doctor would arrive in at least ten hours, and the longer she waited, the harder it was going to be to succeed with her plan.

She reached her wardrobe and pulled out a black cloak so she could blend into the dark night. After she returned to her husband's bedchamber, she waited by his door until she spied Appleton hurrying down the hall. She motioned to him to enter the room.

"Your Grace?" he whispered.

She quickly shut the door and led him over to her husband. "I found him like this fifteen minutes ago."

His expression grim, he said, "I don't know whether to be relieved or not."

"I can't let his brother assume the title," she whispered, glancing at her husband.

With a heavy sigh, he nodded. "That wouldn't be a wise idea."

"It's dark out there. If you wore a covering and we wrapped my husband up in a dark blanket, we could carry him out of here and dispose of his body without anyone seeing us."

He stared at her for a long moment, and she waited for his response, wondering if he'd agree or tell her it was impossible. "What you're suggesting is very unusual," he slowly replied.

She tightened her hold on the edge of her cloak. He wasn't going to go along with it!

"However," he began, causing her heart to leap with hope, "I see no other alternative than to quietly bury him. If he were to take a trip for an undetermined amount of time… Maybe go somewhere special to heal…"

Relieved he was going to help her, she nodded. "We'll do that."

"We also need to take him off this property. No one must ever find him."

"I agree."

"We'll need to take a carriage. There's no way we can carry him as far as we need to."

"Can we risk it without being seen?"

"There is an old carriage that no one uses. It's in the old stable. I'll get that one ready. You find a blanket, and when I get back, we'll wrap him up, and I'll carry him down the servant stairs. No one should see us this late at night."

It sounded wonderful. So wonderful, in fact, it might actually work! While he left the bedchamber, she searched through the room to find a suitable blanket to cover her husband up.

***

Their task was a morbid one. Two hours past midnight, Anna stood beneath a large oak tree in the middle of a forest. She held the lantern up as Appleton finished burying her husband. She shivered and pulled the cloak closer to her, not sure what was worse: the eerie darkness or the chill in the air.

Appleton pounded the new mound of dirt over the grave and straightened his back. "I think we're done."

She stared at the spot where her husband was buried, finally feeling free. Six of the worst years of her life were over. She didn't realize she was crying until Appleton removed his gloves so he could reach into his pocket and give her a handkerchief. Grateful for his everlasting kindness, she thanked him and wiped her face.

"It's over, Your Grace," he said, his voice soothing.

"As long as no one finds out, we'll be all right," she agreed.

In silence, the two turned to the winding path that would take them to their carriage. So much had happened that day, and her exhaustion was quickly catching up to her. Once they reached the carriage, she slipped into it while he discarded his clothes and put on new ones. From there, he led the horses carefully through the forest. Her body swayed from side to side as he navigated them through the rough terrain.

She closed her eyes and rested her head against the back of the seat. She wanted nothing more than to sink into the sweet bliss of dreams where she could forget everything from her tainted marriage to the misery that brought her and Appleton to covering up her husband's death. The entire night kept replaying itself in her mind.

As much as she prayed no one would ever find out what happened, she couldn't help but worry someone would try to find her husband and learn the truth. But maybe by then, she and Appleton could leave the country. They could assume another identity. Maybe by the time people realized her husband was dead, she and Appleton could be long gone.

The carriage came to an abrupt stop. She bolted up in her seat and peered out the window, wondering if someone had caught them. Maybe someone saw them sneak off the estate and followed them into the forest. Her heartbeat accelerated in dread. She closed her eyes and took a deep breath. With a hard swallow, she told herself that whatever happened, she would tell them she forced Appleton to help her. She'd do everything she could to absolve him from guilt.

The carriage door opened. Her eyes flew open, and she saw Appleton's shocked expression. "What is it?" she asked him, tentatively peering out of the carriage to see if someone else was in the area.

"There's a gentleman in the middle of the road, Your Grace," he told her. He held his hand out to help her down. "I can't tell for sure, but he looks a lot like your husband."

Her eyebrows furrowed, she stepped out of the carriage and followed him to where the horses stood. He lifted the lantern from the carriage and knelt by the gentleman lying on his back in the middle of the road. She quickly examined their surroundings and saw no one else in the area.

Taking a tentative step toward Appleton, she whispered, "You said he looks like my husband?"

"He's been beaten, but there's no denying the resemblance."

The gentleman groaned but didn't move.

Curious, she approached him. His eyes were closed and his mouth was open as he struggled for breath. It was alarming to see him covered in blood, a nasty cut on his forehead and bruises lining the side of his face. His clothes spoke of a commoner, but his face was horribly reminiscent of the husband she'd just buried.

She glanced at Appleton before she proceeded forward. While Appleton held the lantern for her to get a better look at the stranger, she bent over him. "Sir?"

He gave no response. Uncertain, she looked back at Appleton.

"He might be the answer to our prayers, Your Grace," Appleton softly told her.

Could he be? She turned her attention to the stranger and examined his blond hair. It was hard to tell in the dim light, but it seemed to be the same shade as her husband's. She inspected the rest of him, sizing up his height and build. If she wasn't seeing it with her own eyes, she would never have believed it. This stranger…this gentleman who was in no way of noble birth…could pass for her husband.

The stranger let out a slight moan of pain, and something in her snapped. "We have to help him."

"I'll get him, Your Grace," Appleton said, handing her the lantern. She stepped back and held it for him as he gently lifted the stranger. "He needs help. If we're not careful, we're going to lose him."

It took her a moment to realize he meant that this stranger could die if they didn't tend to his wounds. "But… Who can we get to help him? No one will believe my husband got beat up like this."

"I have a friend who won't ask questions."

Surprised, she asked, "You do?"

"An old friend. I haven't seen him in years. He went to study medicine while I went to work for your husband's father."

"Will he be upset that we went to him at this late hour?" she asked as he gingerly carried the stranger to the carriage.

"No. I believe he'll be too concerned about this gentleman's wounds."

"But what will we say? We can't tell him we buried my husband and found this stranger on the road."

"I'll tell him this is your husband and he got into a nasty brawl. I don't think he'll ask anything beyond that."

"Then what?"

"Then we ask this stranger if he'll pretend he's your husband."

She halted in her tracks for a moment until she could comprehend what he was saying. She quickly started walking again so she could open the carriage door for him. After she removed her cloak and set it on the seat so it wouldn't stain with the stranger's blood, Appleton settled him along the length of the seat.

Appleton turned to face her. "Do you want to sit with him?"

She studied the stranger. His head was tilted to the side and his eyes were closed. She doubted he would wake up before they reached their destination. "I'll sit in here," she decided. And if nothing else, perhaps she could make sure he didn't slide off the seat.

"If you change your mind, tap on the roof and I'll stop," Appleton replied.

With a nod, she let him help her into the carriage and sat across from the stranger, close enough to help him remain in place if needed but far enough so she wouldn't have to touch him if she didn't have to. As Appleton shut the door, she dared another good look at the stranger. She couldn't see anything but his silhouette, but even so, the likeness between him and her husband sent a chill up her spine. Oh God, let him be a kind gentleman, she prayed. If they could just work out an agreement and get along amiably enough, it would solve all her problems.

The carriage moved forward. She rubbed her eyes and thought of what an exhausting day it'd been. So much had happened and was still happening. She knew her life would never be the same, but the question lingering in her mind was whether it would be better or worse? She turned her gaze to the stranger who remained unconscious. Only time would tell if she and Appleton had made a wise move or a tragic mistake.

Chapter Three

"What do you think? Will he live?" Appleton asked his friend, Dr. Grant, after he tended to the stranger's wounds.

Anna stood up from where she waited in the drawing room with Appleton. Dawn was still a ways off, but she hoped to make it back to Camden while it was still dark so they could sneak back in undetected. Any kind of light might be their undoing. Forcing her attention off the window, she turned to the doctor. She hadn't understood how close the stranger had been to death when they arrived at the doctor's residence, but now that she did, it was a wonder he survived the carriage ride.

Dr. Grant wiped his hands on a clean towel. "Yes, he'll live, but if you hadn't brought him here when you did, he'd probably be dead." He looked at Anna and smiled. "I hate to say it, Your Grace, but your husband knows how to get himself into trouble."

Offering a weak smile in return, she said, "He's a gentleman who isn't afraid to speak his mind." At least that was the truth.

"Apparently not. But luck was with him tonight. He sustained some injuries to his head, ribs, back and shoulder. I'll give you some medicine to help speed his recovery. With enough care and attention, he should be as good as new in due time."

"Can we take him home?" she asked, hoping her desperation to get back didn't show.

Appleton glanced at her before he added, "His Grace is more comfortable at home."

Recalling the old sheets on her husband's bed, Anna decided she'd change them before they let the stranger sleep in that bed.

"I'll help you take him home," Dr. Grant said as he led them out of the drawing room.

She shot Appleton a startled look, so Appleton spoke up on her behalf. "There's no need to go through all that trouble. All that we ask is that you keep tonight's events to yourself. We don't want word to get around about His Grace's undesirable behavior. The last thing we need is a scandal."

"You have my word. I won't tell a soul."

Relieved, Anna followed the gentlemen down the hallway and to the room where the stranger was resting. She still shivered when she looked at him, even though he wasn't her husband. If she hadn't buried her husband, she'd swear this man was him.

To her surprise, the stranger opened his eyes. She shot a startled look at Appleton. All they needed was for him to tell Dr. Grant that he had no idea who they were.

"I see that you're awake," the doctor told him, checking the bandage on his forehead. "You're a fortunate gentleman."

Appleton cleared his throat. "May I have a word with you, in private, Doctor?"

"Certainly." He nodded as he lifted the bed sheet to check the gauze around his ribs. "Everything looks good." With a slight bow, he set the sheet back down. "I'll be back shortly. I'm sure you'd like a moment alone with your wife."

The stranger's eyes darted to Anna, and she nearly froze on the spot. If he said she wasn't his wife, then everything would be ruined. A very tense moment passed before Anna realized he wasn't going to respond to Dr. Grant's statement. Slightly relieved, she finally smiled in an attempt to become friends with him.

Appleton and the doctor left the room. As Appleton turned to shut the door, he looked in her direction, sending her a silent message that wished her luck. She gave a slight nod and waited for the door to close before she went to the stranger's bedside. She pulled up a chair and sat next to him.

She smiled again and was rewarded when he smiled at her in return. Well, that was good. He was at least friendlier than her husband had been. It seemed all he could do was scowl, unless he was having fun at another's expense. Shifting in her seat so she could lean forward, she lowered her voice. "I can't begin to imagine what you must be thinking, but if you'll kindly let me state my case, perhaps we can work out an arrangement that will benefit us both."

He held his hand up to stop her from speaking further and cleared his throat. "You're my wife?"

Her face flushed. "Oh, yes. About that, I—"

"You're beautiful."

She paused, surprised that was his response. He should have been asking her what was going on since he'd never laid eyes on her a day in his life. "Excuse me?"

"I'm afraid I don't remember you."

"No, you don't."

He winced and rubbed his forehead. "I'm afraid I don't remember anything."

Unsure of what he meant by "anything", she decided to help clarify the situation. "I think I can help. I'm a duchess."

"I'm a duke?"

"Well…yes. I mean, if you want to be."

"It's who I am, isn't it? You're my wife, and if you're a duchess, then it means I must be a duke."

Her eyebrows furrowed. "You don't remember who you are?"

He shook his head and reached out to hold her hand. He gave it a gentle squeeze before letting out a low sigh. "I don't remember anything. I can't remember my name, my age, where I live, what I do, or..." He glanced around the room then lowered his gaze to his body. "Or how I ended up here. But you know all of that because you're my wife, right?"

She studied him, trying to determine if he was being sincere or having fun at her expense. His green eyes met hers, and she knew he was telling her the truth. He squeezed her hand again, and she looked down at the way his hand was clasped around hers. It was a soft touch, not threatening and certainly not demanding. She returned her gaze to his. He seemed like the kind of gentleman who'd help her if he understood the situation, but since he didn't remember his past, then perhaps it wasn't necessary to divulge everything.

"Will you excuse me for a moment?" she asked him.

"You'll be coming back?"

"Yes. I won't be but a couple minutes."

He nodded. "All right."

Thanking him, she stood up and hurried out of the room. Quietly shutting the door behind her, she strode down the hall until she came to the drawing room where Appleton was talking to Dr. Grant.

Appleton stood from the chair where he was having tea and went over to her. "What is it, Your Grace?"

Lowering her voice so the doctor wouldn't overhear, she said, "He doesn't remember anything. And when I say *anything*, I mean anything."

"He's lost his memory?" Appleton whispered.

She nodded.

"And if he was beaten and left for dead, then someone out there doesn't like him."

She nodded again, even though she had no idea if that should be a concern or not. He didn't strike her as a bad person.

She'd been intimidated by her husband when she first met him, but she assumed that was because he'd been a duke and she'd been an eighteen-year-old lady having her first Season.

"We'll take him to Camden, and then I'll do a search to see if I can find anyone who knows him," Appleton finally whispered. "In the meantime, I think it's best to limit what we tell him."

That sounded like a good way to proceed, so she agreed.

Appleton turned to Dr. Grant. "I'm sorry, but we can't stay any longer."

"Don't be sorry," Dr. Grant said and faced Anna. "I'm just relieved your husband will be all right. Let me gather the supplies you'll need, and then you can be on your way."

She breathed a sigh of relief. At least this part of the ordeal was over. Now it was a matter of getting him home. From there, she and Appleton would have to decide what to do.

***

By the time Anna and Appleton got the stranger back to Camden and into a clean bed, Anna was exhausted, but she knew their task was far from over. They had to explain his injuries to Dr. Unger who was due by at ten that morning. As dawn came up over the horizon, she glanced at Appleton who tucked the clean bedding around the stranger's body. Fortunately, the medicine from Dr. Grant had made him sleepy so she was spared from having to answer any questions he might have.

She examined the bandages, gauzes, ointments, and medicines on the table by the bed. "Appleton, should we hide these when Dr. Unger comes here?"

Appleton went over to her. "He'll see he's been tended to by another doctor. He'll know something happened. What we need is an explanation for why he has cuts and bruises on his body."

She sighed and rubbed her forehead, willing the ache to subside. "I can't think of a good reason. Can't we just tell him that my husband is well and that his services are no longer required?"

"Not without arousing suspicion."

She groaned and sank into the chair by the table. "What are we going to do? We can't explain something like that when he's been in bed the entire time."

Appleton clasped his hands behind his back and paced the room a few times before he stopped and looked in her direction. "A fall."

"What?"

"If he got out of bed, he could have fallen. A fall that is hard enough can lead to bruises and broken ribs. We can say he fell down the stairs. That kind of fall can do substantial damage."

"And the cuts?"

"He could have caught a few nicks on his way down. He could have scratched himself if he tried to cover his face." He shrugged. "This gentleman also has some bruises on his legs. Whoever did this, they wanted to make sure he was in pain before he died."

She shivered as she thought of the reasons why someone would want to do that. "Do you think we made a mistake in bringing him here?"

"I don't think we had any other choice, Your Grace. At least we know Lord Mason won't be taking your husband's place. If this gentlemen," he motioned to the stranger, "turns out to be an unsavory sort, I think it'd behoove you to live somewhere else. He lost his memory, so we'll tell him that you were only here until he got better."

"All right. But do you think the doctor will believe he fell?"

"I don't know, but he can't prove he didn't."

That was true.

"Everyone is getting up for the day," Appleton said and helped her stand up from the chair. "I need to change clothes and tend to my duties. Try to get some sleep."

Before he could leave the room, she grabbed his arm. "You'll make sure I'm there with the doctor? If he doesn't believe this stranger fell down the stairs…"

"He'll have to believe it because there's no way he'll assume a lady buried her husband in the middle of the night, found a lookalike husband, and brought him back here."

"And these medical supplies?" she asked, turning to them.

"We'll say that it's very fortunate I had a personal friend who was a doctor who came for a stay last night. What a pity it is that he had to leave early in the morning."

"It's too much of a coincidence."

"Maybe, but what are the chances we'd find a gentleman who looks exactly like your husband?"

He had a good point. They were already going to tell one lie. What were a few more? From this point forward, their lives would revolve around keeping their secret safe.

"Your Grace, try to get some rest. When the doctor comes, we'll deal with it then," Appleton softly said.

"You're right." Her hand tightened around his arm. "Thank you."

"You're welcome. I can only hope the new duke will deserve you."

Touched by his care and concern, she smiled before she turned to the door leading to her bedchamber. The night had been a long one, and it was likely that the day would be even longer. But she would get through it. Weary, she slipped into her bedchamber and took a light nap.

***

Three days later, the gentleman woke from his slumber and winced from the pain in his forehead. The door opened, so he turned his head in time to see the lady—his wife—enter the room. She appeared to him every day as an angel with her golden hair framing her head like a halo. He spent all of his time in bed, the medicine making him sleep so he could heal, so he didn't often wake up in time to see her. He was glad he woke up when he did.

Each day, he felt better, but he still didn't remember anything up to the night when a doctor was tending to his wounds. That was the first night he saw her and learned she was his wife. And ever since, she tended to him, cleaning his wounds and seeing to his needs.

As she had the day before, she set down a bowl of clean water by his bed and touched the bandage on his forehead. "How do you feel?" she asked him, her voice soft and tender.

"Better, thanks to you." He tried to sit up, but his strength faltered.

"Please don't strain yourself." She helped him settle back in a comfortable position and fluffed his pillow for him. "You need your rest."

"I get impatient."

"I understand, but I promise these days will pass and you'll be feeling like your old self in no time."

He nodded, knowing she was right. "Mind if I ask what my old self was like?"

She glanced at him for a moment before removing the bandage from his forehead. "I think the ointment the doctor gave us is doing wonders. You'll have a scar but nothing more."

"Why won't you answer my questions? Every time I ask you something, you avoid the topic."

She placed his old bandage on the table and dipped a clean cloth into the bowl. "Do I?"

"Yes. You start talking about my wounds."

With a sigh, she shrugged and turned back to him so she could dab his forehead with the water. "I don't know what to tell you. So much has happened in the past." She cleared her throat and put more ointment on his forehead. "I don't even know where to begin."

That was fair enough, he decided. After thinking it over, he asked, "How did we meet?"

She picked up a clean bandage and placed it over his wound. Her fingers brushed his skin, almost tickling him. "I don't remember all of the details. It happened six years ago."

"What do you remember?"

She sighed. "Isn't there something else you'd rather learn?"

Disappointed since she didn't want to answer his question, he considered other things he wanted to know. He never felt right in forcing her to answer his inquiries, which was why he hadn't had any luck in learning about his past. "All right. I would like to know your name."

"I am the Duchess of Watkins."

"No, not your title. I want to know your name." When she didn't reply, he asked, "Do we refer to each other by our Christian names since we're married?"

"Actually, we don't. We refer to each other as 'Your Grace'."

He frowned. "We do?"

She nodded.

"But why?"

With a shrug, she checked his nose. "Does this hurt?"

"It's a little sore but not too bad."

She turned her attention to his ribs and lightly patted the gauze. "Do you feel any better than you did this morning?"

"Yes. Now will you please answer me?"

Her gaze met his and she shook her head. "You sure are persistent when you're awake."

"Is that something new about me?"

She brought her hands up to his shoulder and peeled back the bandage to inspect his cut. "Just as I suspected. You're bleeding. You need to stop trying to sit up without my help."

He groaned. "I'll sit up right now unless you tell me your name."

"What?" She turned her bewildered eyes to him. "You can't be serious."

Frustrated, he got up on his good elbow to show her that he was, indeed, serious.

"Anna! My name is Anna."

Satisfied, he settled onto his back, relieved his bluff had paid off since he didn't have the energy to sit up. As it was, his head was spinning.

Though she didn't say anything, he could tell she was irritated by the way she threw the bandage on the table.

Wishing he hadn't upset her, he took her hand in his and squeezed it. "I'm sorry. I didn't want to annoy you. I just wanted to know your name."

She relaxed and gave his hand a gentle squeeze before pulling her hand away from his. "It's hard to explain why we don't refer to each other by our Christian names, but we never have."

He hesitated for a moment then asked, "What is my name?"

She bit her lower lip.

"Well?" he pressed.

Bringing the wet cloth to his bad shoulder, she cleaned his wound, and though she was gentle, he winced. "Forgive me. I know it hurts, but I can't think of anything I can do to ease the pain."

"You can tell me my name," he replied through gritted teeth.

For the first time since he started asking her questions, she laughed. "You really don't give up when you want something."

"Does that mean you're going to answer me?"

"Very well. The Duke of Watkins' Christian name is Jason."

His eyebrows furrowed. That was an odd way of answering him. Why didn't she come out and say *his* name was Jason? Were they *that* formal with each other? "I'm sorry."

She dabbed ointment on his shoulder. "Sorry about the name being Jason?"

"No. I'm sorry that I said or did something in the past to make you think you can't be more personable with me."

She paused, and though she didn't make eye contact with him, he detected the unshed tears in her eyes.

"I don't know what kind of husband I've been to you, but I'd like it if we could start over. I love your name, and I'd like to call you by it, if that's all right?"

A tear slid down her cheek, and she quickly brushed it away. "I can't. I'm sorry, but I can't. You must refer to me as 'Your Grace' and I must refer to you as…as…"

"Your Grace?" he filled in for her.

She gulped and finished applying the ointment. Once she placed a fresh bandage over his wound, there was a knock at the door. "I'll be right back," she whispered before she stood up and wiped her hands on the cloth.

He watched her as she left, hoping he hadn't said anything that made things worse. She made her way quietly to the door and opened it a crack. He couldn't see who was on the other side of the door, but he saw her nod and promise the person she'd talk to him shortly. When she turned back to him, she picked up the cloth and placed it in the bowl.

"Are you leaving?" he asked.

"Yes."

"Will you be back?"

"Yes."

"When will you be back?" he pressed.

"Soon."

"How soon is soon?"

She groaned. "Soon."

After a moment, he asked, "You won't stop coming to see me will you?"

"I come in to check on you every hour. What makes you think I'll stop?"

He shrugged. "Because I ask too many questions?"

At that, she smiled. "I'll be back before the clock chimes six. I promise."

Relieved, he returned her smile, glad his angel would be back soon.

Chapter Four

Anna shut the door of the bedchamber and followed Appleton down the hallway and down the stairs. She clutched the bowl and damp cloth, fighting the urge to insist he tell her what he learned about the stranger right away. She dreaded what he might have discovered, but she needed to know. If the stranger already had a wife, he needed to go back to her.

When she and Appleton reached the drawing room, he shut the door and she placed the bowl on the desk. Turning to him, she asked, "What is it? What did you learn about the stranger?"

He shrugged. "Nothing."

"Nothing? But did you show the people who live around the forest my husband's portrait?"

"I did, but no one recognized him. It's like he came out of nowhere."

"Is it possible that you ran across the reprobates who left him in the forest?"

"It's very possible, Your Grace." Appleton took a deep breath and released it. "Since they want him dead, they wouldn't dare mention they know him."

"So there is no wife?"

"No."

Relieved, she sank into a chair and relaxed. She hadn't been aware of how anxious she'd been for the past three days, worrying that someone was going to tell her that she kidnapped the stranger, that his wife and children needed him. Now there would be no reason to send him away, and really, why would it be to his advantage to return if Appleton took him back to the forest? He wouldn't know where to go, and those men who wanted him dead would most likely finish the job.

It seemed that the safest recourse they had was to keep him here. He'd pretend to be her husband and protect her from Lord Mason. She'd give him her husband's title and name, and protect him from whoever wanted to kill him. And the estate would be better off without Lord Mason running it into the ground with his notorious spending habits. Having him here was the best thing for everyone.

"Your Grace?" Appleton asked.

Unaware he'd asked her a question, she turned her gaze in his direction. "I'm sorry, Appleton. What did you want to know?"

"I wondered if we should proceed with our plan and get the gentleman upstairs acquainted with being a duke?"

She nodded and stood up. "Yes. I see no reason to delay it."

"Very good, Your Grace." He picked up the bowl. "I'll take care of this and assure the others that His Grace is on the mend."

Just as she was ready to thank him, the footman opened the door and bowed. "Your Grace, Lord Mason has come by for a visit."

She cringed. Of all times for him to show up! Knowing she couldn't delay seeing Lord Mason without arousing his suspicions, she nodded her consent to let him into the drawing room.

Lord Mason came in and bowed. She gave the obligatory curtsy but refused to make eye contact with him.

"I came to inquire after my dear brother's health," he said, hands clasped behind his back and his eyebrows raised in interest.

She swallowed the lump in her throat and squared her shoulders back. If she was going to lie, she needed to make it as convincing as possible. "You'll be happy to know he's on the mend."

A flicker of disappointment crossed his face before he smiled. "Is he? Then this is good news."

"Yes." She cleared her throat. "Yes, it is." *Though not for you, I suppose.*

"May I see him?"

"Oh, well…" She glanced at Appleton who gave a slight nod. "Of course, you may, Lord Mason. I'm sure His Grace will be delighted to see you." She held her hand out to Appleton. "I'll take the bowl upstairs and dab his forehead with some cool water."

Lord Mason chuckled. "Please tell me you don't do menial tasks as the mistress of the estate."

"I don't consider caring for my husband a menial task," she told Lord Mason as she retrieved the bowl and cloth. "I enjoy it."

He crossed his arms in amusement. "Do you?"

Lifting her chin in the air, she replied, "When it's a task done out of love, it gives one a sense of joy."

"If you say so…" He chuckled again and motioned to the doorway. "Ladies first."

She forced her feet forward, acutely aware of the way his eyes scanned the length of her body as she passed him. Ignoring him, she strode down the hall and up the stairs. She'd given him way too much power in the past. Well, that wouldn't be the case any longer. From now on, she'd never let him see any weakness in her. He wasn't going to take her husband's place. The kind stranger was, and now that she had his protection, Lord Mason couldn't touch her.

She reached the top of the stairs and made it to the bedchamber. Since Lord Mason insisted on walking too close behind her, she didn't bother to pause and check to make sure the stranger was awake before entering the room.

The stranger glanced her way and smiled. "You came sooner than I hoped."

Lord Mason stepped by her and strode over to his bed. "My dear, dear brother! I hear you are feeling better."

He looked between her and Lord Mason who threw his arms wide open as if he planned to hug him then let out a sigh of happiness and dropped his arms to his side.

"To think the last time we talked, you looked as if you were ready to take that first step into eternity. But here you are, and you're on the mend." Lord Mason went over to the table by the bed and lifted the candle so he could get a better look at him. "However, the last time I saw you I don't recall you being covered in bruises. What in the world happened?"

Before he could speak, Anna cleared her throat and took a step toward the bed. "He fell, Lord Mason."

Turning to her, he asked, "Fell?"

"Yes. He developed a fever, and when it was at its worst, he grew delirious. I tried to keep him in bed, but he thought he needed to ride his horse so he could singlehandedly defeat Napoleon."

"He thought he was going to defeat Napoleon? All on his own?"

"I told you the fever made him delirious."

Lord Mason arched an eyebrow. "That's rather strange. When I talked to him, he was rather lucid."

She shrugged. "It happened suddenly. There was no preparing for it."

"All right. So he decided to be the hero and then what?"

Realizing that the stranger was watching her—and believing everything she was saying, she took a deep breath and proceeded with her and Appleton's lie. "He left the bedchamber and fell down the stairs."

"A fall down the stairs?" Lord Mason's eyes grew wide in what she suspected was false horror. "Then my brother is a very fortunate man indeed, for such a fall should have killed him." He turned to the stranger and added, "Usually, a fall down the stairs would break one's neck."

"It seems like I know how to take a fall," he replied.

Anna and Lord Mason turned their attention to him. "Pardon?" Lord Mason asked him.

"It was a joke," he said. "I survived the fall down the stairs because I know how to take a fall." When neither of them laughed, he sighed. "Apparently, it wasn't a very good one."

"I've never known you to joke," Lord Mason replied. With a chuckle, he added, "Now we know why. You're no good at it."

Anna decided if Lord Mason was going to learn about his amnesia, she should do it before the stranger had the chance. "The fall did more damage than you realize. It was because of it that he lost his memory."

"His memory?" Lord Mason asked, his eyes wide.

"Yes. He doesn't remember anything."

Lord Mason leaned over him and furrowed his eyebrows. "This isn't another bad joke is it?"

"I'm afraid not. I don't remember you."

"Really?"

Anna set the bowl down on the table, hoping to break the tension in the room as Lord Mason tried to stare him down in a silent move to intimidate him. "He not only lost his memory, but he tires easily," she said. "Healing is hard on the body. He has several bruises, cuts and broken ribs. He needs plenty of rest."

"I'm sure he does," Lord Mason snickered.

She frowned. She realized he was skeptical over what happened, but it almost seemed like he was playing cat and mouse with them.

Lord Mason gave him a good jab in the side, and he winced. "Oh, forgive me, dear brother. I make it a habit of playfully nudging you in the side. We've done it since we were children. I'd have your wife verify this, but it's something she doesn't know about. It's a shame you don't remember it."

It was on the tip of her tongue to suggest he stop trying to bait the stranger, but she managed to hold her tongue. Anything she said would only make things worse. His suspicions were already raised. She didn't need to add fuel to the fire.

"I won't intrude any longer on your time with your wife," Lord Mason told him. "It's very kind of her to tend to your wounds when a servant could do it. She must love you very much." With a glance in her direction, he added, "Who knew?"

She clasped her hands together so she wouldn't shove him out the door as he left the room. She closed her eyes and counted the seconds until she could hear his footsteps going down the hallway and toward the stairs. Once she did, she shut the door to the room and released her breath. Her gaze went to the stranger who smiled at her.

"You tend to my wounds because you love me?" he softly asked.

Unsure of how to answer that question, she went over to him. "I'm your wife. Caring for your needs is something I do." She reached under his shoulders. "Let's see how your back is healing."

He obliged and aided her and rolled to his side. "Do I like my brother?"

"I don't know." And that was the truth. She had no idea if her husband had ever liked his brother or not. Most of the time, it didn't seem like the two had a good relationship, but how could she know for sure? "Don't worry about it. What's important is that you're feeling better." So he wouldn't ask her anything else about Lord Mason, she quickly added, "You wanted to know about the first time we met?"

As she inspected his back to see how the bruises were healing, he said, "Yes, I would. Are you ready to tell me?"

"Yes." She was as ready as she was ever going to be. "I was in my first Season and enjoying a walk through Hyde Park with a friend when an inconsiderate gentleman insisted on joining us. My friend and I asked him to leave us alone, and though he went his way for a few minutes, he returned."

She wiped one of the cuts along his upper back with a cloth. Even though it wasn't necessary, she added more ointment to his back so she could avoid eye contact with him.

"You noticed that the gentleman wouldn't leave us alone," she continued, "so you politely suggested he find some other form of entertainment. We were grateful for your assistance, and after a brief conversation, we learned we'd be attending the same ball that evening." Blinking back the tears from one of the few good memories she'd had of her husband, she added, "At the ball, you asked me to dance, and it was then that I knew I wanted to be with you."

"So we married because we loved each other?" he asked, glancing over his shoulder.

"I don't know if we loved each other, but I was fond of you and thought that in time…" She decided not to finish the sentence, but if she had, she would have admitted aloud that she thought the Duke of Watkins had been worth loving. And that was the last thing she wanted to think. "Anyway, there's not much else to tell about how we met. We danced, you talked to my parents, and soon we got married in front of family and friends."

"That doesn't sound very exciting," he said.

Unable to resist the chuckle that rose up in her throat, she asked, "And what would have made it exciting?"

"I suppose something exciting would have been if I had saved you from the threat of a wild animal attack or gained control over a horse that you'd been riding which had broken free of your reins and was galloping out of town."

She laughed harder. "Neither of those scenarios are likely to happen in London."

"Hmm.... Then perhaps I could have saved you from a burning building."

"You have lofty ambitions, Your Grace."

"I think if I am going to be someone worth marrying, I ought to do something impressive."

She finished putting the ointment on his back and changed the towel on the mattress so he'd have a clean one to rest on. After he was settled onto his back, she wiped her hands on a clean cloth and sat beside him. "What else do you want to know?"

The more she told him about being the duke, the better off he'd be when he talked to his friends, and now that she knew there was nothing binding him to his past life, she felt safe in moving forward.

"Can I have some water?" he asked. "My throat feels dry."

"Of course." She stood up and filled his glass with water. When she turned back to him, she remembered that he needed to be sitting up and placed his glass back on the table. "I need to help you up."

Once she helped him up, he finished his drink and she settled him back into the bed again, but before she sat in the chair, he patted the spot on the bed next to him. "Will you sit here? I can see you better if you do."

With a nod, she did as he bid. He took her hand in his, and she resisted the urge to pull away from him. He was far too likable, far too gentle, far too appealing.

"What do I enjoy?" he asked. "What are my interests? How long have I been a duke? What do I do as a duke?"

She carefully thought over his questions. The last thing she wanted to tell him was that his favorite activities involved mistresses and gambling. She licked her lips and exhaled. "All right. You like to go to White's when you're in London."

"White's?"

"It's a gentleman's club."

"What do I do there?"

She shrugged. "I don't know. Gentlemen's clubs are for gentlemen only, and what happens there is none of the wife's business."

"I'll have to go there to find out then. Maybe it'll help spark a memory."

"Maybe," she whispered, though she knew it wouldn't. "While in London, you enjoy going to the theatre."

"Are you allowed to go to theatres?"

"Yes."

"Did you go with me?"

She nodded. As his wife, it was her duty to attend social activities with him while in London.

"Do you like the theatre?" he asked.

"Yes, I do." It was the one thing she enjoyed doing, though she couldn't say she cared to do it with her husband. She just enjoyed going there.

"We should do that."

"We'll have to do it when we go to London."

"And when will that be?"

"I'm not sure," she replied. "Maybe next spring."

"What season is it now?"

"Autumn."

"When do people usually go to London?"

"In the spring."

His smiled widened. "Then I should be well enough to go to London when it's spring, and you can take me to the theatre so I can see why I enjoy it."

Despite her apprehension about going to London with him, she felt herself softening and wanting to do what he wanted in order to please him. "All right, but you must be healed enough first."

"I'll be good and get plenty of rest."

"You're hard to say no to, Your Grace."

He sighed. "Won't you call me Jason?"

She shook her head. "I'm sorry, but I can't."

"And you won't let me call you Anna?"

"I think it'd be better if you didn't."

"Why not?" he wondered, his thumb stroking the top of her hand in a way that made her heart give an unexpected flutter.

Wishing to change the topic, she said, "You enjoy horseback riding, fox hunts, and…and…" She struggled to think of another activity her husband liked that hadn't involved drinking, mistresses or gambling, but her mind drew a blank.

"What about my parents? When did I become a duke? What do I do as a duke?"

Deciding those were safer questions to answer, she relaxed and told him all about her husband's upbringing and role as a duke.

Chapter Five

A month later, Jason felt well enough to examine his bedchamber. He saw a small room off to the side of the main room. Curious, he entered it and studied the intricate carving along the edges of the desk. The top was clear, but he thought the drawers might hold some clues to his past so he pulled them open. He sorted through the papers, but given his lack of memory and inability to read, the names and numbers made no sense to him. In one of the drawers was a locked safe. Next to it was a key, which he used to unlock it. More papers. He sighed. How unfortunate it was he couldn't read. He locked the safe and put the key in the cabinet next to his bed since that seemed like a safer place for it. He returned to the desk and resumed his search. In another drawer, he saw a couple bottles of liquor.

The door to his bedchamber opened. Eager to see Anna, he carefully rose to his feet, ready to greet her. To his surprise, a couple of maids followed Anna into the bedchamber, carrying a bathtub and buckets of water. He watched as they filled the tub, and after they left the room, Anna closed the door and turned to him.

"You're in need of a bath, Your Grace," she said as she approached him.

"Do I smell bad?"

"Terribly."

He sniffed himself and coughed. "All right. I agree. I need a bath."

She giggled. "Did you doubt me?"

"No, but I had no idea I was that filthy."

"I wiped you down the best I could when I gave you those sponge baths, but I could only do so much."

His lips curled up at her slight joke. He didn't know why, but he got the feeling that she rarely made a light-hearted comment, let alone tell an outright joke.

She walked over to him and held her hand out. "Do you think you can get into the tub on your own or would you like help?"

Since he welcomed any chance to touch her, he said, "I better not take the chance."

He slipped his arm over her shoulders. A sharp pain twisted in his side, and he stumbled as they rounded the bed. She had to hold him so he wouldn't fall forward. His face warmed from embarrassment. He knew he was having a rough time bouncing back from being ill and injured, but he'd hoped he could manage the walk across the room without incident.

She offered him a sympathetic smile and patted his chest. "There's no need to be uncomfortable around me. I don't mind if you're not graceful."

Even though she meant those words, he still didn't like the fact that he had bouts of weak moments when she was in his presence. "I didn't think to ask this before, but don't I have someone who helps me with getting dressed or with my baths?"

"You did have a valet tend to your needs six months ago, but you dismissed him," she replied as they reached the tub.

"I did? Why?"

She shrugged. "I don't know. You didn't feel the need to tell me."

"But you don't make it a habit of helping me with my baths, do you?"

"No, but then, you've never needed help before. Please undress and get in the tub."

He couldn't argue her logic, so he removed his clothes. He probably shouldn't have been self-conscious since she was his wife. She'd seen him naked many times in the six years they'd been married, except he didn't remember any of it. He was acutely aware that she was standing next to him. He glanced her way as he slipped off his underwear. Relieved that her gaze remained above his waist, he handed her his clothes.

While she put them in a basket for the laundry maid, he grabbed the edge of the tub and gingerly stepped into it. He sank into the water, which wasn't overly hot but warm enough to ease his muscles. He let out a low contented sigh.

Anna picked up a cloth and soap from the table and turned her tender eyes his way. "Feeling better?"

He nodded. "Much. If I'd known how good it'd feel to be in this water, I would have asked for a bath sooner."

With another one of her angelic smiles, she dipped the cloth into the water and rubbed soap on it. "Yes, but I don't think you would have had the strength to sit up. The doctor said you should be able to take brief walks by the end of the week. He doesn't want you to push yourself too hard, but the longer you lie in bed, the harder it'll be for you to heal."

"It almost seems like a contradiction to say that too much rest is bad for me."

She chuckled. "Perhaps, but it's true." She ran the soapy cloth along his back, starting at his shoulders and slowly working her way down. "You're healing nicely. Your bruises are almost gone."

He noticed that even as she used pressure on his back to wash him, she was gentle, preferring to use short strokes to wipe any lingering dirt from his back. She was always gentle with him, taking the time to patiently bring him back to health. Touched by the care and concern she continually showed him, he cleared his throat and whispered, "It's too bad I took that fall down the stairs. If I hadn't, I'd remember everything. I'd like to remember everything, especially you. Like the first time I saw you at Hyde Park or the evening I proposed to you." He glanced over his shoulder and added, "You must have been a beautiful bride."

Her eyebrows furrowed and she stopped washing his back.

"Did I say something wrong?" he asked, wondering why her expression seemed to darken at his words.

With a slight shake of her head, she dipped the cloth back into the tub and rubbed more soap into it. "No. You didn't say anything wrong. I just need more soap, that's all."

He sensed there was something she wasn't telling him but decided it didn't matter. At least not right now. She was probably overwhelmed by everything. Perhaps he'd never told her she was beautiful before. Maybe this was the first time he'd said something that nice to her. He thought to say that he was sorry about the past, that he would try to be the kind of husband who deserved her. He started to tell her this, but when he opened his mouth, he wasn't sure how. He would tell her at some point, but today wasn't the day.

To his surprise, she handed him another cloth and the soap. "For your front," she informed him when he didn't say anything.

"Oh." He took the items and rubbed the soap into the wet cloth. "So I'm going to start taking walks along the property soon?"

"The doctor said you'll be ready next week, and he left a cane to help you."

"Will you walk with me?"

She brought the cloth lower along his back and rubbed it in soothing circular motions. "I will if you want me to."

"Yes, I want you to." Judging by the uncertainty in her voice, he guessed he hadn't wanted to go walking with her in the past. "You can show me the grounds."

"There are a lot of grounds. You'll need to ride a horse or be in a carriage to see all of it."

"Then we can go riding together."

She didn't respond.

Deciding he wouldn't press the issue further, he turned his attention to washing his chest and legs, glad that there were enough suds in the water to hide his erection. The bath wasn't something he considered overtly erotic, but being in close proximity to Anna while naked had an unexpected effect on him. He forced his thoughts back to washing himself off. To his surprise, after she finished washing his back, she washed his hair. Now this proved to be a very relaxing experience, so he closed his eyes and sighed.

She chuckled. "I thought you might enjoy it if I washed your hair."

"Did you?" he murmured.

She massaged his scalp and hummed a tune. Not being familiar with it, he focused on the melody, wondering if he'd heard it before. It was pleasant with a touch of melancholy to it, something that didn't surprise him. There was an underlying sorrow he sensed beneath her smiles, and suspecting he had something to do with that sorrow wasn't easy to think about. But she dutifully came to his bedchamber to help him, and since she was nice to him, she must be willing to forget the past and start over. Perhaps losing his memory was the best thing that happened to them.

When she was done, she retrieved a towel. "Once you dress, I'll have the laundry maid change your bedding."

He eased out of the tub, careful to mind his aching joints. He accepted the towel from her and wrapped it around his waist. She picked up another towel, and he thought she was going to hand it to him but she wiped the water off his chest and back.

Afterwards, she handed him the towel and set out his new clothes on a chair. "Do you feel up to eating more than soup tonight?"

As he dried his hair with the towel, he nodded. "Yes. In fact, I'd love more substantial food. What do I usually eat?"

"Your favorite meal is roast quail."

"All right. Can I have that?"

"Of course. While you dress, I'll talk to Cook."

She left the room, and he hobbled over to the window, aware of the ache in his ribs. He pushed open the curtains further to let more light into the room. He took a moment to inspect the grounds. From his vantage point, he saw a well-groomed landscape that was surrounded by trees. His gaze went up to the sky, and he noted how clear it was. Not a single cloud in sight. He smiled. The future stood before him and Anna, and he had a feeling it was going to be a good one—much better than whatever had been in their past.

He turned to his clothes and dressed, taking his time since he had to stop a few times when his sore muscles protested. Recovery was taking time, and he had to remind himself that he needed to be patient. Once he was done, he checked his reflection in the mirror. He hadn't seen himself since he lost his memory, so it wasn't any surprise that nothing seemed familiar. Most of his face was still bruised, but he noted the broad nose, the dimple in his chin, the high cheekbones, and high forehead. His blond hair fell in waves to the shirt's collar.

He stared at his reflection, hoping something—anything—would spark a memory, even if it was brief. But nothing came. With a shake of his head, he turned his attention to inspecting the rest of his body, noting his tall frame and slender build. He was Jason Merrill, the Duke of Watkins, and he lived at Camden. He closed his eyes and repeated what Anna had told him several times. When someone knocked on the door, he opened his eyes and answered it, glad to see Anna had returned.

He wasn't sure what to make of her slight intake of breath, so he asked, "Is something wrong?"

She blinked several times before she offered a weak chuckle. "No, not at all. You look good, Your Grace." She entered the room and gestured to the laundry maid. "Since you're decent, I'll let her change the sheets."

"Of course," he replied and quickly stepped aside to allow the maid into the room.

The maid went into the room. Anna went over to the window and opened the curtains wider than they were. "I see you looked at some of the grounds."

"Yes." He approached her and turned his attention to the green landscape. "I like lots of sunlight in the room."

"Do you?" she asked.

"Did I not tell you this in the past?"

She hesitated for a moment and cleared her throat. "In the past, you've always had the curtains drawn."

"I did?"

She nodded, but she didn't explain further. Instead, she said, "There are a couple of hills on the other side of the estate, and a path that winds through a group of trees. I think you'll enjoy walking on that path. It leads to a beautiful fountain."

"You like that path a lot," he whispered, noting the wistful look in her eyes.

"I do. It's like being in another world."

"It sounds romantic. We'll have to walk it."

She peered around him, so he turned to see what caught her attention. The laundry maid had removed his old sheets and was putting on the new ones. She looked back at him and asked, "Do you feel up to coming downstairs for dinner tonight?"

"No, not yet. I did good to walk around this room today." After a moment of silence passed between them, he ventured, "Will you eat dinner with me tonight?"

"I don't know," she whispered, breaking eye contact with him.

Hesitant, he wondered if he should proceed or not. She

hadn't had any meals with him, and since he'd been eating nothing but soups, he thought nothing of it. But tonight he was going to have a real meal, and the fact that she didn't want to share it with him made him uneasy. It was yet another indicator that things between them hadn't been what he wanted them to be.

"I'd like to have dinner with you," he insisted, his voice soft. "I promise I won't chew with my mouth open or spit when I talk." As he hoped, she chuckled at his joke. "How can I get you to eat with me? Should I stand on my head or attempt a backflip?"

Her eyebrows furrowed. "Those are odd things you'd think to do."

"They were the first things that came to mind, but I'll do them or anything else you request if it means I can secure your company for dinner."

She sighed. "Why do I get the feeling that you're not one to give up easily?"

"Haven't I always been that way?" he asked.

He expected her to say that it was, but she cleared her throat and stepped around him. "The bedding is done. I'll inform the footman to bring both of our dinners up here."

As she led the laundry maid out of the room, he couldn't help but wonder if there was something important he didn't know but should? And did he dare press the issue when it was clear their marriage had been on shaky ground prior to his illness? It seemed to him the best recourse was to start fresh, to make this a new beginning for them both, and if he was going to make that new beginning, he couldn't afford to rehash the past. Closing his eyes, he promised himself that he wouldn't think of the past anymore. From now on, he'd focus on the future and see where it'd take him and Anna.

Chapter Six

A week later, Anna played her favorite melody on the piano in the drawing room. Many times, this tune brought her a sense of peace, and right now, it seemed to be the only escape she had from her worries. Her fingers pressed down on the keys as she closed her eyes. As in times past, she tried to conjure up a world she often imagined—a world where she was alone in a cottage near a stream surrounded by wildflowers and sunshine. It was her special place, and she didn't dare tell anyone in case they laughed at her. She was a duchess, a wealthy one at that. Why would she have need to escape to a better place? But if people understood how shallow money was when one was miserable, then perhaps they wouldn't think it so strange that she loved her daydreams as much as she did.

A tear slid down her cheek, and she stopped playing so she could wipe it away. Today her mental escape to the cottage with the gentle flowing stream wasn't coming. For the life of her, she couldn't get the stranger out of her mind. It shouldn't grieve her that he was so nice. She should have welcomed it after years of feeling like she was walking on eggshells to accommodate her husband. And yet… And yet, he terrified her. She didn't know how to respond to him.

It was her fear someone might realize he wasn't her husband and track down her husband's body rotting in the ground of the forest that compelled her to tend to him as much as she did. As long as she could keep them from getting close, they might not suspect anything was different. And the stranger was different. It was easy to explain the lack of memory for things her husband had known and did. But how could she explain why he hated quail or playfully joked around or asked for things instead of barking out orders? It was so obvious that he wasn't the same person. Someone was bound to notice, or so she feared.

"I hoped you would finish the music," Appleton said as he entered the room.

She blinked back another tear and took a deep breath so he wouldn't notice her weakness. It was ironic how he'd seen her at her weakest in the past when it came to her husband, but she didn't dare let him see how much the stranger unnerved her. She straightened her back and cleared her throat. "I think I missed a note as I played," she finally replied and picked up from the beginning of the piece.

"We can't get it right every time, Your Grace," he replied. "I thought you might like to have tea and scones."

"Has it already been an hour since you came in to ask if I wanted them?" She turned to the mantle above the fireplace and looked at the clock.

"Yes, it has."

She turned her attention back to him and sighed. "I'm afraid I'm not in the mood to eat or drink anything. I'll just wait until dinner."

"As you wish. I also came to inform you that the gentleman upstairs would like to see you."

Her heart pounded in a mixture of excitement and dread. "Oh?"

"I suspect he's getting restless staying in his bedchamber all day."

"Yes, he probably is." She ran her fingers over the smooth keys of the piano and tried to decide if she should wait or go up there immediately.

"You can't keep him away from the world forever," Appleton kindly said, his voice low.

"I know."

He offered her an understanding smile. "I realize it's easy for me to say that since I'm not in the precarious position you are, but it is comforting to know he's a good gentleman."

"But since he is a good gentleman, are we condemned for lying to him? We're making him a liar right along with us."

Appleton sat on the bench next to her and kept his voice low so no one would overhear them. "And what would be the alternative? Lord Mason becoming the duke? Then what?"

Of course, he was right.

"Wherever the gentleman upstairs is from, it's not from around here," he said.

"I don't suppose we'll ever know what brought him to the forest that night or why someone wanted him dead."

"Probably not, but I see no reason to worry about it. Whatever he did to end up in the forest, I'd rather have him be the duke than Lord Mason. At least he'll treat you well."

The sound of someone coming toward the drawing room caused them to stop talking. She cleared her throat and faced the piano while Appleton hastened to his feet and approached the doorway. To her surprise, the stranger entered the room. Even if he had a cane to assist him, she didn't think he should be so careless.

She bolted from the bench and hurried over to him. "Your Grace, you shouldn't push yourself so hard."

"I feel well enough to walk. As long as I take it slow, I'm fine," he assured her, glancing at Appleton. "Am I interrupting something?"

"No," she quickly replied. "Appleton was just telling me that you wished to see me."

"Yes. I got impatient waiting for you, so I figured I'd

come down to see you." He smiled in his usual disarming way. "I hope you don't mind."

"No, no I don't mind. I just don't want you to get a relapse, that's all."

Appleton cleared his throat. "Shall I bring in some tea?"

"Yes, please," she replied.

After he left, the stranger turned to the open book on the piano. "Do you make it a habit of playing this melody?" He motioned to the songbook.

She closed the book and placed it on top of the other two books. "Yes. Are you sure you feel well enough to be down here? The doctor says you're making excellent progress, but I don't think you should push yourself too hard."

"I told you I'm fine." With a smile, he added, "Do you like to play music?"

"It's something I do to pass the time." She didn't know why, but she didn't want to talk to him about it since she enjoyed it so much. Maybe it was something that was too personal. For sure, she had no intention of playing anything when he was in the room. She moved away from the piano and pulled aside the curtains. "It's a pleasant day. If you feel up to it, perhaps we should venture for a walk. Nothing long, of course, but a brief one should be all right. Some fresh air might do you good."

His gaze lingered on the piano, and she thought he might press her about her music. But to her relief, he nodded and hobbled toward the settee. She noted how much he relied on the cane and wondered exactly how extensive his wounds were. She could only imagine what the men who beat him and left him for dead did to him, but considering the fact that he didn't remember and Appleton's friend hadn't disclosed the details to her, it'd always remain a mystery.

He eased onto the settee and let out a breath. With a chuckle, he glanced her way. "I hope this won't get me in trouble, but I have to admit that sitting isn't as easy as it looks."

Her eyebrows furrowed and she took a step toward him. "Are you in pain?"

"Only a little." As she opened her mouth to suggest he take something for the pain, he added, "It's a minor thing. I'm already feeling better."

She wasn't sure if he said that so she wouldn't send him right back upstairs to rest in bed. He shot her a smile, and she averted her gaze.

Appleton came into the room and set the tray with the tea and scones on it. "Is there anything else you require of me?"

The stranger looked at her, so she shook her head. "That will be all for now, thank you."

Appleton bowed and exited the room, closing the door behind him.

"Will you sit?"

Blinking, she turned her attention back to the stranger. Though he patted the spot next to him on the settee, she opted to sit in the chair across from him. "I can pour the tea better if I sit here," she quickly explained before he asked her why she chose to sit away from him.

"All right."

Even if he accepted her excuse, he had to know it was a lie. She could reach the tea just fine from the settee. But there was no way she could sit next to him. Not when being near him was starting to stir up emotions she'd long ago forgotten she could feel.

She poured their tea and dared a look in his direction. She knew she couldn't keep thinking of him as "the stranger", but she couldn't think of him as Jason either. Perhaps it was time she settled on thinking of him as "His Grace". He was here to be the duke, after all, and it was appropriate she start thinking of him as such. She realized putting him in her husband's place wasn't easy, but it was something she agreed to when she brought him here.

Releasing her breath, she handed him his cup, hoping he

didn't detect the slight trembling of her hand. As long as he didn't realize how nervous he made her, she could handle it.

He accepted the cup and scanned the room. "I take it this is primarily your room."

"Really? What makes you say that?"

"The flowers. They're all over the place."

Curious, she turned from the tray and inspected the room. "They aren't all over the place. I only have two vases with flowers in them."

His smile widened. "Exactly."

Realizing he was joking, she relaxed and giggled. "If you think that's too much, just wait until you see all the flowers outside come spring."

"The grounds are littered with them?"

She picked up her cup. "You might feel faint if you think two vases full of flowers are too much. I'll bring the smelling salts when we go for walks."

He laughed. "I'm relieved to be in the hands of someone so practical. I bet you've even figured out how you'll carry me back into the house if I should faint."

"I wouldn't carry you. I'd have the footman or," she stopped herself before she referred to Appleton by name in front of him, "the butler do it."

"As I said, you have it all figured out. I am fortunate to be in such capable hands."

She took a sip of tea. "I trust you will manage during our brief walk. Hopefully, you'll manage the fallen leaves better than flowers. You wouldn't want to be known as the duke who was defeated by such delicate things."

"No, you're right. I'd most likely be the laughingstock of noblemen everywhere."

Her lips curled up at the way he shuddered. She drank more tea, glancing at him as she did so. The resemblance between him and her husband was still disturbing, and she had to remind herself the two weren't the same person.

He reached toward the tray and picked up a scone to eat. "It's quite a strange thing, don't you think?"

"What's strange? That you can pick up your own scone?" she asked, unable to resist teasing him.

"No." He grinned and ate it. When he finished, he added, "That's a good scone. Did I always enjoy them?"

"I think so." She couldn't recall her husband ever saying he didn't like them, so it seemed like a safe answer.

"I don't like quail like I used to, but I like scones. I also still like baked eggs and roast chicken. So some things I used to like, I still do, but for some reason, my favorite meal—quail—is no longer my meal of choice. I find that hard to understand."

She shifted in her chair and shrugged, breaking eye contact with him as she did so. "I can't explain it, Your Grace." And really, she couldn't. Not without causing a lot of problems—problems she'd rather avoid.

"I suppose it doesn't matter. What matters is that I still enjoy eating."

She nodded and finished her tea. "Eating is a good thing." She rose to her feet. "Are you ready for that walk?"

"What about the scones? Don't you want some? They really are good."

"I'll eat a couple when we return. You won't be able to take a long walk, Your Grace. We won't be more than a few minutes."

He took another swallow of tea and set the cup on the tray. "Very well. I will do as you suggest, Anna."

She clenched her hands together. Whenever he said her name, it made her heart speed up, and that wasn't something she wanted to experience. As he stood up, he lost his balance. She ran over to him and wrapped her arm around his waist to help steady him before he tumbled to the floor. "Your Grace, are you all right?"

"A bit clumsy, I'm afraid, but I'll manage," he said with a wry grin. "Though this is rather nice, don't you think?" He put his arm around her shoulders and gave her a light squeeze.

Her face grew warm and she hastened to retrieve his cane. Handing it to him, she said, "You'll need this, Your Grace."

He took the cane.

Ignoring the disappointed look on his face, she turned from him and headed for the door, ready to open it.

"You're very kind, Anna," he softly said.

Her hand on the doorknob, she paused, acutely aware that he was watching her. The heat of his stare made her tingle in excitement as much as it frightened her. Unable to look back at him, she opened the door and managed to keep her voice surprisingly calm as she replied, "Kindness has nothing to do with it, I assure you." Then, before he could respond, she slipped out of the room.

She took a deep breath to settle her nerves as she stood in the hallway. It would take him a moment to catch up with her, and she was thankful for the reprieve from him, even if it only spanned a few seconds. He was just a gentleman she found on the side of the road who needed healing as much as she needed a husband to ward off Lord Mason. She needed to go back to thinking of him as the stranger. It was the only way she could keep the distance she needed from him. Maybe Appleton could let him slip into the role of her husband easily, but she couldn't do it. She just couldn't open herself up to him that way.

She closed her eyes and swallowed the lump in her throat. This was necessary. She had no choice. Lord Mason must never be the duke, and the stranger was the answer to her prayers. As soon as he was well enough, he'd start going to the gentleman's club, hunt, horseback ride, and do other things gentlemen did to fill up his days. She wouldn't always have to be around him so much. And at that time, the distance between them would be sufficient so he could slip into his role as a duke and she could continue being the duchess, much like she and her husband had done before. The only difference would be that she would be treated well. Surely, she could handle that.

"Oh good, you're still here," the stranger said as he hobbled out of the room. "I was afraid you already took off running to enjoy the sunny day."

Her emotions settled, at least for the time being, she turned to him and offered a polite smile as the footman approached with their cloaks. "The gardener takes good care of the grounds, Your Grace. On occasion, the visitors have commented on how beautiful the grounds are."

"Do they?"

As the footman helped her with her cloak, she nodded. "Yes. It's a lovely sight."

"Well, then we're wasting time standing here talking, aren't we?"

Just as she was about to respond, the footman asked her, "Will you require a parasol, Your Grace?"

"Surely, you don't want one of those on a perfectly good day like this," the stranger told her.

"It's to protect my eyes from the sun," she informed him and nodded to the footman to indicate she'd take it.

"A hat for you, Your Grace?" the footman asked him.

"No thank you." As the footman retrieved the parasol for her, the stranger let out a regretful sigh. "Don't you want to feel the sun on your face?"

"I'm not particularly interested in it."

"That's a shame."

She accepted the parasol from the footman when he returned but waited until the stranger had his cloak on before she left the house. She opened her parasol and slowed her steps so he could keep up with her. "Why is it a shame that I don't want the sun on my face?"

"I was on the veranda outside my bedchamber earlier

today, and you know what I discovered?"

Though she suspected he'd tell her even if she didn't say it, she asked, "What?"

"The sun feels great."

She shifted her parasol to her other arm and peered up at him, noticing the way he tilted his face back and grinned. She paused and waited as he stood still and soaked up the sun. In all her years of marriage to her husband, he never once smiled the way this man was smiling now. This man enjoyed life. She wondered what it was like to embrace life with such abandon.

He opened his eyes and turned his gaze to her. "Put down the parasol and feel the warmth of the sun."

"I don't need to lower my parasol for that. Even with the chill in the air, I can feel how warm the sun is."

Though he sighed, his smile didn't falter. "Why do I have a feeling that you'll fight me every step of the way?"

Her eyebrows furrowed. "Fight you? I don't recall us having an argument."

He started walking down the path that led to a fountain, so she joined him, allowing him to determine the pace they'd be walking. "While it's true we haven't had an argument," he began, "you seem reluctant to do what I ask."

"I don't understand. I've been eating meals with you, and I'm walking with you as we speak."

"But you hesitated when I extended the invitations, and just now, you hesitate to let the sunlight grace your face. I don't blame you, Anna. Whatever I was like in the past, it's made it difficult for you to trust me."

"How do you figure that?"

"It's in the way you hesitate. I had to convince you to eat with me, and if I hadn't come down the stairs today, would you be walking with me right now?"

"We didn't often eat together in the past, and we never took walks. You spent a lot of time detained in London, and I spent a good portion of my time here at Camden."

"Why?"

"I don't know," she lied. "It's not a lady's place to ask where her husband spends his time."

"I'm sorry."

"There's nothing to be sorry for."

He held his hand up to stop her. "I might not remember what I did, but I'm intelligent enough to see the result of my actions. You're my wife, and you've treated me with much kindness. Kindness, I realize, that I don't deserve. I might not be able to change the past, but I'd like to do what I can to give us a good future."

What could she say to that? He was innocent of everything her husband had done, and yet he was promising her something she'd desperately wanted for so long. She did the only thing she could think of to do: she nodded. Seeming content with her response, his smile widened.

His gaze went to the fountain which was surrounded by red, orange, and yellow leaves. "Ah, I see I've stumbled upon the first batch of leaves."

"No, that's not the first. If you look behind us, you'll see we passed by some leaves close to those trees."

He glanced in the direction she pointed to. "How did I miss those?"

Because he'd been watching her the whole time, but she didn't dare tell him that. Instead, she said, "In the spring and summer white flowers surround the red ones in front of the manor, and if you look at them as you come here from the road, you'll see the red ones spell 'Camden'."

"Do they?" he asked, looking intrigued.

"They do."

"I'd like to see that."

"You will. Come spring, we'll go for a carriage ride, and I'll make sure to point them out to you."

With one of his disarming smiles, he said, "I look forward to it."

"In the meantime, do you feel well enough to walk to the fountain and back to the house?"

"Yes. It feels good to be outside after being cooped up inside for over a month."

"Remember, don't overdue it. You don't want to regret walking too much when tomorrow comes."

"I'll be sure to take it slow."

Satisfied, she turned to the fountain and enjoyed the rest of her walk with him.

Chapter Seven

Two weeks later, Anna was playing an upbeat tune on her piano when Appleton entered the drawing room with something in his hand. She stopped the music and focused on him.

"I can't recall the last time I heard a melody so cheerful in this house," Appleton commented.

She shrugged and stood up so she could approach him. "I thought I'd try something different today. Is that letter for me?"

"For you and His Grace. It's an invitation."

By the hesitant tone in his voice, she gingerly accepted it, her face going pale when she realized it was from Lord Mason. As much as she didn't want to see what the contents of the invitation contained, she opened it and read it.

Lowering his voice, Appleton said, "You don't have to accept it, Your Grace."

"But if I don't, he'll get curious and come out here again." And her newfound peace would be ruined.

"What is that?" the stranger asked.

Appleton stepped away from Anna.

Anna looked up from the invitation in her hands as the stranger entered the drawing room. "You're without your cane?" she asked him.

"I don't need it anymore," he said.

She glanced at Appleton. "Will you be so kind as to ask

the footman to get our cloaks?"

After Appleton nodded and left, the stranger turned to her. "You mean I don't have to ask you to go for a walk with me today?"

"That's not fair, Your Grace. We went for a carriage ride yesterday, and that was my idea."

"Only because you thought I was doing too much walking."

"Does that matter?"

He shrugged and smiled. "I suppose not. It's actually a compliment that you worry about my health as much as you do. Will we be discussing what you're holding in your hands during this walk?"

"Yes, I suppose we should."

"It doesn't look pleasant."

She sighed. "It's not."

Appleton returned with their cloaks and asked him, "Will Your Grace be going without a hat?"

As they slipped on their cloaks, he grinned. "I can't refuse the opportunity to go without one. I find them bothersome."

That was yet another difference between this gentleman and her husband, but she chose not to dwell on it or the possibility that Lord Mason might pick up on the fact that he wasn't really his brother.

"Very well, Your Grace." Appleton bowed and led them to the front door where the footman waited for them before he opened it and handed her the parasol.

Once Anna and the stranger were outside, she almost didn't open her parasol right away so she could get an idea of what made him enjoy the sunlight touching his face as much as he did. But he turned his gaze to her, an action which made her self-conscious enough to open it. He shot her one of his charming smiles, and she tightened her grip on the handle of the parasol, praying he didn't detect her uncertainty. She must keep thinking of him as the stranger she and Appleton found that night they buried her husband.

As long as she thought of him as the stranger, she could keep an emotional distance from him. Each day, it was getting harder and harder to do that, and several times, she had slipped and almost thought of him as Jason. But she hadn't even thought of her husband so intimately. It was the stranger's persistence on calling her Anna that made her feel closer to him than she wanted to be.

"Will you escort me to the fountain?" He offered his arm and looked at her with that hopeful expression that made her afraid she'd give him anything he wanted.

She swallowed and debated whether she should take his arm or not. Up to now, she hadn't touched him, except when she had cleaned his healing wounds.

He took her hand and placed it on his arm. "There. Now I can feel like a true gentleman and let you escort me to the fountain."

Despite her apprehension at being so close to him, she chuckled. "You'll let me escort you? If you were a true gentleman, you'd be the one escorting me."

"Hmm… You have a good point, though to be honest, I don't mind it when you take the lead. As long as you let me come with you, I'm content."

"At least you're not hard to please."

"I try to be accommodating," he teased.

"You are."

After a moment of silence passed between them as they strolled down the path to the fountain, he asked, "Is now a good time to ask about the invitation you received?"

"Yes," she softly replied, thinking if she was going to do it, it might as well be now. "You remember Lord Mason?"

He nodded. "My brother."

She winced and hoped he didn't notice since the parasol

partially obstructed his view of her face. "Yes. He came to visit you shortly after you lost your memory." She cleared her throat. "He's having a dinner party in a week and we're invited to attend."

"What happens at dinner parties?"

"Not much, really. You catch up on the latest gossip, eat, play a few games, and go home."

"It doesn't sound like you enjoy them."

"It depends on who attends the dinner parties."

They stopped at the fountain, and she sat beside him on the bench. She fingered the invitation and glanced at him. Considering the clothing he'd been wearing when she and Appleton found him, she wondered if he could read it. If he could, then he'd understand, by the way Lord Mason worded the invite, what kind of gentleman he was. Otherwise, it was hard to explain.

"Can you read?" she asked him.

"I don't know."

As a duke, he should be able to, and it suddenly occurred to her that if someone were to find out he couldn't, then problems might arise, even if he did lose his memory. To find out if he needed to be taught to read, she showed him the invitation. "Can you read this?"

He studied the script and shook his head. "No."

She turned so she could face him. "This is very important. You must not let anyone know you can't read. Even if you've lost your memory, you don't want them to know you're illiterate." She took a deep breath and willed the image of Lord Mason's smirk from her mind. "Some people don't care who they hurt."

"Are you talking about my brother?"

Choosing her words carefully, she replied, "Lord Mason isn't someone I'd voluntarily spend time with."

"Why not? What has he done?"

Breaking eye contact with him, she shrugged and faced the fountain. "He hasn't *done* anything, exactly. I don't know how to explain it, but even though he's of noble birth, he's not what a gentleman should be." And how it pained her to even think of him as a gentleman, but because of his status, she had to. She cleared her throat. "As long as you don't let him get any power over you, you'll be fine."

"I don't understand. How could he get power over me? Did he manage that in the past?"

"No. You've never given him the opportunity." At least, her husband hadn't. "Try not to show him your weaknesses." He furrowed his eyebrows, and she knew he wasn't sure how to follow her advice. "If he makes you uneasy at all, leave the room."

After a moment, he nodded. "All right. I can do that."

She really hated to go to the dinner party. It was akin to sending him to the wolves since there would be times when he'd be alone with the gentlemen while she would be with the ladies, but she didn't know what else she could do without arousing Lord Mason's suspicions.

"Do you worry I won't be able to handle him like I did in the past?" he softly asked.

She couldn't tell if he was hurt by the possibility she might think that or if he was worried about it, too. She opened her mouth to assure him that she was confident he could handle it, but it would be a lie. And ironically, despite the many lies she'd already told him, this was the one lie she couldn't. With a sigh, she admitted, "You're nothing like the Duke of Watkins I used to know. You're gentle and kind. You're much better in ways I don't think you'll ever appreciate." Her voice trailed off and she closed her eyes before her voice wavered. God help her, but it was hard to keep thinking of him as *the stranger*.

"You worry my brother will take advantage of who I am now because I'm not as hard as I used to be," he finished for her.

She took a deep breath to steady her emotions and nodded. Yes, he was so gentle and kind, he might not be able to stand up to Lord Mason.

"I can do it, Anna," he whispered, resting his hand on her shoulder.

Startled by his touch, her eyes flew open and she looked at him. Her heart leapt in excitement. She didn't want to enjoy it, but no matter how much she willed herself to scoot away from him, she couldn't. He released her shoulder, and though she knew she should be relieved, she also felt disappointed. A lady could get used to the kind of touch he'd just blessed her with. Apparently, years of coldness and rejection left her more vulnerable to gentleness than she cared to admit.

"Since you warned me, I'll be prepared and act accordingly," he told her.

She nodded, hoping he was right, but the only way either one of them would know was for him to try it.

"Would you do me a favor?" he asked.

"What is it?"

"If you can't refer to me as Jason, would you please call me Watkins? I don't want to be 'Your Grace' all the time."

She winced before she could stop the reaction. He didn't ask her an easy thing. If he had any idea how difficult it was, he wouldn't ask it at all. "There's nothing wrong with me referring to you as 'Your Grace'. It's your due as a duke."

"But it feels unnatural to do that every time. I suppose if you were a stranger or an acquaintance, it would suit, but I'm your husband."

"I don't know if I can."

"Sure you can. Open your mouth and say Watkins."

She got ready to shake her head, to deny she could even do that much, but he leaned forward and kissed her cheek. His lips were soft and warm, just as gentle as his touch, and despite her better judgment, her resolve weakened. "All right. I'll call you Watkins." Perhaps if she stuck with that, it wouldn't be so bad. Perhaps she could still keep enough distance from him so she wouldn't get too attached.

He smiled and wrapped her hand in his. "Thank you."

He turned his attention to the fountain, but she couldn't think of anything but the terrifying prospect of what calling him Watkins and allowing him to touch her so intimately might mean. It seemed to her she was quickly approaching a bridge—one that she'd not only cross but one that might possibly be her undoing.

***

Jason couldn't help but notice the way Anna kept fidgeting next to him in the carriage, and it got worse as they got closer to Lord Mason's estate. He considered holding her hand or putting his arm around her shoulders to offer her some kind of comfort, but he sensed she didn't want him touching her so he refrained.

He turned his attention to the window, his mind wandering to nothing in particular. When the estate came into view, he straightened in his seat. From the other carriages pulling up to the front, he estimated that Lord Mason had invited five other couples.

Beside him, Anna rubbed her forehead and sighed.

"At least it's only for three hours," he said.

"Three hours can seem like an eternity when all you want to do is go home," she replied, her hand falling to her lap.

He reached over and clasped her hand in his. "You said if we came here, then he wouldn't feel the need to come out to Camden, correct?"

She nodded.

"Then think of it as three hours spent to avoid having to see more of him."

A smile crossed her face. "That's a better way of thinking about it."

He wondered just how dreadful his brother was. With a shrug, he figured he'd find out soon enough. For sure, fretting over the evening wasn't going to change the outcome. Whatever was going to happen was going to happen. All he could do was as Anna suggested and not let Mason bother him.

The carriage came to a stop, and he waited for Mason's footman to open the door before he left the carriage and held his hand out to help Anna down. Her grip tightened around his hand to the point where he thought she might cut off his circulation. His eyes widened but he gave no other indication that he was surprised by the fierceness of her anxiety.

Once her feet hit the ground, he offered her his arm, which, to his relief, she accepted. Her grip was still tight around his elbow, but at least the feeling had returned to his fingers. He followed the other couples to the entrance, slowing his steps to accommodate for Anna's hesitation.

As they walked up the steps, someone called out to them. Her hand clenched even tighter—something he didn't think possible—before he turned to see who it was. He didn't recognize the couple, of course, but he smiled a greeting.

"Jason," the gentleman said with a bow, "I heard you made a full recovery."

Jason encouraged Anna to face the couple and bowed to the gentleman in return. "Yes, thanks to my wife who took care of me. Unfortunately, I took a fall down the stairs, and I lost my memory."

"Mason stated as much," he replied. "You don't remember it, but we're good friends. I am Ian Daniel, Lord of Hedwrett, and this lovely lady is Candace, Lady of Hedwrett."

"It's a pleasure to," he stopped himself before he said 'meet' since technically he already knew them, "see you in attendance at this dinner party."

"You wouldn't fare well to miss one of Mason's dinner parties," Ian said in a tone Jason suspected was part amusement and part warning. "We shouldn't dally outside when there's wine and food waiting."

With a nod, Jason urged Anna to turn around, and they entered the manor where the butler took their cloaks and led them to the drawing room. Jason scanned the room where his brother was telling jokes to three couples and a lady who laughed. Jason and Anna followed Ian and Candace into the room and sat on a settee.

Mason chuckled and waved his hand dismissively to the group. "That's nothing, I assure you. Her sister was even more dreadful." Mason turned his gaze to Jason and clapped his hands. "My dear, dear brother! I tell you," he told the others, "he was on the verge of death. In fact, you could say Death was knocking on his door, but my brother defied Death and sent him back to where he came. Death's loss is our gain."

The others nodded their agreement, but even so, Jason sensed his brother wasn't sincere. Beside him, Anna clenched her hands in her lap but showed no emotional reaction on her face.

"We are fortunate indeed," one of the gentlemen said, giving Jason a polite nod.

"However, it's not all good news, I'm afraid," Mason added with a regretful sigh. "My brother doesn't remember any of us, even me. And to think I gave him the best years of my life while we were growing up."

The group chuckled, and Jason couldn't tell if they laughed because they wanted to or if they had to.

"Fortunately, you have Lady Templeton to comfort you," Ian said.

Mason glanced at the lady sitting behind him and smiled. "And what a privilege it is to be comforted by someone so lovely."

"You flatter me, my lord," she replied, shooting him a coy smile as she waved her fan in front of her face.

"Not unnecessarily so."

Anna sighed softly. At first, he thought she wished he would talk to her in the same way Mason was talking to Lady

Templeton, but as he noted her clenched hands and gritted teeth, he realized it was a sigh of impatience or irritation. If he'd been alone with her, he'd ask her which one it'd been. Perhaps it'd been both. Whatever the cause, she wasn't as happy to be here as the others in the room were.

The butler entered the room and announced that dinner was ready.

Jason joined the others and stood up. When he realized the gentlemen offered their arms for their ladies, he turned to Anna and did likewise. She remained sitting for a long moment before she stood and slipped her arm around his. As they headed for the dining room, he couldn't help but notice her steps were slower than the others. If she hated coming here so much, why didn't she refuse to come? Surely, she could have written no and had him sign it, especially since he could now write his name. But she'd been insistent they come. Now it was his turn to sigh. Whether he'd lost his memory or not, he doubted that he could understand the way a lady's mind worked.

Once everyone sat around the dining room table, Mason proceeded to tell everyone about his venture to British India. Jason tried to pay attention, thinking that since he was Mason's brother, it was his duty to take an interest in what he did, but as Mason droned on, his mind kept wandering to the oddest things.

He noticed the way one of the lady's feathers kept coming loose from her hair. She had to keep putting her fork down to put it back in its proper place. Then there was Ian who made it a habit of stealing glances at one of the ladies who wasn't his wife. To her credit, the lady ignored him, but she snickered when the other ladies took a second portion of the veal when the footman offered it to them. Jason didn't know what to make of her, but he supposed it didn't matter. A gentleman across from him had some food stuck between his teeth, which wouldn't have been bad if he hadn't laughed at every joke Mason made. Jason made eye contact with him at one point and motioned to his teeth, but the gentleman shrugged and turned back to Mason.

"My kind brother!"

Startled, Jason took his eyes off the food in-between the gentleman's teeth so he could address Mason. "What is it?"

Mason took a sip of sherry and set the glass on the table. "Will you be going to British India?"

Jason glanced at Anna to see if it was something he had planned to do before he lost his memory. She gave a slight shake of her head.

Mason laughed. "I don't believe it. You're not basing your decision on the opinion of a lady, are you?"

Unsure of how to respond to that, especially since everyone was watching him, he cleared his throat and shrugged. "I don't remember if British India interested me or not…before I lost my memory."

"You could have asked me that. We are brothers, and considering how close we were, I know your interests more than her."

He wanted to look at Anna to see whether or not this was true, but he didn't dare. Not with everyone watching him.

"You needn't be shy about asking me questions," Mason continued. "I grew up with you. I know things about you she doesn't."

"I'll keep that in mind," Jason finally replied, not sure what else he was supposed to say.

"Please do. I want to help you. We're blood. Family. That's what matters most."

He nodded but decided to keep quiet.

"And yes, you were very interested in going to British India. In fact, we discussed going together before you lost your memory."

Since Mason waited for him to respond, he said, "In light of the situation I find myself in, I think it's prudent I stay home. I don't want a relapse."

"Of course not. No one wants that. But maybe in the future you will feel well enough to go. I promise you it's worth the trip. They don't call it 'the Jewel of the Crown' for nothing."

Ian set his fork on the plate with a loud clatter and wiped his mouth with his napkin. "I hear it includes a great amount of land."

"It does." Mason turned his attention to Ian and started listing off the territories the British Empire controlled in India.

Jason breathed a silent prayer of thanks that Ian spoke up when he did. He didn't care for the way Mason was prodding him, as if he was testing him. What did Mason expect? He lost his memory. He wouldn't remember if he wanted to go to British India or not.

He turned his attention to the dessert as the footman served it, grateful he could focus on something pleasant. He glanced at Anna who refused the dessert and gripped the cloth napkin in her lap. She hadn't relaxed once since they stepped out of the carriage. For the first time that evening, he hoped they could go home soon. Whether it was Mason's annoying questions or Anna's anxiety, he couldn't help but think that he should have insisted she write the letter declining the invitation to this dinner party. Next time, he would insist on it, even if he had to ask Appleton to write it for him.

Chapter Eight

Anna didn't want to leave Watkins when the dinner was over, but considering the gentlemen and ladies had separated, she didn't have a choice. She bit her tongue on her protest and joined the ladies to the drawing room. As long as she didn't arouse anyone else's suspicions, she might manage through the rest of the dinner party unscathed. It was bad enough that Lord Mason insinuated Watkins needed her in order to say whether or not he wanted to go to British India. It hadn't been her intention to put Watkins in such an awkward situation, but he'd looked over at her and she'd hoped the silent shake of her head would be subtle enough for Lord Mason to miss. But it hadn't been. To her dismay, very little got past him, and that worried her.

There was nothing she could do now but hope Lord Mason wouldn't notice anything else that was amiss about her husband. She stopped her thoughts and took a deep breath. No. The stranger wasn't her husband. He was filling a role, pretending to be her husband. Her real husband was buried in an unmarked grave beneath the forest floor. She must think of him as Watkins and nothing more.

"Anna, is something troubling you?"

Anna jerked and turned her attention to Candace who sat next to her on the settee. Across the room, the other ladies hovered over something and giggled. From where she was sitting, she couldn't make out what it was because the piano hid it from view.

Anna swallowed and turned to face Candace, praying her voice would be steady when she spoke. Of all the people she would lie to, Candace would be the hardest since she knew her better than the other ladies did. "I'm fine. I'm just...overwhelmed," she finally managed.

"Overwhelmed your husband still lives?" Candace softly asked, her sympathetic tone bringing back all the times she had confided to her about how awful her marriage had been.

Here it came. If she wanted her lie to be believable, she needed to get it over with. "I would have said yes before he lost his memory, but since he did lose his memory, he's a different person." There. She said it. With any luck, Candace would accept it.

Candace seemed to consider Anna's words before she spoke. "I did notice something different about him at dinner."

Heart racing, Anna nodded. "Yes, he's a lot nicer now."

"Very much so. I can't imagine he'd let Lord Mason speak to him in such a way before."

"No, he wouldn't." And that was another strike against Watkins. She wondered if she had any chance of pulling the ruse off. Watkins was innocent of any wrongdoing, so it'd be on her head if the lie was exposed. Forcing the possibility aside, she said, "I like the person my husband is since he lost his memory. It was the best thing that's happened to him." *And to me.*

"I wish my husband would lose his memory if it meant he'd become a better person," Candace whispered so the other ladies wouldn't overhear.

"I'm sorry."

"Why should you be sorry? You weren't the one who arranged my marriage? It was my greedy brother who did the vile deed. I'm just glad I finally conceived so Ian won't come to my bed anymore."

Anna inwardly shuddered. She knew all-too-well how awful it was to have a brute of a husband in her bed. "I can't blame you for being relieved. I never got such a reprieve, but at least mine was always quick."

In fact, Anna estimated it took her husband a total of five minutes from the time he entered her bedchamber to when he left. She used to count down the minutes to distract herself at first, and after a while, she counted them to assure herself it'd soon be over.

She reached for Candace's hand and squeezed it. "I hope you have a son." And she hoped Ian wasn't the type of gentleman who wanted two sons in case one died. "You do realize you can live apart from him if you have a son."

"That's what I'm hoping for. He only wanted an heir. Otherwise, he wouldn't have married, and any lady would've suited as long as she wasn't associated with scandal."

"What irony it is when our pristine reputations attract the wrong kind of gentleman."

"A cruel twist of fate might be a better way of stating it."

Anna let go of Candace's hand and smiled. "You're always welcome at Camden should you need a place to stay while you seek out your own home."

"Thank you, Anna. You've always been a good friend. I had a feeling you'd be dear to me when I first met you at the engagement party."

"Ian and my husband knew each other since their school days. It was natural you and I were bound to meet."

Lady Templeton approached them with three ladies following close behind. "You two don't make it a habit of keeping to yourselves during all of Lord Mason's dinner parties, do you?"

"Oh, they do," Helen replied. "If you marry Mason, you'll get used to it."

Anna's cheeks warmed. Helen often chided her and

Candace for removing themselves from the other ladies on several occasions. "My husband almost died. It's been a hard ordeal."

"Then why did you agree to attend this dinner party?" Lady Templeton asked.

Anna couldn't tell if she was trying to bait her or if she was honestly concerned. "Lord Mason is my husband's brother. It'd be improper for us to neglect attending the party."

"Hmm..." She shrugged. "I suppose that line of reasoning works as good as any."

The other three ladies giggled and whispered amongst themselves.

Anna frowned. All right. So Lady Templeton was hoping to bait her. That being the case, she would fit in very well with those three cackling busybodies hovering around her. Anna turned her attention to Lady Templeton who looked overly impressed with herself. "So you and Lord Mason met while he was in British India?"

Lady Templeton sat in a chair and, like a bunch of puppies, the other ladies followed suit. "One might term it that way, but I prefer to think of it as me taking the initiative to get something I need."

Anna glanced at Candace who gave a slight shrug. "I'm afraid I don't understand your meaning, my lady."

"You weren't supposed to," Lady Templeton replied with a snicker.

Her skin bristled, and she knew right then and there that she didn't like Lady Templeton. Such a thing wasn't necessarily bad. At least if Lord Mason married her, the two would be an equal match.

"Was he as dashing as he claims he is when meeting the fairer sex?" Helen asked, her lips curled up in mischief.

Lady Templeton chuckled. "Is that what he claims? While I wouldn't exactly call him inadequate, I will disclose that I was far more charming than he was." As Helen stifled another giggle, she touched her arm and added, "We must never tell the gentlemen this, of course. You know how much they pride themselves on their prowess when obtaining our affections."

"That is the way gentlemen are," Helen replied.

Anna sighed and glanced at Candace who looked just as eager to get away from them as she felt. Before the others could notice her friend's unease, Anna cleared her throat. "Lady Templeton, I'd love to hear your version of how you and Lord Mason met."

"Oh yes!" Helen eagerly nodded as the other ladies turned to Lady Templeton in interest. "Please tell us!"

"All right," Lady Templeton agreed as she shifted into a more comfortable position on the seat. "First, however, I must assure you that every part is true." With a wicked grin, she continued in a sly voice, "Especially when he fell at my feet and swore his undying devotion to me."

Resisting the urge to roll her eyes, Anna put on a polite smile and listened as the lady continued with her endless drivel of how she impressed Lord Mason.

***

"And this is the sword I acquired when I traveled to China," Mason told his brother as he turned the object over in his hands, admiring the way the silver blade glistened next to the firelight in the den. "Would you like to hold it?"

Jason shook his head. "No, I'd rather not."

"Come now, my brother. You never could resist the opportunity to touch a weapon, especially a sword as magnificent as this."

From across the room, two gentlemen played chess and the others watched. Though Jason didn't remember anything about the game except that Mason had told him he loved it, he would have preferred to have been over there at the moment instead of here with Mason.

Now as Mason held the sword out to him, Jason reluctantly took it in his hands, waiting for something to trigger his memory, but his mind was blank. "You said I used to enjoy holding this?"

"I didn't say you enjoyed it. I said you couldn't resist the opportunity to hold it."

Mason laughed and gave him a hearty pat on the back, an action which caused him to stumble forward and knick his hand on the blade.

"Jason, you shouldn't be so clumsy. Look what you did to my blade." He took the sword from Jason in an abrupt way that almost caused Jason to get another cut. "I'll have to get this cleaned. Immediately."

While he went to pull the cord to alert the butler to enter the room, Jason sucked on the small cut in the palm of his hand. It took him a moment to recall his handkerchief. He quickly grabbed it and pressed it to his wound. Compared to what he'd been through with the fall down the stairs, this was a minor thing. Unfortunately, he wished he could say the same thing about Mason. He didn't know why, but Mason seemed to have a vindictive streak. And for some reason, it was aimed directly at him.

The butler entered the room, and Mason gave him orders to clean the sword. Jason glanced over at Mason, and for a moment, he thought that Mason scowled at him. But in the next instant, Mason smiled. Jason blinked and shook his head, not sure of what to make of the whole thing. Surely, Mason understood he hadn't meant to get blood on the sword, and truth be told, he wouldn't have if it hadn't been for Mason giving him a good swat on the back.

"Don't stand there looking as if you've lost all your friends," Ian called out in a jovial tone. "Pull up a chair. The game is getting good."

If for no other reason than to have something to do, Jason made his way to the chess game where the two players were studying the pieces. Jason retrieved a chair, found a free spot to sit and breathed a sigh of relief. He hadn't realized he'd been nervous around Mason.

The butler left, and Mason went to the wall of his prized collection of weapons and brushed a pistol with a cloth. Jason turned his attention back to the game. Even if he didn't remember the rules, he thought watching the two men strategically move their pieces across the board was more entertaining than Mason's ramblings. The men remained quiet, and the spectators upped their bets on who they thought would win. According to Ian, it was a close game. Jason could only nod and continue to watch as the men played.

He didn't know how long he was watching the game until his mind wandered off, but the butler's voice jolted him back to the game. "Brandy, Your Grace?"

Jason straightened in his seat and turned to the butler who presented a tray with glasses full of brandy on it. "Yes, thank you."

He went to reach for one glass, but the butler turned the tray slightly to the right and said, "Perhaps this glass might be better."

"I don't think it should matter," Jason replied.

"Lord Mason requested you have this particular glass."

Jason's gaze went to Mason who was examining the sword. Turning his attention back to the butler, he whispered, "I'll make do with this one."

He tried to reach for another glass, but the butler stopped him. "Excuse my boldness, Your Grace, but Lord Mason was quite adamant you receive this glass instead." He lifted the glass and held it to him.

Jason hesitated, but then Mason glanced in his direction and he knew he had to accept it. He settled the glass on his lap and watched while the other gentlemen took whichever glass they wanted. Studying the glass in his lap, he tried to figure out if something was in the brandy that shouldn't be there but knew he wouldn't be able to see anything suspicious in it. Mason was much too clever for that.

"Are you sure you don't want to place a bet?" Ian asked, drawing Jason's attention back to the game.

"No," he replied.

"I've never known you to resist the chance to make some easy money."

"It appears that Jason is a different person ever since he lost his memory," Mason said.

Not realizing Mason had walked up behind him, Jason jerked.

Mason laughed and placed a hand on his shoulder. "My goodness, dear brother, you're as squeamish as a lady. First the sword and now this. I hope you haven't lost your taste for liquor as well or we might have to send you to the drawing room so you can sip tea with the ladies."

Most of the men chuckled, but Lord Basemore—if Jason remembered right—shook his head. "He's been ill and lost his memory, Mason. There's no need to be so critical of him."

"You're right," Mason replied, appearing appropriately contrite. "It's just that the old Jason would have put me in my place. Even if that was aggravating at times, I rather miss it. But," he shrugged, "there you have it." He looked down at Jason and though he smiled, there was no mirth in his eyes. "Like I said, you're a different person. I'll have to get to know the new you, hmm?"

Jason frowned. What did he mean by that?

"You can't blame him for what happened," Lord Basemore muttered and turned back to the chessboard where he waited for his opponent to make the next move.

Mason's grip tightened on Jason's shoulder for a second

before he released his hold on him. Finally, Mason walked away from him, and Jason relaxed. He was starting to detest Mason, which was a shame since Mason was his link to his childhood and the only one who could tell him all about it. Now all the questions he'd consider asking his brother vanished. Even if he asked Mason the questions, he had no way of knowing if his brother would tell him the truth.

He glanced down at the glass. There might not be anything in it. For all he knew, Mason was playing cat and mouse with him, but he didn't dare take the chance. A careful scan of his surroundings showed him that he was within reaching distance of one of Mason's plants.

Lord Basemore moved his piece, causing a cheer from the gentlemen who betted on him. Since Mason was looking at the chessboard, Jason poured the contents of his glass into the plant's soil, making sure no one saw what he was doing. Having managed the task undetected, he breathed a sigh of relief and settled back into the chair to watch the rest of the game.

Chapter Nine

"You want to what?" Anna asked at breakfast the next morning, the watermelon halfway to her mouth.

"Get married again," Watkins replied before biting into his eggs.

She glanced around the room, conscious that the servants were watching them. None of them gave any indication as to what they thought of his odd statement. Forcing her gaze to his, she cleared her throat. "We should discuss this when we're alone." Despite the awkward moment, she ate the watermelon and managed to swallow it without incident.

"Oh."

Startled by the disappointment in his voice, she turned her gaze back to his. Perhaps a change in topic might ease things. "Do you feel like going for a horse ride today?"

He shook his head. "No."

"But don't you want to learn? Riding a horse is something gentlemen often do."

"Maybe some gentlemen do it."

Curious by his hesitation, she pressed, "But not you?"

He ate another forkful of eggs and shrugged. "Is it a requirement that all gentlemen ride them?"

Gripping the fork in her hand, she struggled for the best response she could come up with. He was taking the place of a gentleman who went horseback riding almost every day. The fact that he didn't seem to care for it marked yet another difference between him and her husband, and she didn't know how much she could keep expecting people to believe he was the same person she and Appleton buried. Surely, even if a gentleman lost his memory, he should maintain most of the same interests he had before.

After careful consideration, she ventured, "I'll tell you what. I'll discuss the matter of a," she glanced at the servants and lowered her voice, "a wedding while we ride horses."

He frowned, not seeming happy with the bargain but nodding. "All right."

Relieved, she offered him a tentative smile. There. That was simple enough. The only reason Watkins didn't like the idea of riding a horse was because he hadn't done it. Or, if he had done it in the past, he didn't remember how much he enjoyed it. Surely, he enjoyed it. All gentlemen enjoyed riding horses.

When breakfast was over, she went to her bedchamber and allowed her lady's maid to change her outfit.

"Your Grace, you've lost some weight since you last went riding," she said. "I'll have the seamstress make the necessary adjustments so your next ride will be more comfortable."

Though Anna had no intention of riding again unless she had to, she nodded. She didn't care for the activity herself, but her love went to music where she immersed herself in daydreams the songs provoked as she played the piano. On occasion, she'd compose a short piece and play it, but more often than not, she was content to enjoy the melodies composers far greater than she had created.

Once her lady's maid pulled her hair back and secured them with pins, she thanked her and left the room. On her way down the hall, she passed Watkins' bedchamber and jerked when the door opened. She noted the way her husband's riding clothes fit perfectly on him, and for a moment, it truly seemed as if her husband had come back to life. The blood drained from her face.

In an effort to cover up her reaction, she let out a nervous laugh and placed her hand over her pounding heart. "I didn't expect you to open the door as I was passing by," she quickly said, hoping he wouldn't suspect more than that.

"This doesn't feel right," he replied, glancing at his riding outfit. "I can't explain it, but the clothes feel too restrictive."

"Do they? They don't look tight on you."

"That's not what I meant. I..." He shrugged. "I'm not sure how to explain it. It seems too formal."

His comment made her wonder—for the first time—what his life had been like before he lost his memory. She knew he didn't have a title, and to be honest, she didn't even think he was part of the middle class.

"The sooner we do this, the sooner we can discuss a wedding," he said but stopped before he took his first step toward the stairs. "That is, unless you'd rather discuss it over a cup of tea or a relaxing walk?"

Ignoring the hopeful grin on his face, she headed for the staircase. As she assumed, he followed her. It was yet another small difference between him and the gentleman she'd buried. Watkins would compromise with her. He would listen to her and take her thoughts into consideration. He wouldn't force his will upon her or punish her for disagreeing with him.

She slowed her steps and waited for him so they could finish going down the stairs together. "You don't need to be so nervous about riding a horse. It's easy."

"If you say so..."

She glanced at him to see if he'd continue the thought, but he didn't. Sure that he'd feel better once he was on the horse, she led him out to the stable. Once the stable master and stableboy turned to them, she told them to get their horses ready and quietly waited next to Watkins as they performed the task.

Watkins shifted from one foot to the other, and it took

her a few seconds to realize that he dreaded riding the horse. She knew he'd be anxious, but she had no idea he'd be scared. She studied his profile, noting the tightening of his brow and the way he swallowed the lump in his throat. Her gaze lowered, and she saw him clench and unclench the gloves in his hands. Looking back at the stable master, she watched as he and the stableboy finished saddling the horses.

As the stable master and stableboy led the horses to them, she whispered, "It'll be all right," but Watkins didn't bother to acknowledge he heard her.

The stableboy helped her onto her horse, and as soon as she settled into the sidesaddle, she checked on Watkins' progress. She frowned. Watkins no longer looked scared. Now he looked terrified.

"I can help you onto the horse, Your Grace," the stable master told him.

Watkins finally glanced in her direction, and her heart went out to him. Never did anyone try so hard to please her. She sighed. Perhaps today wasn't the time to force him into riding his horse. She cleared her throat to get the stable master's attention. The stable master turned his head in her direction, and the horse took a step toward Watkins, neighing as it did so. To her surprise, Watkins cried out and stumbled back. He proceeded to lose his footing and fell on the stable floor.

The stable master and stableboy hurried to help him up. "Your Grace," the stable master said as he brought him to his feet, "are you all right?"

Anna quickly got down from her horse and went over to them. "His Grace must not be feeling well today." She handed the stableboy the reins to her horse and turned to Watkins. Removing her gloves, she touched his face, and though she already knew it would be cool, she said, "Thank goodness. No fever. I feared he might be getting ill again. I suppose we ought to take it easy. Maybe we'll go for a ride another day."

Watkins glanced from the horse to her, his breathing faster than normal and sweat covering his brow. Thankfully, the stable master and stableboy were already unsaddling the horses, so they were distracted. She slipped her arm around Watkins' and led him out of the stable, eager to get him away from prying eyes. Never in all the times she'd known her husband did he show any kind of fear. God willing, the servants wouldn't think it strange that Watkins could be easily startled by something as simple as a horse.

Once they were down the path leading to the fountain, she relaxed. "What did the horse do that spooked you?"

"I-I don't know," Watkins muttered, not looking at her.

She struggled for something suitable to ask, something that might give her insight into why a horse should scare him. It had to be something to do with his past. "What were you thinking when you saw the horse coming toward you?"

"I didn't think anything. I just wanted to get out of its way."

"Out of its way?" That didn't make any sense since the horse hadn't been threatening him.

"I can't explain it. I just knew it wasn't safe."

She considered his words and wondered if he fell off a horse while going through the forest, but that didn't make sense since he'd suffered injuries that only another human being could inflict on him. No. Whatever it was about the horse that scared him had nothing to do with the incident that led to him ending up in the forest.

They reached the bench by the fountain and sat down. At least his breathing had returned to normal and his face wasn't pale. Getting away from the horse was a good thing in that regard, but it did little good when she thought of how difficult it'd be to explain why her husband no longer loved horses. Had her husband fallen off a horse, her task would be much easier.

She stared at the fountain for a long moment before asking, "Would you be willing to walk the horse?"

"Walk the horse?"

"Just hold onto the reins and lead it around. You don't have to ride it."

"You want me to do this today?"

"No." She understood by the way he squeaked the question that he was in no shape to do it today. "I was thinking in a week. In the meantime, we can make several trips out to the stable, and you can get to know your horse."

He fidgeted uneasily on the bench. "I'd rather not. I have no desire to know any horse."

Her heart plummeted. Short of forcing him out to the stable against his will, she had no idea how she was going to convince him to get over his fear of horses.

He turned to her and smiled. "This is a bad way to start talk of our wedding, isn't it?"

Refusing to meet his gaze, she shook her head. "It's unnecessary. We're already married. Everyone was there. Your being sick changes none of it." The lie was a bitter pill to swallow, but she had to say it. Under no circumstance could she admit the truth.

"Maybe I was there, but I don't remember it."

She looked away from him so he wouldn't pick up on her wince. It was getting harder and harder to hide her feelings around him. And that terrified her because she knew what it meant. God help her but she wasn't as strong as she wanted to be.

He sighed. "Why do you continue to pull away from me? If we are husband and wife, aren't we supposed to become closer?"

She shook her head and turned to face him, silently pleading with him to understand, even when she knew deep down, he couldn't. Her only hope was that he'd relent. "It's not that easy."

"Isn't it?"

"No. You yourself should understand that. You couldn't get on a horse today, but you have no idea why. So can't you accept the fact that I can't marry you again?"

The first emotion to flicker across his face was hurt. The second was anger. She held her breath and waited for him to respond. The cold hand of fear wrapped its way through her body as she recalled the times her husband had looked at her in anger…and what happened to her afterwards.

"I don't understand why I need to walk a horse around so I can eventually ride it while you don't have to at least explain to me why you refuse to marry me again," he said.

She waited for more, to see if he'd lift his hand against her, but he didn't. Instead, he let out a frustrated sigh and rubbed his eyes. Relieved, she released her breath.

"I really want to do this," he softly told her. "I'm willing to overcome my fear of horses for you. Why can't you oblige me and let me remember our wedding?"

"It isn't done," she argued, though her voice was weak as a part of her relented.

"So just because other people don't do it, does it mean we can't?"

"What you're asking is more than a simple afternoon event. Weddings require time to prepare and bans to read. People must be notified, a breakfast prepared, outfits tailored. It's a lot of work, and I'd have to explain to everyone what happened to you. Then there will be endless questions to answer because they'll want to know all the details. After everything that's happened over the past couple of months, I don't have the strength to go through all of that."

With a reluctant sigh, he relented. "I suppose it doesn't matter. Not really. As you said, we're already married."

Shoving aside the sting of guilt that crept over her, she reminded herself she was doing it for him. If Lord Mason was asking questions, then others would, too, and she could only do so much to protect him from people who might know the difference between him and her husband. "It's for the best," she finally said, wondering if he'd agree or not.

He nodded but didn't respond. Not knowing what else to do, she sat by him in silence and watched the water as it fell from the top of the fountain.

Chapter Ten

Two weeks later, Anna glanced up from her piano when she heard someone enter the drawing room. She assumed it was Appleton, but to her surprise, it was Watkins. He went over to the settee and looked expectantly at her. Her fingers paused on the keys.

He smiled and motioned for her to continue. "I enjoy listening to you play."

"You do?"

Giving her an annoyingly charming grin she still hadn't gotten used to, he nodded. "You can be assured I meant every word I said." Then he leaned back and placed his hands behind his head, never once taking his eyes off her.

Her face warmed under those intense green eyes of his. So much like her husband and yet so different. With her husband, those eyes made her shiver in dread. With him, it made her shiver in delight. Forcing the observation aside, she resumed her playing. If he wanted to come in here and listen to her play, the least she could do was oblige him.

But the matter was easier said than done, for her fingers kept slipping on the keys. After the fifth time she missed a note, she gave up and closed the songbook.

"Why did you stop?" he asked, straightening in his seat.

She offered a nonchalant shrug. "I was done with the song."

There was no way she'd tell him the truth, that he unnerved her and that whenever he was around, all she could think of was how wonderful he was. Yes, he was attractive, too, just as her husband had been, but it was his sweet temperament that called to her, insisting she throw caution to the wind and fall in love with him.

She cleared her throat. "Perhaps I'll go for a walk."

With a disappointed sigh, he asked, "Must you? I was enjoying what you played."

It was on the tip of her tongue to say that because of her mistakes, there was no way he could have enjoyed the melody, but then she realized he had enjoyed it because she played it. She could have hit every wrong key, and he would have liked it. "You're much too kind," she finally told him.

"I don't see how being honest is being kind, but if you say so…" She stood, so he quickly added, "I meant what I said. I'd like to hear you play. You spend so much time at that piano, but I only get to hear snippets of your music. Would you grant me the privilege of at least two more songs? Then if you still wish, we can go for a walk. I'll even take the horse along to get used to it."

She sat back down. "You strike a hard bargain, Your Grace."

"I didn't think you'd continue playing any other way."

He was right, but she chose not to admit it. Instead, she opened the book. "Do you prefer it to be light or dark?"

"I prefer music."

It took her a moment to pick up on his joke, and when she did, she shot him an amused grin. "You know what I meant."

He chuckled. "Play something cheerful and romantic."

Arching an eyebrow, she said, "I didn't think gentlemen preferred romantic."

"Of course, we do, especially in the presence of a beautiful lady."

"You speak like a rake, Your Grace."

Without waiting for his reply, she turned her attention to the book and picked out a melody he'd probably enjoy. Fortunately, it was also something easy to play, which would mean fewer mistakes.

Or at least that was the theory. As she played, she was acutely aware that he was watching her. At one point, she dared a peek in his direction and saw that he was smiling at her. But it was more than a smile. It was the way he smiled, as if he saw everything lovely and perfect in a lady when he looked at her. This shouldn't have caused her greater unease, but it did and the resulting jumbled mess she played made her wish she had picked something short. This song was much too long. She grimaced her way through the rest of it and was relieved when it finally came to an end.

She breathed a sigh of relief and closed the book. If she had to go through that horror again, she might give up on playing anything for the rest of her life. She stood and, pretending she hadn't noticed the way she butchered the song, said, "I think we should walk without the horse this time."

He rose to his feet. "That was very well done. I hope you'll let me listen to you play again in the future."

She settled for saying, "Maybe," and left it at that. Who knew? Maybe twenty or thirty years from now, she could play for him without botching up the whole thing. "I'll need to change into more suitable shoes. I'll be back soon." Before he could talk her into another song, she hurried out of the room.

***

By the time Anna showed up at the door of the drawing room, Jason was tapping the keys of the piano. He smiled when he saw her. She was a vision of loveliness, just the kind of thing that made a gentleman's blood come to a boil. His initial thought was to chastise himself for thinking of her in such a way, but she was his wife. He had every right to think of her in sensual terms. They'd shared a bed together in the past. It was a shame he didn't remember it.

But he reasoned that they'd be sharing a bed again. Maybe not right away but soon enough, or at least that's what he hoped. Whatever he'd done to make her unhappy, he hoped that he could redeem himself.

"Are you ready for the walk, Your Grace?" she asked, still waiting for him in the doorway.

Forcing his attention off her figure, he tapped a key on the piano and asked, "Did I ever play the piano?"

"No."

"Why not? It looks like fun."

Her lips curled up into a smile and she entered the room. "I enjoy it immensely."

"I gathered that much by how often you play it. You needn't be so worried about playing in front of me. I love to watch you play." And *watch* was the keyword. He much preferred to look at her while she played instead of standing in the hallway and listen to her. "In addition to you and Appleton teaching me how to read, would you like to teach me how to play something?"

She clasped her hands in front of her. "I don't know."

"Why? Did I used to hate the piano?"

"No, it's not that."

Noting the hesitant tone in her voice, he pressed, "Am I an undesirable pupil when it comes to reading and writing?"

"No. You've been an excellent one."

"So why won't you explain what these silly looking things are?" He held up one of the songbooks and pointed to the bars with different dots on them. "The only thing I recognize is the words at the top of the page."

"That's the title."

"Oh. Good." He set the book in front of him. "Now that we've established that, how do I play the song?" He patted the spot on the bench next to him. "You lead; I'll follow."

She let out a sigh, and he couldn't tell if it was from frustration or because she detected his ploy to get close to her. Either way, it didn't matter since she sat next to him. He noticed she left enough space between them so they weren't touching, but he quickly corrected that oversight and closed the gap between them.

"Watkins," she said, a hint of warning in her voice.

In an effort to distract her, he tapped a black key. "What do the black ones do?"

"Those are for flat or sharp notes."

"What do flat and sharp notes do?"

"They enhance the music when they're played at the right time."

"Oh well, that's good." He tapped a white key. "So these white ones don't enhance the music?"

She giggled. "They do. It really depends on the melody and how all the notes go together." She picked up another book and placed it in front of him. "If you want to start playing the piano, you need to start with the basics. These notes on the page form a C-major scale: C, D, E, F, G, A, B."

"It almost sounds like the order of the alphabet."

"Well, it is in a way, but the note you start with depends on what type of scale you're using." Before he could ask another question about scales, she motioned to the keys. "This is where the C-major scale begins. As you go up the scale, you can think of the alphabet. Remember that when you get to 'G', you go back to 'A'. Here's how you play a C-major scale."

He watched as she played each key. "You're good at this."

"It's not hard to play a scale."

"Then I should try it." He followed the path her fingers had gone up the piano and let his hand brush hers since her hand was still resting on the keys. "How was that?"

Her face grew pink as she pulled her hand away. Clearing her throat, she replied, "You did very well, but next time you need to also look at the sheet music in front of you so you can remember which note goes with which key."

"Where are the sharp and flat notes?"

"That's not covered in this lesson. What you need to do is get familiar with the notes."

"Oh." He glanced at the sheet music and the keys. "Just how long does that take?"

She shrugged. "It depends on how much time you put into it. The more you practice, the faster you'll pick things up."

He frowned.

"What's wrong?" she asked, peering up at him.

"I thought I was going to play a song today. Is that not going to happen?"

She chuckled and shook her head. "I'm afraid not. You need to learn the basics before you can play one of the songs."

"But you make it look so easy."

"I've been doing this for twenty years. I learned the basics when I was a child."

"And you play something every day," he thoughtfully stated. "It'll take me twenty years to play what you do today?"

"Not quite. I've been playing those songs for years. I enjoy them more than others, so I play them often."

He played the scale, and though he was looking at the music sheet in front of him, he was paying more attention to how close her hand was to his. Though she wasn't playing anything, her hand remained on the keys, something he guessed was as natural to her as breathing. "How long did it take until you learned to play one of your favorite songs?"

"I don't remember. I think I was twelve or thirteen when I played one."

He ended the scale and brushed his hand against hers. She didn't pull away from him, but he noticed the way she slightly stiffened against him. He quickly went down the scale, and as he suspected, she relaxed. It was a shame. She was so soft and kind. He'd have to have a heart of stone to not love her. If only he knew what he could do to break through her wall.

"I think that's enough practice for today," she said and stood up from the bench.

"But I only did the C-major scale."

She didn't look in his direction but focused on closing the songbooks. "We can practice another time if you wish. I'd rather go for a walk if you don't mind."

"No, I don't mind," he softly replied and stood up. "I'm willing to walk my horse."

She turned her gaze to his. "I only played one song for you. You aren't under any obligation to do that."

Taking her by the elbow, he led her out of the drawing room. Once they put on their cloaks, they left the manor, and he said, "I'm ready to try it." And considering how important it seemed to her that he learn to be comfortable with a horse, he wanted to show her he was making an effort.

"In that case, I should've worn my riding outfit," she said.

"You'll be fine," he assured her and gave her elbow a reassuring squeeze. "You're not riding the horse. You're just helping me walk it."

"I would like to be with you in case you need assistance."

"You do care about me," he teased.

Though she sighed, a smile formed on her lips. "Watkins, I didn't say no about marrying you because I don't care about you. You understand that, don't you?"

"I know. You just don't feel it's necessary since we're already married." Since she didn't reply, he added, "I understand,

Anna. Please don't think I'm complaining because I'm not. I was joking. I know you care about me. You wouldn't have helped me after I got ill if you didn't care."

Though she nodded, he wondered if he said something that upset her. She never voiced a complaint about anything he'd done in their past, and he understood she had cause to be wary of him. It seemed to be a fine line to tread. At times, he sensed they were drawing closer and at other times, like now, he sensed she was pulling away from him. He just wished he understood why. If he did, he might be able to do something to rectify things.

When they reached the stable, his attention turned from her to the horses, specifically his horse which was in its stall. He didn't realize his grip had tightened on her elbow until she winced. "I'm sorry," he quickly apologized and put his hand to his side.

"It's all right." She offered him an understanding smile before telling the stable master to get his horse ready for a walk.

As the stable master hurried to perform the task, she glanced at him and whispered, "Are you sure?"

Jason swallowed the lump in his throat. "It's just a walk. I won't get on it. I'll be fine."

Even as he said the words, his heart rate picked up and his breathing grew shallower. He wiped the sweat from his forehead and wondered why he should have such an intense reaction from being near a horse. It didn't make any sense. If he had to have this reaction, it should have been from the stairs. After all, he'd fallen down those. He hadn't suffered an injury from a horse.

"Let's wait outside," Anna whispered and led him out of the stable. "There's no reason to stay in there when the weather is nice enough to enjoy."

He took a deep breath of the crisp air to settle his nerves. "I can't explain it. I don't know why horses frighten me as much as they do."

"I don't know either."

He wished she did. Without his memory, there was no way he could figure out what incident caused him to be this way. The stable master arrived with the horse, and he took a step away from it.

"I'll take the reins," Anna told him and accepted them from the stable master. "We can walk down that path." She motioned to the trees along the property. "We haven't been down there yet."

Forcing his eyes off the horse, Jason joined her as she headed for the trees. "It might be a nice change of pace." Especially since all the fountain did was remind him that she wasn't interested in marrying him again.

She walked beside him, and it didn't go unnoticed that she stood between him and the horse, something he was grateful for since it lessened his anxiety. He looked at the way she held the reins and made a mental note to do the same thing when it was his turn.

"He's an easy horse," she said. "He's been well-trained."

"I know. I can tell that." He studied the horse which showed no signs of aggression.

"I'm proud of you."

Surprised, he turned his gaze to her. "Why?"

"You're afraid of the horse, and yet you're pushing through your fears. I admire that about you."

"Well, when you've been on the brink of death, I suppose there's not much to stop you from doing anything."

Further surprising him, she reached for his hand and held it. "I'm glad you lived. Even if it may not seem like it, I'm thankful you're here."

Her confession thrilled him to no end, and despite his better judgment, he encouraged her to stop walking so he could face her. "That's a wonderful thing to say."

Lowering her gaze, she softly replied, "I only said it because it's the truth."

"Which is why I appreciate it all the more."

He brushed her cheek with his free hand, and when she looked up at him, he tilted her head back and kissed her. It wasn't something he had planned to do when he agreed to walk with her, but the moment seemed right. She was opening up to him, revealing a part of herself he hadn't seen before—at least not that he could remember, and all he wanted to do was show her how much she meant to him. Even if he couldn't say the words, he could still reveal his feelings.

After a moment's hesitation, she responded to him. Her lips were soft and warm, and he wanted nothing more than to stay like this forever. She was wonderful. Absolutely and completely wonderful. But too soon, she pulled away from him and brushed a tear from her cheek.

"Anna?" he asked, wondering why a kiss should make her cry.

She shook her head and turned from him. "I can't. It's not right."

"What do you mean it's not right?" he pressed. She led the horse further down the path, so he hurried after her. "I don't understand. We're married. What could be wrong with us sharing a kiss?"

"I can't explain it."

"You can't explain it?"

She stopped walking and faced him, her eyes begging him to understand something she couldn't tell him. "You're better off not knowing. I'm sorry."

He stared at her for a long moment, wondering if he should press the issue or let it go. The only reason he relented was because he was afraid if he didn't, her wall would go right back up, which was the last thing he wanted after the progress they made that afternoon. "All right," he softly replied. "I'll take the reins now."

She glanced at the reins and then at him. "Watkins, I…" She released her breath. "Why do you have to be so nice?"

Of all the things she could have said, he didn't expect that. Laughing, he took the reins from her, and despite his apprehension, he stepped around her and stood next to the horse. "I don't see why being nice should be a problem."

Giving a slight grin, she replied, "It's not. It's just…" She shook her head and rubbed her forehead.

"You're not used to it," he filled in for her, his laughter dying down. "I'm sorry about that." Before she could respond, he took her by the arm with his free hand. "All I have to do is walk this horse by pulling the reins, correct?"

"Yes, that's all there is to it."

"Then there should be nothing to worry about." Hoping he didn't give away his fear of the animal, he stepped forward, and the horse followed. Realizing his grip had tightened on her arm, he apologized and loosened his hold.

"This might be more appropriate." She brought his hand to hers and clasped it. "We'll take it slow. There's no need to rush things."

He nodded, and together, they headed back to the stable.

Chapter Eleven

It was the middle of February and Anna decided she'd play a melody she hadn't played for a couple weeks. It was her favorite one, but as she played it on this particular day, it didn't soothe her troubled mind as it had in the past. Nothing she tried eased the conflicting emotions she felt at knowing Watkins was hurt, and worse, that she was the cause of it.

Even now, he was outside walking the horse. It bothered him to do it. She saw him from the window of the drawing room before she sat down to play music. He was keeping the horse at a good distance, and when the horse neared him, he jerked a bit and reestablished the distance that made him the least uncomfortable. She had offered to go with him as she had the other day, but he insisted on doing it himself.

She wondered if his desire to do it alone had more to do with being away from her than from showing the others that he didn't need his wife holding his hand. She really couldn't feel more awful if she tried. Here he was, doing what she wanted despite his fears, and she was refusing to marry him.

Though he hadn't said more about it after their talk at the fountain, she noticed he wasn't as cheerful as he used to be. Oh, he was pleasant and sweet, but some of the enthusiasm she'd come to expect from him was gone. She had no idea two gentlemen who looked exactly alike could be so different. In some ways, it would have been easier if Jason wasn't so nice. She gritted her teeth and stopped playing the melody. No. He wasn't Jason. He was Watkins. She must not think of him by his Christian name.

She closed her eyes and picked up from where she left off. She managed to finally slip into the world where only her imagination could take her. The swell of the music embraced her soul, and she gave herself to the experience of feeling. No more thinking. No more wondering if she was right or wrong.

For the moment, she was lost in her solitary world where she sat in a gazebo with nothing but fog surrounding her. Snow fell around her but the gazebo remained untouched, and in her mind, there was no bitter chill. There was just the peace of being alone in a place where no one could find her. But then someone emerged through her protective barrier, and it took her a moment to realize who it was as the fog dissipated around him. Jason.

Gritting her teeth, she banged the keys in frustration. No. He wasn't Jason! He was Watkins.

"Your Grace?"

Startled, her eyes flew open and she saw a concerned Appleton standing next to an amused Lord Mason. Biting back a groan, she turned to Appleton. "Yes?"

"Lord Mason is here to see His Grace," he replied.

As if she didn't have a care in the world, she resumed playing the melody. "Well, he can't. His Grace is out with his horse."

"I haven't known you to be so dismissive of me," Lord Mason spoke, a slight warning in his voice.

"My husband is no longer ill, Lord Mason," she replied with more bravado than she felt. "While I appreciate the concern you've shown him during that time, you may go back to seeing him a couple times a year."

She realized the more she talked, the harder her fingers hit the keys, but something about Lord Mason's visit struck her the wrong way. Not that his visits were ever welcome, but today, it seemed unnecessary. Why couldn't the scoundrel leave them alone?

"In light of my brother's lack of memory, I thought I'd do him a favor and tell him about his past. You weren't there when he was growing up. It's to his benefit he knows everything, don't you agree?"

Her fingers paused on the keys and forced her gaze in his direction. "I suppose you'll insist on it no matter what I say."

Appleton's eyebrows furrowed, and she knew what he was thinking. Never, in all the time that insufferable oaf of a husband had been alive had she dared to talk to Lord Mason this way, but she was tired. Tired of who she used to be. Tired of trying to maintain an appearance of her old life. Tired of Lord Mason scanning her up and down as if she were nothing better than a prostitute who was there to service him. Tired of tolerating the harsh way Lord Mason and her husband had treated her. She wanted nothing more than to be free. Free to be who she truly was and free to love who she wanted to. She wanted to love Jason. She closed her eyes and took a deep breath. No. It was Watkins.

"Is Her Grace feeling well?" Lord Mason asked Appleton.

"She's fine, my lord," Appleton replied, placing his arm around her shoulders and leading her to the settee. "It's something common to ladies. A little rest and some tea, and she'll be back to her old self."

Lord Mason's eyebrows rose in interest. "Something common to ladies? Is this good news for my brother?"

Her head shot up, and she glanced at Appleton who shrugged. "It's not that. I'm not expecting a child. I'd explain, but the matter is of a private nature."

Lord Mason nodded and bowed. "My apologies, Your Grace. I had hoped it was good news."

She highly doubted he'd be happy if she were expecting a

child since it would mean he'd never secure her husband's title, but she gave a polite smile as if she believed him. Let him think her time of month was upon her. It excused a lot of things, especially her foul mood. She sighed. Once, just once, she'd love to wipe that satisfied smirk off his face. Often, she imagined giving him a good slap. She didn't think he could retaliate since Jason…since Watkins was alive.

"I'll take my leave," Lord Mason began, "but if I happen to see my dear brother, I'll have to greet him. It's only proper."

She let out a weary sigh as Appleton showed him out. Why wasn't he leaving her and Watkins alone? He was never that interested in his brother. Sure, they attended each other's dinner parties and spent some time together when they were in London, but Lord Mason hadn't made it a point to visit on a regular basis. It seemed that ever since she and her husband returned from London because her husband took ill that his brother paid frequent visits. At first, she assumed it was because he wished to know if he'd be the next duke, but now—with Watkins' good health—she suspected another motive.

Standing from the settee, she walked over to the window and searched the grounds. She didn't see Watkins anywhere, but that didn't mean Lord Mason wouldn't see him and insist on talking to him. She took a deep breath and released it. At some point, she had to trust that Watkins could hold his own against the likes of Lord Mason.

***

As soon as Jason saw his brother, he halted in his steps along the grounds. The horse he was leading brushed his shoulder with its nose, causing him to jerk away from it. He tightened his grip on the reins and wondered for the millionth time why the beast should give him such unease. The horse wasn't difficult. It followed his commands without a fuss. But there was something frightening about it. And it wasn't just this horse. All the horses made that cold shiver of dread crawl up his spine. The only thing that walking the horse around seemed to do was enable him to be near it without dropping the reins and running for his life.

He took a deep breath to steady his nerves as Mason approached, riding his horse as if he didn't have a care in the world. How Jason envied him that level of comfort on the animal. But now wasn't the time for petty jealousies. It wouldn't do well to show any sign of weakness in front of him. Jason didn't have to remember him to understand he was a dangerous gentleman. In an effort to appear brave, he headed in Mason's direction, glad the horse willingly changed their course.

"Ah, it's a fine day for a ride, isn't it?" Mason called out as soon as he was within hearing distance.

Jason waited until he slowed to a trot before he spoke. "I thought I'd take a break from riding and walk for a while."

"Walk? You?" Mason threw his head back and laughed. "Since when do you walk?"

"Since I had a near miss with death. Walking is good exercise."

Mason pulled the reins so that the horse stopped. "So is bedding a lady who likes it rough and running before her husband shows up to her bedchamber, but I only do that in moderation."

Jason was too shocked by his brother's bluntness to respond right away, and when he did, he laughed. "You're telling a joke."

"If you say so." He shrugged and examined his gloves. "These were a gift. Like them?"

Glad for the change in topic, Jason nodded. "They're nice."

"They're from British India. It's fine craftsmanship like this that makes me glad I went there. It's a shame you missed such a marvelous opportunity, but perhaps we'll get a chance to go together in the future."

"Perhaps," Jason said, though he had no intention of it.

"I didn't come out here to talk of exercise or gloves. I thought you might find it profitable to learn about your past, and while your wife can fill you in on some parts of it, I can tell you everything. Why don't you get on that fine animal, and we'll go for a ride?"

Struggling not to give away his apprehension, he said, "I need to take him back to the stable." He turned to lead the horse toward the stable, hoping that would be the end of this part of the discussion.

Unfortunately, Mason urged his horse forward so he could keep pace with Jason. "You can ride the horse back to the stable."

"I know. I just don't want to. I want to walk."

"You are nothing like the gentleman you once were. The Jason I knew would never degrade himself by walking a horse."

Ignoring the taunting from his brother, Jason decided he wouldn't give him the satisfaction of making him get on the horse. If he did, then his brother would know he could twist things around so he did his bidding.

"Very well," Mason said, sounding bored. "I'll go at a very slow pace to keep up with you."

Jason refused to look in his brother's direction. He decided to slip around the other side of his horse so he wouldn't be trapped between both horses. As it was, the one he owned was hard enough to manage without panicking. Without bothering to glance in Mason's direction, he asked, "You wanted to tell me about my past?"

"I figured it'd be the right thing to do, given I'm your brother and all."

"All right." Jason doubted he could stop him from telling him about his past if that's what he wanted to do, so the sooner he went along with it, the sooner Mason would leave. "Where do you want to start?"

"Now this is something I do remember about you. You were always one to get right to the point."

Surprised since nothing else he did seemed to be the same as how he'd once done things, he peered around his horse to see the amused look on Mason's face. "I was?"

"Yes. With you, it was either say it or stop wasting your time."

Jason nodded. He'd have to take Mason's word for it, but he had a feeling that given Mason's tendency to draw things out, he most likely lost patience with him long ago.

"You needn't worry. I'll get on with it," Mason said, not disturbed by the silence on Jason's end. "Has Anna told you when you were born and where?"

"September 2, 1784, right here at Camden."

"Yes. I hear that our parents were very protective of you and refused to let anyone—not even our relatives—see you until a week after you were born. Such was not the case when I was born three years later. They invited everyone to see me almost as soon as I took my first breath, and it's reported that you worshipped me immediately."

Jason resisted the urge to roll his eyes at his brother's joke.

"Apparently, you lost your sense of humor when you lost your memory." Mason shrugged. "Mother had another child, a girl, but she was stillborn. After that, she bore Father no more children. You and I grew up side by side, making friends at the boarding house. We met the gentlemen who attended my dinner party there."

"All of them?"

"Yes. Some sooner than others, and we ended up attending Eton together."

"What were my interests?"

"You loved riding horses," Mason pointedly stated.

He sighed. Granted that was the case, and Anna had already made that clear. He didn't know why he had such an aversion to them now, and when he asked Anna about it, she couldn't give him an answer. Maybe Mason would. "Did I fall off a horse?"

"No. You were always good on one."

Jason sighed in disappointment. So much for finding out why horses bothered him as much as they did.

"The good news is that you took a fall down the staircase and survived," Mason commented. "Considering your injuries and how long that staircase is, I'm surprised it didn't kill you."

Frowning, he peered around the horse again and noticed the dark expression on Mason's face. Mason glanced his way, and he quickly turned his attention back to the stable, which was close up ahead. The sooner he could get to the stable, the better.

"But you asked about your interests, so I'll tell you," Mason continued, his tone now pleasant. "Besides horses, you love the theater, music, dancing, chess, gambling, drinking, White's… You like things other gentlemen enjoy. What we need to do is go through the desk in your bedchamber. You keep important papers there."

Jason recalled the papers but said, "We can do that another day." They reached the stable and he handed the reins to the stable master, relieved the ordeal with the horse and Mason were finally over, at least for now. "I must go back to the house."

"Oh, then I should join you. Perhaps we can share a glass of brandy? You never turn down a glass of brandy."

He removed his riding gloves. "Maybe next time. I think I'll rest for a while."

"Rest? After a walk?"

"It was a long walk." And there was more truth to that than Mason would understand. He didn't think the ordeal with the horse would ever end. "It was a pleasure to see you again." He gave the obligatory bow and waited for Mason to return the farewell with a nod before he headed for the manor.

Chapter Twelve

Anna tapped the window, watching as Watkins bowed to Lord Mason and stepped away from the stable. She would have given anything to know what the two had just discussed. The distance between her and the two gentlemen was too great for her to see their faces. If she could, their expressions might clue her in to whether their conversation had been pleasant or not.

Someone cleared his throat, so she turned from the window. Appleton set a tray of tea on the table. "Are you feeling well, Your Grace?"

"I'll be fine." She went to the settee and poured the tea into her cup. "Do you want some?"

"No, Your Grace." He waited until she took a sip of the tea before he added, "I can't help but notice you seem unhappy. Is there something about His Grace that I should know?"

Catching his meaning, she shook her head. "He's done nothing to hurt me. In fact, he's the kindest gentleman I've ever met, besides you."

"Ah, I think I understand the conflict. He's an easy person to like."

"Too easy." Her throat constricted on the confession. Up to now, she'd kept her swirling emotions from him, but now they were screaming for attention. "I don't like it."

With a chuckle, he asked, "Why not?"

"I think you know the answer to that," she whispered, afraid to speak the words.

"If it eases your mind, I've seen the way His Grace looks at you, and a person would have to be blind not to see that he cares for you very much. I dare say he might even love you."

She forced down another sip of tea, blinking back her tears. "Yes, that's what I'm afraid of."

"Why is it something you should fear?"

"Because it wasn't supposed to be like this. He was supposed to fill a role, nothing more."

Sighing, he sat across from her and turned his tender eyes her way. "You were miserable with your husband. There was a time when you wanted so desperately to find a way out of the marriage that you tried to take your own life."

She settled the cup in her lap, her gaze settling on the scars at her wrists, forever a reminder of the lowest point in her life.

"Don't you owe it to yourself to find what little happiness life has to offer?" Appleton softly asked. "There's so much sorrow in the world, why turn your back on the chance to experience joy?"

A tear slid down her cheek, but she didn't brush it away. "I don't deserve him. I've been lying to him all this time. He wants to get married so he can have the memory of our wedding, but it'd be another lie because we wouldn't be getting married again."

"No, you wouldn't be getting married again. You'd be marrying him for the first time, but isn't that in your best interest? Wouldn't it set your mind at ease to know he's really your husband? Then that would be one lie you wouldn't have to live with anymore."

She shook her head and took another sip of the tea. "I don't feel like reading the Banns and waiting for someone to object before the priest would marry us, if he'd even agree to do it. I don't think Lord Mason will sit by and let the marriage happen. I think he'd suspect something was wrong."

"You don't have to make it a formal event."

"You think I should consider a special license?"

"Or you could make a trip to Gretna Green," Appleton quietly suggested. "Then he would have a memory of the wedding. Granted, it would be a simple affair, but you will exchange vows with him. Lord Mason doesn't need to know. And it'd offer you the security of knowing you are truly married to him."

She sighed. He made several good points, but if she married Watkins, she'd be getting too close to him. Right now knowing he wasn't really her husband was the only safe thing she had to hold onto. "I can't," she whispered.

She expected him to protest, but he didn't so she finished the rest of her tea and set the cup on the tray. Footsteps crossing the threshold alerted her to Watkins' presence in the room. Eager to find out what Lord Mason told him, she rose to her feet and approached him. "Your Grace, is all well?"

Watkins' gaze went to Appleton before settling on her. "Yes. I managed fine with the horse."

That wasn't what she meant, but she didn't think it was wise to question him about Lord Mason until they were alone. "Would you like some tea? It's got a dash of peppermint in it."

"No, not right now." He glanced at Appleton again. "I think we should take a walk. I'll wait here while you change into a suitable dress."

It took her a moment to understand he was dismissing her. Her eyes widened when she realized he wanted to talk to Appleton alone. She looked at Appleton who stood by his chair, quietly waiting for their instructions. Appleton would never betray her. The secret burial of her husband would die with him. Turning back to Watkins, she nodded. "I'll return shortly." With nothing else to say, she left the room.

***

Jason waited until Anna was climbing the stairs before he softly closed the door to the drawing room. He turned his attention to Appleton and crossed the room until he was standing in front of the butler. "There is something I've been meaning to ask you, and I require you to be frank with me, even if you know I won't like the answer."

Appleton's expression remained impassive, giving no indication if Jason's solemn tone worried him or not. "What is it, Your Grace?"

"I notice that you and my wife are close, closer than it seems a butler and Her Grace should be."

Appleton's eyes lit up with understanding. "Oh, you mean to inquire about my relationship with her?"

He nodded.

"You have no need to worry, Your Grace. I think of her as a daughter, nothing more."

Relieved, he relaxed. "May I ask how such a relationship came to be?"

"When you married Her Grace, things were different from the way they are now. There were times when it was best if she wasn't alone with you. I learned to always be nearby in case she needed help."

"In case she needed help. You mean, in case she needed *your* help?"

"I'd rather not go into details about the past. It's not pertinent to how things are with you and her today."

"If it's my past, I have a right to know what happened."

After a moment of silence, Appleton slowly said, "Suffice it to say, alcohol gave you a terrible temper, and if you weren't happy, you had a tendency to take it out on her."

The hairs on the back of his neck stood on end. "How bad was I?" he softly asked, afraid of the answer even as he needed to know it.

"Let's just say she wouldn't be here today if I hadn't caught her late one night at the gazebo."

"Gazebo? There's no gazebo on these grounds."

"Not after I had it burned, Your Grace. It was the one place where she sought comfort. On one particular night, I was returning from the stable and thought I saw someone in the gazebo. I expected an intruder, but it was Her Grace and there was blood running down her hands."

"Blood?" Jason swallowed and squeaked out, "Did I stab her?"

"No, but she had bruises. I didn't realize it until after I carried her to the house and wrapped her wrists. She didn't angle the blade right, and that was to her advantage since it's why she didn't die that night. After that, I stayed by her side. It didn't happen again."

Jason collapsed into the nearest chair, sure he was going to be sick as it occurred to him what kind of person he'd been. No wonder Anna didn't want to talk about the past, and no wonder she didn't want to marry him again. It was a marvel that she wanted to spend any time with him at all.

"Your Grace," Appleton began, once again choosing his words carefully, "I wouldn't hesitate to leave you alone with her. You're not the same gentleman."

Head bowed, Jason didn't respond. How could he do something like that? He didn't think he had it in him to be violent that way, especially to someone as sweet as his Anna.

"Is there anything else you require?" Appleton softly asked.

He shook his head, relieved when Appleton left the room. He didn't know how he could face Anna after everything he'd just learned. He placed his face in his hands and tried to think of a way—any way at all—he could rectify the damage he'd done.

The door creaked open, and he looked up in time to see

Anna enter the room.

Without thinking, he fell to his knees in front of her and took her hands in his. "Anna, I don't know what to say. Appleton just told me the truth."

The color drained from her face. "He…he…what?"

"Will you forgive me?"

Her eyebrows furrowed. "Forgive you?"

"I am so sorry." Unable to maintain eye contact with her anymore, he lowered his head and swallowed the lump in his throat. "I was a brute, a loathsome creature. I readily admit it. If I could go back and undo the damage I've done, I'd give my life to do it. Appleton told me about the way I was, how I hit you, why you tried to end your life… I don't deserve a second chance, but if you'd grant me one, I promise I'll never be harsh with you again."

"Please stop," Anna finally said and pulled her hands out of his.

He couldn't blame her. His apology came too late. There was no way she was going to open herself to him again. He should be glad she'd even be willing to talk to him.

After she closed the door, she returned to him and leaned over him. "Stand up, Your Grace. You have nothing to be sorry about."

"Even if I don't remember, I'm still responsible for the abhorrent way I behaved."

"No, no you're not."

She wrapped her arm around his shoulders and urged him to stand, but he couldn't bring himself to face her. With a sigh, she knelt by him and took his face in her hands, forcing him to look at her. His eyes teared up and he shook his head. Her grip on his face tightened.

"Jason, I order you to look at me." She released her breath and closed her eyes for a few seconds before opening them. "I can't explain everything. You'll just have to take my word for it, but here goes… You're not the same person I married. What that person did is not your burden to bear. You have nothing to be sorry for. You are a gentle, kind, and caring gentleman. I don't want to think about the past. I want to embrace the future. For the first time in my life, I can do that, and I don't want what happened back then to taint what I have now. Can you do that for me? Can you forget what Appleton told you?"

"That seems to be a question more appropriate for you to answer given the way you suffered."

"Yes, I can forget. I have forgotten." Her eyes filled with tears, but she blinked them away. "When I look at you, I don't think of any of it. I only think of how much better things are now."

He cupped her face in his hands and brushed her cheeks with the pads of his thumbs, wondering what he'd done to be blessed with a lady who was so willing to forgive him. "I make you this promise: I will never do anything to hurt you again."

A tear trickled down her face, and he gently wiped it away. He leaned forward and kissed her forehead. He felt another tear fall down her cheek and lowered his head so he could kiss it away. She lowered her hands and held onto his arms. At first he thought she meant to pull him away but soon realized she had tightened her hold, a silent encouragement for him to stay close to her. And honestly, there was no other place he'd rather be. He didn't know if she brought her lips to his or if he brought his lips to hers, but his heart leapt at the intimate contact. It was so wonderful—so completely wonderful—to be with her this way. He might have taken this for granted before, but he wouldn't again.

When their kiss ended, he pulled away from her so he could look at her and smiled at the joy he detected on her face. So that's what she looked like when she was happy. Since his health improved, he'd noticed the sorrow in her eyes, but now there was no sorrow there and it gave him a feeling of elation to know they really could start over.

"I want to marry you," he whispered. "Even if it is foolish, I feel it'd be a new beginning for us. Please say yes."

She let out a light chuckle and brought her arms around his shoulders. "Yes. I want nothing more than to marry you."

His heart ready to burst, he pulled her into his embrace and kissed her again. The past was the past and could stay there. From now on, it would be the future. And he could think of nothing that could ruin it.

Chapter Thirteen

Anna's hands shook as she collected her comb and hand mirror and placed them in her valise. It was hard to focus on what she needed to pack when her heart was beating so fast she thought it might jump out of her chest. She stopped for a moment and took a deep breath to help ease her nerves. She couldn't believe she was doing something this rash. It seemed like a dream. To be sure, she pinched herself. No. She was still awake.

"Your Grace, you ought to let me pack your things," her lady's maid said as she entered the bedchamber.

"I know. It's just that I…" She blushed and took another deep breath. She didn't feel comfortable with her enough to say that she was too excited by Jason's kisses to have fetched her to pack on her behalf.

Her maid smiled. "I think I understand, and it's about time you enjoyed life, Your Grace."

Unsure of what to say, Anna changed the topic. "I'll select something to change into before I leave."

"I'll help you with it."

With a nod, Anna turned to her wardrobe to select her traveling outfit. Once she did, her maid helped her into it and styled her hair.

"I'll pack my things, Your Grace," she said when she was done. "I won't be long."

"No," Anna quickly replied. In her haste, she'd forgotten her maid would plan to prepare for the trip as well. Good heavens but her mind wasn't what it should be. Her thoughts were one big jumbled mess. Clearing her throat, she added, "His Grace and I want to make this a private affair."

"You don't need to explain to me, Your Grace, but I'll add that I think it's terribly romantic."

"Yes, it is, isn't it?"

And that made Anna's stomach tighten even more in a mixture of fear and anticipation. She wanted nothing more than to marry Jason, but in the back of her mind, she worried that someone would discover that he wasn't the real Duke of Watkins. And if he found out, what then? Would he still want to be with her? Pushing aside her worries, she pulled the cord that would notify Appleton her things were ready.

"I hope you have an enjoyable trip," her maid called out as she left the bedchamber.

By the time Anna turned from the cord, her maid was already gone. Anna went over to her vanity and checked her reflection. She couldn't recall how long it'd been since she cared about her appearance, but she wanted to please Jason so she studied her hair to make sure not a strand was out of place. Then she pinched her cheeks to give them more color.

"You have something for me to take to the carriage, Your Grace?" Appleton asked, his lips curled up into a grin.

"I take it you're happy," she replied as she turned away from the mirror.

He stepped into the room and shrugged. "I might be a slight bit relieved you're showing good judgment."

Resisting the urge to let him know that his answer amused her, she motioned to the items she planned to take with her. As he picked them up, she lowered her voice and said, "His Grace blames himself for things he never did."

Appleton sighed. "It wasn't my intention to let him know,

but when he asked why you and I are closer than a butler and the lady of the house are supposed to be, I had to explain to him that my interest in you goes no further than that of a father and daughter."

"So he knows about that night you found me in the gazebo?"

He nodded. "But I didn't tell him about your husband's mistresses or illegitimate children."

"Those things aren't unusual for a duke to have."

"No, they aren't, but I didn't wish to burden him with all of your husband's indiscretions."

"Maybe he'll find out anyway."

"Maybe, but not today."

He was right. Considering Jason's reaction to finding out as much as he had, it was best not to give him another reason to experience undeserved guilt.

"I'll take these down now," Appleton softly said and left her bedchamber.

She watched him as he left, thinking it would have been better off if Jason had never found out about that part of her past. It wasn't right he should bear the guilt of another gentleman, and yet, it was his guilt that pushed her over the edge. She'd fought her feelings for as long as she could, but knowing how deeply he wanted to protect her crumbled what was left of the wall that she'd carefully constructed around her heart. And now she would love him forever. She didn't know if it saved her or doomed her, but she knew the course was set and she'd follow it, wherever it led.

***

The new valet presented Jason with his comb, and as Jason ran it through his blond hair, a knock came at his bedchamber door.

"I'll get that, Your Grace," the valet said.

Jason nodded and turned his attention to the mirror. He couldn't stop thinking about the new start he and Anna were making. It was a huge step they were taking, and he'd always be grateful she was willing to do it.

The valet returned to him. "Is there anything else you wish to take for your trip? Appleton is ready to take your valise to the carriage."

"Just this." He handed the valet the comb and looked at the doorway where Appleton stood. No longer seeing the butler as a threat to his relationship with Anna, Jason smiled. "I'll be down soon."

As Appleton came into the room, Jason turned to the valet. "You may go."

The valet bowed and headed out. Jason waited until Appleton carried his things out of the room before he went to the small room off to the side of the bedchamber. It'd been a curious thing that Mason should mention the desk in this room. He glanced back at his empty bedchamber. If he was going to take a better look at the contents in that desk, now was a good time. Besides, if he didn't, it would be on his mind during his trip, and he'd rather be focusing on Anna than thinking about this desk and Mason's curious interest in it.

He sat down at the desk and opened the drawers, wondering what it was that he should be looking for. There were many papers, and they were neatly divided up into categories. Since he was still learning to read, most of the script looked like a jumbled mess, but he did come across a list of numbers.

Numbers were far easier for him to understand, so he took it out of a stack. The name at the very top was his father's name. He ran his finger along the top column and softly sounded out the few words written on it. Then he ran his finger along the left side and down the rows. Excited, he realized this was the list of salaries his father used to pay the servants. A careful study of the list, however, made him frown.

Two and a half months ago, he recalled going down the staircase at a slow pace, afraid if he went too fast, he'd do more harm to his body and delay a walk with Anna. He hadn't had the patience to wait for her to decide it was a good time to see him, so he was on his way to see her. As he made his way down the stairs, he listened to her play on her piano, her music blocking out the sound of his footsteps.

When he reached the bottom of the staircase, he noticed that the footman and steward were in a heated discussion further down the hall. Their heads were bowed together but their gestures indicated a difference of opinion. Something about it bothered him, and in that instant, he knew that he shouldn't let them see him. He lifted the cane and made his way down a nearby corridor so they wouldn't hear him. He gritted his teeth at the pain that pierced his side, but he was rewarded for his effort when he realized they were arguing over their wages.

Now as he studied the numbers on the sheet his father had written long ago, he understood their contention. He hadn't been paying them as much as his father had. He slipped the paper back in its proper location and went to the cord along his wall to summon the steward. Anna had explained that the steward handled the finances, so he was the right person to talk to.

As he waited for the steward, Anna opened the door adjoining their rooms. Pleased she chose the private way to come see him, he smiled. "I hope you're not having second thoughts about running off to Gretna Green with me."

Her cheeks grew pink and she shook her head. "No, Your Grace. I was ready to head downstairs and wondered if you wanted to join me."

He sighed and brought her into his arms, loving how soft she was against him. "I thought we moved beyond this 'Your Grace' thing. You should be calling me Jason."

"I can call you both," she insisted. "Your name is Jason, and your title allows me to refer to you as 'Your Grace'."

"You have an answer for everything, don't you?"

"It's the correct one, Your Grace."

Then she brought her arms around his neck and kissed him. He pulled her closer to him and deepened the kiss. Now that he'd gotten a taste of what kissing her was like, he didn't want to stop. Her lips were warm and inviting, and when her tongue brushed his, a jolt of excitement surged through him. He couldn't remember what being in bed with her was like, but he couldn't wait to explore the pleasures waiting for them.

She ended the kiss and drew away from him. "In private, I can refer to you as Jason, but in public, we have to be more formal."

Disappointed she was no longer in his arms, he replied, "I won't call you Anna in public."

"I know. I'm just explaining why I won't when others are around."

"But you just referred to me as 'Your Grace' a moment ago, and we're alone."

"But I meant it as a term of endearment."

Well, there was that. A knock came at the door, directing his attention to the steward who waited for his permission to enter. He turned to Anna. "I'll be down shortly."

She nodded and left the room.

He motioned for the steward to enter before he asked, "Did you bring the ledger?"

"I do every time you summon me, Your Grace," he replied, his voice almost hesitant.

"Good. I'd like to know what everyone's wages are." He held his hand out.

The steward handed it to him.

Jason opened it and turned to the sunlight coming through the window to get a better look at the columns and rows. It took him a couple minutes to get a firm grasp on what was happening with the finances. Turning back to the steward, he said, "It appears that my father paid you and the others more than I do."

The steward furrowed his eyebrows. "Your Grace?"

"Is that an accurate assessment?"

"Well, yes."

"When did I make such a decision?"

"Shortly after you acquired the title."

Jason ran his finger along the page in the ledger. "So that is almost seven years?"

"Yes, Your Grace."

Jason's gaze returned to the page and settled at the bottom where the balance was. He couldn't do the calculation in his head, so he went to the desk in the other room and wrote down the numbers until he came up with the proper back payment plus raises due the staff. When he returned to the steward, he handed him the ledger and the paper. "I believe I owe you and the others your back wages and the appropriate raises for your services."

His jaw dropped. "Your Grace?"

"Do you have a problem with accepting the money rightfully yours?"

"No, no I don't."

"You can see according to the household balance that I have more than enough."

"Yes."

Jason waited for the steward to continue since he opened his mouth to say something, but then he closed his mouth and took another good look at the paper in his hand. "I must be going," Jason said. "I trust you'll relay this to the servants."

The steward's shock gave way to a hearty chuckle. "Yes, Your Grace. Of course."

"Good."

Feeling much better to right yet another wrong in his past, Jason followed the steward out of his bedchamber so he could be with Anna.

Chapter Fourteen

When the inn at Gretna Green came into view, Jason turned from the carriage window and saw Anna peering out her window. "It's too late to change your mind," he told her in a playful tone. "We came all the way to Scotland." He took her hand in his and squeezed it. "You have to marry me now."

With an amused smile, she said, "I don't recall suggesting we turn around and go back home."

"I just wanted to make sure you didn't consider that an option."

"I wouldn't think of it."

"Good." He pressed his lips to her cheek. "I promise I'll be good to you."

"I know you'll be," she whispered and squeezed his hand.

The carriage came to a stop at the inn, and they went in to secure their room. Though his stomach growled and it was the dinner hour, he didn't feel like waiting to get married.

He turned to Anna as she laid her belongings on the small vanity in their room. "I'll see what I can do about getting a priest."

She placed her brush by the mirror and glanced at him. "You don't want to eat first?"

"The priest might be busy. I want to make sure we get married tonight."

"Once you set your mind to something, there's no stopping you."

"With a lady like you, can you blame me for being impatient?"

Though she sighed, a smile hinted at her lips. "You're far too charming for my own good."

Secretly pleased, he said, "I'll be back as soon as I secure an appointment."

"I imagine you won't rest until you do."

"Of course not." He went over to her and kissed her. "I've been looking forward to this for a very long time."

Before she could comment, he hurried out of the room. After he went to the innkeeper and found out where one of the priests lived, he left the inn. On his way down a path, someone called out the name Alastair. He didn't think anything of it until the person got more insistent. Wondering who was calling out the name, he stopped and turned to the person. To his surprise, the gentleman was heading straight for him.

Jason waited for him to catch up to him. "Is there something I can help you with, sir?"

"Sir?" The gentleman laughed and patted him on the shoulder. "You and I were friends since we were children, and you address me so formally?"

"I'm afraid I don't know what you're talking about."

He laughed again. "Oh, Alastair, you always did have a sense of humor. Good thing, too, considering the lot you were given in this life. But never mind all that. You look good. I take it they were gracious enough to let you go. Or did you escape?"

Jason didn't know what to make of the gentleman's strange ramblings, but he knew they were meant for someone else. "I'm not Alastair. I'm Jason Merrill, the Duke of Watkins."

The gentleman stopped laughing and studied him. "But the resemblance…" He motioned to his face and then the rest of him. "You don't recognize me? I'm Don. You know, the 'fire eater'?"

Jason shifted uneasily from one foot to another, not sure what to make of the nonsense the gentleman was saying. "I'm sorry, sir, but I don't know what else to tell you. Perhaps Alastair is at home."

"No, Alastair doesn't live here." He scratched his head and examined him again. "You're really not Alastair?"

He shook his head. No, he wasn't Alastair, and the fact that this stranger assumed he was perplexed him. "Maybe you'll see him again. At least, I hope you will." Obviously, it was important to this gentleman that he did. "I must be on my way."

His face fallen, he nodded. "I'm sorry, Your Grace."

"Think nothing of it."

He turned to take a step away from the gentleman when the gentleman said, "It's ironic. That's something Alastair used to say."

Unsure of how to respond, Jason shrugged and continued on his way to the priest's residence. He didn't know what to think of the strange encounter except that there was someone out there who looked just like him. Whatever the situation, it didn't concern him. His thoughts returned to Anna, and he forgot all about the gentleman.

***

Anna stood by Jason an hour later. When she'd married the first time, there had been a large group of people who watched. The unmarried ladies were envious that she managed to snag a duke. Even she had been in awe that she would be a duchess as soon as the wedding was done. Back then the title was so important to her and her family and friends. What a silly thing a title was. It didn't lend itself to happiness or safety. It was meaningless when one woke up trapped like an animal in a cage, when one day passed slowly into the next, when death was the only means of escape.

But her second marriage wouldn't be like that. Jason, who'd come out of nowhere, had something more important to offer her than a title. With him there would be love and security. She had no doubt about that. So it was with gratitude she promised herself to him. This would be the first day of the rest of her life. What was once lost had been found. She'd been given a reason to enjoy life again, and she decided that she would embrace all of it. Appleton was right. There was so much sorrow in life; it was foolish to deny a chance to be happy when the chance came along.

After they were married, Jason said he wanted to get something for her. Despite her curiosity, she resisted the urge to follow him and returned to their room so she could get ready for bed. She felt a flutter in her stomach at the knowledge it was time to be intimate with him. She spent more time than necessary brushing her hair at the vanity table and recalling their exchange of vows. It couldn't have been better. Even without all the splendor, it was better than her first wedding. Her lips curled up into a smile. What could be more wonderful than the joy at knowing she was safe with her husband?

The door to the room opened, and Jason entered it, hiding something behind his back. She took in his mischievous grin and put the brush on the table.

"What are you hiding?" she asked, trying to see what was behind his back.

He laughed and turned so that her effort was in vain. "I'll show you if you give me a kiss."

Amused, she approached him, aware that her shift caressed her body as she walked forward.

His gaze traveled down the length of her. "You're beautiful."

Ignoring the nervous thrill that shot through her, she stepped up to him and kissed him, aware that her breasts lightly brushed his chest. She cleared her throat. "Will you show me now?"

"Show you what?" he asked.

"What's behind your back?"

He blinked and chuckled. "Oh. Right. I almost forgot." He took the roses from behind his back and presented them to her. "I got these for you from a merchant."

"They're lovely," she whispered and touched the soft pink and red petals. "Thank you."

"She told me if you hang them upside down, they'll dry out and you can keep them forever."

"I'll be sure to do that."

She kissed him again, and this time he brought her into his arms and deepened the kiss. The roses still in hand, she wrapped her arms around his neck and pressed her body against his. He groaned and let his hands fall down her back and to the curve of her rear end. He parted his lips, and she responded in kind, inviting him into her mouth. His tongue caressed hers, claiming her mouth. A swell of excitement coursed through her. It was such a wonderful feeling to be desired so passionately.

He pulled away from her and took the roses so he could place them in the vase on the table. When he turned back to her, she decided to beat him to it and remove his clothes for him. She found she enjoyed the process, peeling off layer after layer, slowly exposing more of him. Where such boldness was coming from, she didn't know. She wouldn't have believed herself capable of being this way before, but with Jason, it was easy to forgo her inhibitions. She wanted to be intimate with him, for his body to claim hers, to be consumed by his love.

He didn't deny her the exploration she craved. If anything, he encouraged it. He shrugged off his clothes to help her and guided her hands from his shoulders to his stomach. She hesitated along the scars that reminded her of the night she and Appleton found him in the forest.

It was a double-edged sword to be angry with whoever hurt him while being grateful they left him for her and Appleton to find so she could be with him now. She blinked back her tears in case he assumed she didn't want to be here with him. The truth was she wanted to be here. There was nowhere else she'd rather be, nothing else she'd rather be doing. Even the joy of music failed in comparison to this moment.

Jason brought his hands to her shoulders and gently massaged them. His lips went to her neck and she moaned. She tilted her head to the side while her hands traveled further down his body. She wrapped her hands around his erection, noting its strength. The area between her legs ached for him. Even if she hadn't enjoyed her time with her first husband, she'd discovered that she was capable of pleasure and wanted to experience it with him. She ran her hands down his length and brought them back up. He softly moaned and squeezed her shoulders.

She let go of him and pulled the shift over her head. Before she had time to toss it to the floor, he was cupping her breasts and studying them. She would have chuckled at his impatience had he not brushed her nipples with his thumbs, an action which made her knees grow weak.

"Let's go to bed," she whispered, her voice raspy.

He didn't argue as she took him by the hand and led him to the bed. Together they settled on it, and he gathered her into his embrace and kissed her, his lips no longer gentle but determined. He rolled on top of her, and she wrapped her legs around his waist aware that the male part of him was nestled at her entrance. But he didn't enter her as she thought he would. He moved his hips, his erection stroking her sensitive nub, and she gasped from the stimulation. Enjoying the way he was teasing her, she rocked her hips with him.

He lowered his head and kissed her neck, flicking his tongue along the path to her ear, making her squirm in delight. She felt moisture build between her legs as he continued to stroke her nub with his arousal. She could so easily take him into her, but he broke the intimate contact in favor of getting on his knees so he could get a good look at her body. He took his time in studying her, first with his hands and then with his mouth. He explored her breasts, circling her nipples with his thumbs before he brushed them with his tongue. She groaned and murmured his name. His response was to bring one of his hands between her legs and insert two fingers into her so he could stroke her core.

It wasn't long before she realized the pleasure mounting deep inside her meant that she'd climax soon, but she wanted him to be inside her when she did. She quickly removed his fingers and rolled him onto his back. He helped her straddle him before he entered her. She moved above him, her sensitive nub rubbing against his body. Looking down at him, she saw him open his eyes and smile at her. Smiling in return, she closed her eyes and gave into the urge to pursue her climax. Nothing else mattered at this moment except that they'd both find satisfaction in this act. And it wasn't long before she reached the peak, her body clenching around him as he stiffened beneath her and released his seed. She gasped and remained still, lightly groaning as wave after wave of pleasure consumed her.

When they both descended back to Earth, she collapsed in his arms. Out of breath, they remained silent, and she listened to the soothing beating of his heart.

"Thank you," he whispered.

She lifted her head so she could look at him. "For what?"

"For marrying me again. Now I have this memory to look back on and enjoy."

"I do, too."

With a smile, she kissed him, and it wasn't long before they were making love again.

Chapter Fifteen

As Anna and Jason returned home in the carriage, she narrowed her eyes when she realized Lord Mason was talking to the footman. She couldn't be sure, but it appeared as if they were having an argument. The footman shook his head and threw his hands up in the air in a manner that indicated he'd had enough of their discussion before he hurried into the manor.

She expected Lord Mason to leave, but he didn't. He turned in time to see the carriage and headed for the front entrance. Her grip tightened on the reticule resting in her lap.

"What's wrong?" Jason asked, peering out the window to see what caught her attention.

"It's Lord Mason," she grumbled. Leave it to him to ruin her good mood.

"He is my brother. I suppose he's coming by because we're family?"

"Maybe." She wasn't sure. Something about his frequent visits made her uneasy. "If you don't mind, I'd like to have a word with him."

"You think he's intruding?"

Wondering how much she could tell him without arousing his suspicions, she decided to say, "Before you became ill, he made it a habit of stopping by two or three times a year. Then suddenly, he started coming by once a week."

"That often?"

"When you were sick, I thought…" She paused, not sure if it was necessary to tell him more or not.

"You thought what?" he pressed.

She sighed, not sure if it made a difference or not but decided it didn't do any harm to tell him. "I thought he was waiting for you to die so he could take your place."

Jason frowned. "You mean, he was eager to see me die?"

"A title avails a gentleman much, and the better the title, the more it's desired."

"I understand."

Noting the hurt in his voice, she slid her arm around his and kissed his cheek. "That's the way Lord Mason is. He doesn't care about anyone but himself. It has nothing to do with you."

He sighed. "I'm not surprised. He's done nothing to make me think he's my friend."

"He hasn't?"

"No."

She wondered if he'd disclose more than that, but the carriage came to a stop. She released his arm and got ready to confront Lord Mason. She'd had enough of him. Appleton understood the situation and would help her. Now that she had Jason, Lord Mason had no power over her.

The coachmen helped them down, and Lord Mason waited for them near the carriage door. "I understand congratulations are in order," Lord Mason said, his hands behind his back. "A second wedding. I suppose it was necessary, given the circumstances."

His gaze darted to Anna who froze in place next to Jason. Lord Mason knew her secret. No, he couldn't know. Not for sure. She and Appleton were careful the night they buried her first husband. So he didn't know. But he suspected. And that made him more dangerous than he'd ever been. Whatever she did from this point forward, she must not raise his suspicions further.

Jason turned to him. "To what do we owe the pleasure of your visit?"

"I came to talk to you," Lord Mason said, directing his attention back to him.

It was on the tip of Anna's tongue to protest, but she knew she couldn't. Not without making Lord Mason question why she was suddenly protective of Jason. She bit her tongue so she could keep quiet. It was hard to do—painful even—but she managed.

Jason nodded. "I suppose a brief walk might be good after a long ride back." He gave Anna's arm a squeeze. "I'll return to you shortly."

Again, she used all her willpower not to say something as the two gentlemen left together. The only saving grace in this situation was knowing that Jason didn't remember anything. Since he really did have amnesia, then Lord Mason couldn't catch him in a lie. Even so, she wished Jason hadn't run off with him. Sure, her first husband could stand up to him, but Jason was so gentle and kind, she wasn't sure what to expect.

"Your Grace, did you have a good trip?"

She turned in time to see Appleton approaching her. Her shoulders relaxed, and she smiled. "Yes, I did."

"I'm glad to hear it," he replied.

She waited until the coachman departed with the carriage before continuing. "Lord Mason is here."

"Yes, I know. He came to see His Grace, but I told him His Grace wasn't due back until later today. You came sooner than I expected. You say everything is all right?"

"Yes. It couldn't be better. I never knew marriage could be so wonderful."

"It seems to me that marriage is neither good nor bad, but it's the people in it who make it so."

She chuckled. "That's true. The right person makes all the difference."

"It's nice to see you laugh." He grinned and motioned for her to go into the house. "I'll have your favorite tea and biscuits made for you."

"Thank you, Appleton."

As she walked toward the steps that would take her inside, she heard a horse neighing. Hopeful, she turned to see if Lord Mason was heading off the property, but to her dismay, he wasn't. Instead, she saw him and Jason riding their horses.

"Appleton?" she asked, turning to him.

"It's not my place to tell His Grace he shouldn't ride a horse," he softly told her.

"But you know how much it scares him."

"And he knows it, too."

"Lord Mason is baiting him," she weakly said, her heart pounding anxiously in her chest.

"You'll have to trust that His Grace can take care of himself. If he went on the horse, then there's a good reason for it."

He was right. She knew he was right, and yet, she wanted nothing more than to run out there and demand he return the horse to the stable at once. After six years of being miserable, she was finally happy, and Lord Mason was threatening to take that away from her.

"It's best to let His Grace handle things," Appleton told her, his tone sympathetic.

"All right. And it's not like he knows the truth."

"That's to his benefit."

And he must never know. She didn't have to say it. Appleton understood. As long as Jason didn't know, he was safe from anything Lord Mason might try to do.

***

"One would never think you've ridden a horse before," Mason

called out.

Jason couldn't be sure if Mason's tone was teasing or mocking, but he was focusing too much on his horse to care. It wasn't that it felt unfamiliar to be on it. In fact, it felt as if he had been on it in the past. But something about the animal made his stomach turn, as if it was determined to see him harmed. It was nonsense, of course, since it had been the fall down the stairs that injured him, but it was still an unsettling feeling.

"You say you don't remember how to ride a horse?" Mason asked, trotting beside him.

"I did lose my memory," Jason said, hoping his voice didn't betray how nervous he was.

Why did he let Mason talk him into riding a horse? He never should have agreed to it, but there was something about Mason that made him want to prove he could perform any task, no matter how dangerous. And that wasn't good.

"You forgot how much you love to ride that magnificent stallion," Mason said. "It's your pride and joy."

"It is?" The horse stepped into a slight dip and Jason's grip tightened on the reins. It's all right, he thought. He wasn't going to fall off and be run over by the thing. He gulped, wondering why he should even imagine the animal running over him. Glancing at Mason who was scanning the landscape with mild interest, he asked, "You said I never had any trouble with horses?"

Mason chuckled. "I should say not. They knew better than to defy you. You were a formidable gentleman…before the memory lapse."

Jason caught the silent challenge in Mason's stare, but he couldn't hold his gaze. He had to focus on the path his horse was traveling, and that required far more attention than he cared to admit.

"You don't remember falling down the stairs?" Mason pressed.

"No. How could I? That's why I lost my memory."

"And you fell down the stairs leading to the main entrance?"

"Yes." That's what Anna told him, and he had no reason to doubt her.

"So while you were deathly ill with a fever, you stood up and tried to walk down the stairs."

"Right."

"Hmm…"

"Hmm, what?" Jason snapped, not appreciating whatever Mason was hinting at.

"There's no need to be touchy with me, dear brother. I'm merely wondering how a fall of that magnitude didn't break your neck."

"It was probably because of the way I fell," Jason replied, heat rising up to his face. "Are you calling my wife a liar?"

"Most certainly not. I just never heard of a gentleman who fell down the stairs and survived."

"Well, now you have."

"Yes. I have indeed."

Jason let out a frustrated sigh. As much as he tried not to show Mason that he could bother him, it didn't work. Mason knew exactly how much he was upsetting him, and by the smirk on his face, he took a fiendish delight in it.

"Let's not tarry," Mason said. "The whole point of being on a horse is to ride it, is it not?" He gave him a wink and urged his horse into a full gallop.

Jason decided he should get over his fear of the horse, and the sooner, the better. He wouldn't give Mason any more reasons to taunt him. With more courage than he felt, he snapped the reins and joined Mason. It wasn't so bad now that he'd adjusted to the way the horse moved, but he couldn't stop the feeling that he'd fallen off of it at some point in his past. Maybe he did and no one else knew about it.

Sweat broke out across his forehead. He felt the world tilting around him for a brief instant, but he blinked and refocused. To his surprise, Mason wasn't taking the trail but was veering off toward a group of trees. He gripped the reins and fought the urge to turn back toward the fountain where it would be safer. If Mason insisted on going this way, then he'd do it.

"Now do you remember why you loved riding?" Mason called out.

"I told you I don't remember anything," he shouted, breathing heavier than he knew he should be.

The ride wasn't that strenuous, but his mounting apprehension about those trees was making it harder to breathe. He gulped and put pressure on the stirrups, slightly lifting himself off the horse. He had no idea what he was doing or why, except it seemed natural to do it. They came closer to the trees. So close, in fact, he wondered if they'd have enough time to stop.

Mason made a smooth turn and ran alongside the trees, and since he urged the horse to go faster, Jason fell behind, unwilling to go faster than he already was. He didn't like this. His horse was going under the trees, and the branches seemed too low. Heart racing, he tried to fight the sensation of falling off the horse, but the sensation was too strong.

Something in him snapped, and he knew he couldn't stay on the horse anymore. He reached up, grabbed one of the thicker branches, and swung up on it. His horse neighed and bucked back, hitting the branches, but Jason leapt over to another branch before he lost his balance. Mason pulled the horse to a stop while Jason's horse ran off in the direction of the stable. Gasping for air, Jason turned his attention to Mason who looked up at him with a surprised look on his face. He gripped the bark of the tree in his hand, his shock making it so that he couldn't speak.

"How did you do that?" Mason asked.

Jason gulped and shook his head. "I don't know. Did I ever do this before?"

"I've never seen you do it." After a moment, he threw his head back and laughed. "Bravo, dear brother. You did a splendid job. But I am wondering if you can get back down?"

"I don't know."

"Well, let's see if you can do it."

Seeing as how he had no other choice, he swung down the branches until his feet hit the ground. He looked up at the highest tree branch he'd been on and wondered how he reacted in time to get up there. He didn't think he made it a habit of climbing trees. For some reason, that didn't seem right. But somehow, he had done something similar. He turned his attention to the ground. While up there, he hadn't been afraid of the height, and he wondered if that should be a surprise.

"Marvelous. Absolutely marvelous." Mason clapped his hands. "I wouldn't have believed it if I didn't see it with my own eyes. You must come to my estate. I'll have a dinner party, and you can tell everyone about it."

"Oh, I don't think that's necessary."

Mason slid off his horse and led it over to him. "Not necessary? After a fine show like that, you deserve a round of applause. I insist on inviting our friends over so you can receive the praise you deserve. Now, I won't take no for an answer. You are my brother, after all, and I can't wait to see the look on Ian's face when he finds out how you did that."

"Lord Hedwrett?"

"Yes. You do remember we called him Ian at my last dinner party?"

"There were many names I had to remember that night."

"I understand. I'm sure we overwhelmed you. Fortunately, you will be able to see everyone again, and this time, we won't be strangers." Mason patted him on the shoulder and led him and the horse in the direction of the manor. "It'll be good for you. Anna will enjoy it, too. Candace will be there. I hear the two get along so well they forget the other ladies are in the room with them."

He knew Anna wouldn't like the idea, and he liked it even less. Before he could reply, he caught sight of Anna hurrying in their direction. "Excuse me, Mason." Worried something was wrong, he ran to meet her.

She slowed and waited for him to reach her before she came to a stop. "I saw your horse go by and thought you were hurt."

Pleased she worried about him, he grinned. "No, I didn't get hurt."

"But why did the horse run off?"

"I left it in favor of a tree branch."

"What?"

He glanced over his shoulder and saw that Mason was almost within hearing distance of them. "I'll explain later. My brother wants us to go to another one of his dinner parties."

She grimaced and shook her head. "Jason, I'd rather not."

"I know." Since Mason had come close enough to hear them, Jason turned to him. "I regret to inform you that my wife and I will be detained for a time, so we are unable to attend your dinner party. We are enjoying our time as a newly married couple, or at least newly married from my perspective. I trust you understand."

Mason glanced from her back to him and bowed his head. "Forgive me for imposing. Of course, you need time to be with her. I'll send an invite at another time. Then you can tell everyone your marvelous act while we were at the trees." He hopped up on his horse. "At a more convenient time."

Jason waited until Mason left before turning back to Anna who visibly relaxed. "He really bothers you."

She shrugged and crossed her arms. "He's not the nicest of gentlemen."

"I understand that," he replied and pressed his hand on the small of her back to lead her to the manor.

"I wish he wouldn't come by so often. It wasn't pleasant when he came by a couple times a year, but it's disturbing he keeps coming by as often as he does now."

"That's why I told him we prefer to spend time alone. Perhaps he'll stay away longer this time."

"I hope so." After a few moments, she asked, "Will you tell me what happened at the trees?"

With a chuckle, he nodded. "I have to admit it was a surprising display of my agility. I had no idea I was capable of such a thing."

"What thing is that?"

"When I rode close enough to a tree branch, I swung up on it as if I'd done it all of my life. Do you recall me performing such a task before?"

Her eyebrows furrowed and she shook her head. "No, no I don't," she whispered, an uncertain tone in her voice. "What do you think it means?"

"I have no idea. I suspect I've done something similar in the past. I must have if I knew what to do, don't you think?"

Biting her lower lip, she nodded but didn't say anything.

"Perhaps it's something I learned before I met you. I think what surprised me the most was how natural it was, as if I was born doing it. I know that sounds odd since I obviously didn't do it often, but it feels like I did."

She glanced at him, and he thought he saw a worried look in her eyes.

"Anna, are you all right?"

Taking a deep breath, she offered him a tentative smile and slipped her arm around his. "Yes. I'm fine. I…I'm just relieved you're all right. It doesn't sound like jumping on a tree branch while riding a horse is a safe maneuver."

"Probably not. That's why it seems like I shouldn't know how to do it, and yet I do."

"Well, neither one of us know why, so I suppose it's not

worth thinking about anymore."

He grinned and kissed her cheek. "You're right. I'd rather think about us instead."

Her body relaxed against him. "I agree. What do you want to do today?"

"I wouldn't mind seeing if everything has been put away in your bedchamber." He wiggled his eyebrows suggestively.

Her cheeks grew pink as she caught his meaning. "I'm sure everything is fine, but if it makes you feel better, we can do that."

"It would. Plus, we need to get out of these clothes."

"Yes, indeed we do."

Catching the teasing gleam in her eye, his smile widened as they continued their stroll to the manor.

Chapter Sixteen

*I*n April, Anna woke up in her bed, wrapped in Jason's arms. Ever since they married, he'd slept in her bed, something that pleased her though she wouldn't tell him. It was wonderful to be loved so well. The past six years were now a blur to her, and if she had to go through it all again so she could be with Jason, she would.

She studied her husband as he slept. In sleep, he looked happy. Of course, he looked happy while he was awake, but she fancied that in sleep, he always had good dreams. She brushed aside the lock of blond hair that had fallen over his eyelids and noted the silky strands between her fingers. Then she traced his cheek and his jaw, enjoying the rough sensation. He would shave it away, but she liked the masculine appeal it gave him.

His eyes opened and he smiled. "Good morning," he murmured and drew her closer to him before he closed his eyes.

"Good morning, Your Grace," she whispered. "Did you have good dreams?"

"I did. Then I woke up and realized they were all true."

Pleased, she gave him another kiss. "What can I do to make you happy today?"

"Take me to London."

"Why London? Aren't you content to remain here?"

"I am." He opened his eyes and cupped the side of her

face with his hand. "I enjoy every moment we have together. I just remember what you said about London. The theatre, the balls, a walk in Hyde Park, the museum... There are so many things to do there. I want to go to them. I want to experience everything. I want to embrace life."

Taking in the enthusiastic tone in his voice and the excitement in his eyes, she knew she didn't have a choice. He'd been hiding from the world in this place. She sighed. "You're right. I've been selfish to keep you here all to myself."

He chuckled and kissed her. "I wouldn't say selfish. It gave us a second chance. I'll never regret that."

She wouldn't either, but she wondered if it was wise to send him to London where people knew her first husband. Undoubtedly, Lord Mason would be there this time of year. She took a deep breath to steady her racing heart. There were far too many things to fear, and now she had to worry that someone in London would figure out Jason wasn't the duke. God help her if that person knew Lord Mason. She released her breath and hoped Jason didn't pick up on her increased heart rate.

"We'll have a wonderful time there, Anna."

Jason's soothing tone helped her relax, but only a little.

"You'll see," he continued. "We'll go to London and see the sights and dance. We'll have some great memories that we'll bring back with us to warm us up during the cold winter months. And if the memories don't warm you up, I'll be happy to help."

Despite her apprehension, she found herself laughing at his joke.

"There. That's better," he said and hugged her.

"I can't deny you anything," she replied.

"That's a good thing," he insisted and kissed her again.

Wrapped protectively in his arms, she could only hope the decision to go to London wouldn't be the wrong one.

***

Jason sorted through the desk that was in the room off to the side of his bedchamber. Now that he could read, he wanted to see what documents were in the desk. He wiped the sweat from his forehead and checked to make sure the small window in the room was open. It was and the breeze wafting into the room was cool.

Someone knocked on the door, and he looked up, surprised to see Anna standing in the doorway. "I thought you wished to play a few songs on the piano before you retired for the night," he said.

"I planned to, but then I thought of something I need you to do. Will you come to my bedchamber when you're done in here?"

If she wanted to make love to him, all she had to do was say so, but he thought it was charming she was too embarrassed to come out and say it. With a wink, he said, "I'll be there soon."

Though she seemed confused by his reaction, she shrugged and nodded. "I'll be waiting for you. I'll have everything ready. There's not much time to waste."

He chuckled. "I didn't realize you were so impatient for me."

"Well, it's something that needs tending to, and the sooner, the better."

"In that case, do you want me to join you right now?"

"No. I'm not that impatient. I can wait until you're done in here."

He watched her as she left the room and grinned. It was nice to be wanted so badly. His gaze went to the open drawer in the desk. It was the last one he had to examine. He collected the papers and a safe and set them on the desk. Sorting through the papers, he learned what assets came with the estate, and after reading through those, he picked up the safe. He studied the lock and recalled the key he put in his cabinet.

Placing the safe down, he went to the cabinet near his bed and opened it. He searched the bottom of the shelf and found the key. Once he returned to the room, he sat at the desk and inserted the key into the lock. After he opened it, he pulled out the documents and studied them. With a frown, he put them down and opened a drawer so he could pull out the paper where the family lineage was documented.

"This doesn't make sense," he whispered as he set the paper beside the family tree he'd found in the safe.

The paper was nearly identical, except for one thing. He traced through the lineage to compare the two pieces of paper. Everything was the same except for one thing: one person was missing from the family tree. That person happened to be his twin brother.

Setting the paper aside, he searched through the other papers in the safe and discovered a notice of death. He sighed. His poor parents, especially his mother. He recalled that Mason said their parents refused to have visitors shortly after Jason was born and now it made sense. Their parents were grieving the death of the first twin, his older brother of three minutes who was never named. The cause of death was reported as a stillbirth.

He sighed and picked up another piece of paper. It was a letter from his father instructing Jason to never mention the death of the unnamed boy. Jason put the paper down and debated whether or not such a thing was necessary. Why keep the infant's death a secret? There wouldn't be anything to gain from it.

He sat back in his chair. He should tell Anna, shouldn't he? Drumming his fingers on the desk, he thought over the pros and cons to both options. Sighing, he rubbed his eyes. He didn't like the idea of keeping anything from Anna, but telling her wouldn't change things. It certainly wouldn't bring his brother back. Looking at the safe and papers around it, he decided he would honor his father's wish and not tell anyone about his twin brother. He put everything back in the desk before he returned the key to the cabinet.

His attention went to the door connecting his bedchamber with Anna's, and he smiled. He'd kept his wife waiting long enough. The poor lady went through all the trouble of telling him how much she wanted him in bed with her. The least he could do was oblige her.

He decided he wouldn't bother his valet this time and dressed for bed. When he secured the straps of his robe, he went over to the door and entered Anna's room, pleased to see that she was also in her robe. She sat in front of her vanity and brushed her hair.

His smile widened and he tiptoed over to her. He covered her eyes with his hands. "Guess who?" he whispered.

"Umm…" She tapped the brush in her hand. "Can you give me a hint?"

Chuckling, he removed his hands and kissed her cheek. "Does tall, strong, and handsome sound familiar?"

"No, not really."

"You're charming." He kissed her neck, and she giggled. "Now, what did you want me for when I was in my bedchamber?" Even if he already knew, he'd like to hear her to say it.

"I need you to read that book."

He waited for her to say she was joking, but she pointed to her desk, which was on the other side of the room. Just to make sure she wasn't kidding, he humored her and walked over to the desk. His eyes grew wide. Indeed, she hadn't been joking. The book sat on top of the desk, opened to the first chapter as if mocking him. At least there weren't papers beside the book this time or else he'd be expected to practice his writing as well. He knew she took the task of teaching him to read and write seriously, but this was ridiculous.

"Why did you call me to your bedchamber if you had no intention of using me for your pleasure?" He turned from the desk and watched as she brushed her hair in front of her vanity mirror. "I won't be able to concentrate on reading while we're in your bedchamber. You would have done better to take me to the library like you usually do." He crossed his arms. "A gentleman can't focus when there's a bed in the room."

She finally glanced his way and gave him an amused smile. "I thought you'd be more comfortable reading in here than in that stuffy library. The chairs in this room are more comfortable."

"Well, I'm not going to be comfortable in here if all I'm going to do is sit in a chair and read."

"I assure you that I won't leave you unsatisfied, Your Grace, but we already delayed your progress by spending too much time in intimate pursuits. You still have things to learn about being a duke."

He groaned and plopped down in the chair by the desk. "I fail to see what the urgency is. I lost my memory. People will understand if I don't do everything perfectly."

"Regardless of whether you lost your memory or not, there are certain expectations you must fulfill in polite society. You don't want to do anything that causes a scandal."

He glanced at the book. "And a book this gigantic is going to prevent me from causing a scandal?"

"Those are etiquette guidelines, and yes, it's important you read them."

With a grimace, he brought the book into his lap and flipped through it, picking out random passages to read. "If a gentleman passes a lady he is briefly acquainted with, he must not tip his hat or greet her unless she first acknowledges him. When walking up the stairs, gentlemen must go first. When walking down the stairs, ladies must go first." He placed the book back on the table. "I don't see how those things matter."

"They matter a great deal, Jason. You must take everything in that book seriously. You'd be surprised at how little it takes for gossip to circulate through London, and the Ton can be unforgiving if you upset the wrong person."

"Have you been the victim of gossip?"

"No, I haven't, but I've seen others who have been, and it's not pleasant. Candace had to settle for marrying Ian because no other gentleman would have her. Candace made the mistake of making a morning call without the proper allowance from her superior. The superior in question happened to be Lady Cadwalader, and she has a lot of influence with the Ton. Had it not been for that social blunder, Candace could have married someone far better than Ian. Ian's one of the few gentlemen who won't let the Ton dictate what he can or can't do. He needed a lady to give him an heir so he offered his suit, and her brother arranged the marriage on her behalf." Her voice drifted off as she inspected the brush in her hands.

Curious, Jason leaned forward. "You don't like Ian?"

"He's Lord Mason's friend, and people are often known by the company they keep." She turned her attention to the mirror and resumed brushing her hair. "So you see why it's important that you read the book. If we're going to London, you need to be acquainted with the proper etiquette." She glanced his way and smiled. "Besides, the book isn't gigantic like you claim. You can read it in one sitting if you wish."

"I'm sorry, Anna, but I have no intention of staying up all night reading. I'll humor you and read some of it tonight, but I have something far more interesting to study than what the Ton wants me to do or not do."

Her face grew pink at his meaning, and she averted her gaze from his. Finding her reaction to intimate talk adorable, he stood up and approached her. He took the brush from her and gently brushed her silky blonde hair, which fell to the middle of her back.

"What are you doing?" she asked, turning her head in his direction.

He turned her head back to the mirror and continued to brush her hair. "Brushing your hair."

"All right. Perhaps I should have worded the question differently. Why are you brushing my hair?"

He shrugged. "I thought it'd be a good way to start studying you."

She chuckled. "I think you already know everything about me."

"There's always something new to learn." He lifted her hair and kissed the back of her neck, noting that she shivered in delight. "Ah, I see I found a sensitive spot right there."

He kissed her again and grinned when a soft moan escaped her lips. Letting go of her hair, he brushed it a few more times before placing the brush on the table in front of her. He brought his hands to her shoulders and, noting how tense her muscles were, massaged them.

"You needn't worry about London. I'll behave myself as required," he promised. "And if I'm not sure about something, I'll ask you."

"You will read the book, won't you?"

"Yes." He laughed and worked his way down her back. "I'll read and memorize every painful word."

"Painful?"

"You have to admit that reading an etiquette book isn't exactly the most stimulating way to spend one's time."

"No, but it's necessary."

He knelt beside her and kissed her cheek. "I know it's necessary. I won't do anything to embarrass you."

She turned toward him and clasped his hands. "Jason, it's not about being embarrassed. I just don't want people to think you're different from the way you were before. You used to know all the etiquette rules and obeyed them."

"And I'll obey them this time. But can you explain why gentlemen walk in front of ladies when going up the stairs and why they walk behind ladies when going down the stairs?"

"That is simple. It all has to do with the ankles. The gentleman must never see a lady's ankles. When a lady goes up or down the stairs, she might need to lift the bottom of her dress ever so slightly to avoid tripping on the hem. It's possible that a gentleman might see her ankle in such a situation, but if he walks in front of her while going up the stairs and behind her while going down, he can't see the front of her dress."

With a wicked grin, he slid his hand under her robe and touched her ankle. "So seeing your ankle would be scandalous?"

"Not in the privacy of a bedchamber, but I wouldn't recommend you take a peek at my ankle while we're in public."

"Then it's a good thing we're in your bedchamber." He traced the curve of her calf and brought his hand up her thigh. She parted her legs, and he accepted her silent invitation and lightly brushed the inside of her thighs. "I promise I won't lift your dress to see your ankle when we're in public."

As he hoped, she laughed at his joke, but her laughter died down when he leaned forward and kissed her neck. She shifted in the chair and spread her legs so he could touch her more intimately. He brushed his tongue up to her earlobe and left a trail of kisses from where his tongue had been. His fingers teased the folds of her flesh before he inserted a finger into her, noting her soft warmth. She moaned and gripped the arms of her chair.

Now this was more like it. He'd rather be doing this than reading a book. He slid another finger inside her and stroked her core in the way he knew she liked. She rewarded him with another moan and rocked her hips. His thumb found her sensitive nub and he caressed it using circular motions he knew she liked best.

Up to that point, they'd always been undressed when enjoying each other's bodies, but he couldn't deny the thrill of doing this while they were still clothed. He continued kissing the side of her neck, mindful to brush his tongue over the sensitive area that made her squirm in pleasure. She gasped and moved faster, an action which motivated him to use more pressure on the bundle of nerves in her core.

She was getting wetter with each stroke, and his erection throbbed in anticipation as he continued to caress her tender flesh. Her moans grew louder, something that aroused him further since he knew she was almost at the peak. He loved giving her that experience, knowing it was him who was giving her the height of sexual pleasure. And when she cried out and her flesh clenched around his fingers, he groaned, pleased he had succeeded.

After she relaxed, she took his face in her hands and kissed him, her tongue brushing his lips, prompting him to open his mouth for her. He obeyed and her tongue interlaced with his. She deepened the kiss, and his fingers continued to lightly tease her flesh. Moaning, she shuddered and ended the kiss.

"You feel good," she murmured, leaving a trail of kisses from his jawline to his ear.

"You do, too," he whispered in a raspy voice, thinking there was nothing more wonderful than a lady's body.

She nudged his fingers out of her and motioned for him to lie down on the rug. He did as instructed and smiled as she pulled his robe open, exposing his erection. She turned so she was facing away from him and straddled him. Intrigued, he lifted her robe, pleased by the view of her backside as she guided him into her body.

He loved the initial contact as he entered her, loved how her flesh surrounded him with its moist warmth and drew him deeper into her. He murmured his appreciation and held onto her hips as she rocked them back and forth. The position required her to do everything, something that left her in complete control, something he certainly didn't mind. His body tightened as he felt the familiar tension building up inside him. When he finally reached the peak, he cried out and released his seed. She waited until he relaxed before she got off of him and turned to face him. With a smile, she gave him a lingering kiss.

He sighed in contentment and pulled her into his arms. "Now that's worth coming to your bedchamber for."

She giggled and nudged him in the side. "Don't forget to read the book."

"I won't. I'll start it in a few minutes."

"All right."

"You should stop worrying, Anna. You're much too nervous about London. Everything will be fine."

After a few minutes, he kissed the top of her head and helped her to her feet. He adjusted his robe and led her over to the desk. "I'll start reading the book, and you can sit on my lap and keep me company."

Without waiting for her response, he set her on his lap, wrapped his arm around her waist, and picked up the book. She settled against him, and he started reading.

Chapter Seventeen

Two weeks later, Anna sat in the drawing room of her London townhouse. She'd never been more grateful for the calming presence Appleton provided. While Jason changed into new clothes so they could go to the museum, she drank tea, grateful she had a chance to talk to her friend. She looked over at Appleton as he dusted off the piano.

"You don't think anyone will suspect Jason's not the duke, do you?" she quietly asked, mindful to listen for footsteps in case someone was on their way to the drawing room.

"I doubt it, Your Grace." Appleton turned his caring eyes in her direction but wiped off the keys. "He looks just like the duke, and now he can read and write fluently. He can play chess and knows everything the duke did. He's prepared for this."

She nodded and took a sip of tea. It'd been quite the process to teach him everything he needed to know, but since they found him in the forest, they'd dutifully tended to the task and now they would see if their efforts had been in vain or not. She prayed their efforts hadn't been in vain. It was one thing for Lord Mason to be suspicious, but if others were as well, then what would stop Lord Mason from investigating further? Whatever might be said of Lord Mason, she wouldn't accuse him of being a fool.

"You should enjoy yourself while you're here," Appleton

finally said.

"Yes, I know," she whispered.

She wished she could follow his advice. She really did. For once in her life as a duchess, she was happy. Truly and completely happy. It was too good to be true. Nothing this good could last forever, could it? She placed her empty cup down and rose to her feet. Taking a deep breath, she smoothed her dress and put her hat on. She studied her reflection in the mirror. No one would suspect how anxious she was, which was good. As long as she kept her feelings beneath the surface, no one should question things.

She tied the ribbon under her chin and adjusted the hat so it was comfortable. "I suppose the only way to get over my fear is to go outside and face the people my first husband knew."

He paused and straightened up, and she caught sight of his concerned expression. "The only way you're going to feel better is if you do the same things you always did while in London."

"Wish me luck?"

He offered her a tender smile. "All the luck to you and your husband."

She could do this. Jason could do this. Appleton was right. They couldn't have done anything else to prepare Jason for London. He knew all the etiquette rules. All she could do now was hope other people would believe he was her first husband. She gave Appleton a tentative smile before she left the drawing room. She was ready to head up the staircase leading to their bedchambers when she saw Jason bounding down the steps.

"It's a lovely day to go out, isn't it?" Jason asked when he reached her.

"Yes, it is. It reminds me of the days we walked to the fountain," she replied.

He kissed her on the cheek and grinned. "We'll take more walks when we get back. In the meantime, we'll enjoy everything London has to offer. The museum is first, correct?"

They turned to the door, and she nodded. "Yes. It'll be a good way for you to see the portraits of royalty so you can match their names with their faces."

"I'm looking forward to it."

As the footman opened the door, she left the townhouse first and descended the steps. She waited for him to catch up to her before she accepted the footman's help into the carriage. Once Jason settled next to her, the footman closed the door. She waited until the coachman urged the horses forward before she took Jason's hand in hers and squeezed it. "You amaze me. I've never seen anyone embrace life the way you do."

"With you as my wife, I have a good reason to. I'll never give you a reason to regret giving me a second chance."

He kissed her, and his lips lingered on hers. If only it could be just the two of them forever, secluded from the rest of the world. Then her life would be complete.

The kiss ended all too soon, and she was, once again, aware of the other carriages that passed them by. If nothing else could be said for London, she had to admit that it was full of excitement. There was something to do for everyone. But she decided they would do what Jason wanted. As long as she was with him, it didn't matter what the activity was, but she suspected their calendar would soon be full since she'd left the necessary calling cards at their friends' and acquaintances' residences.

"This evening we'll go to Hyde Park?" he asked, putting his arm around her shoulders and drawing her closer to him. "From five to six, is it?"

"Yes."

"Will we see anyone we know there?"

"I'm sure we will," she replied. "Are you nervous about meeting them?"

"No. Should I be?"

She sighed. How she envied his ease with new situations. "I wish I could be more like you."

"I like you just the way you are."

The carriage came to a stop, so he put his arm back at his side and looked out the window. "The museum is bigger than I thought."

"London has a rich history to celebrate."

"Indeed, it does."

The coachman opened the door, and they stepped out of it. When they reached the entrance of the museum, she caught sight of Lord Mason. She narrowed her eyes at him. There was no way he'd follow them…was there?

"What a surprising coincidence," Lord Mason greeted. "I didn't know you were in London." Glancing her way, he added, "It was rather rude of you to not leave me a calling card."

"I did," she lied. "I suppose it got misplaced once your butler took it."

His smile stiffened. "I must have a word with him so he'll be more careful in the future."

"Yes, you must," she replied, turning her attention to her gloves and acting as if she didn't have a care in the world.

"What brings you to the museum?" Jason asked his brother. "I didn't think portraits interested you."

"And how would you remember that?" Mason's gaze went to Anna. "Did she tell you I'm not a cultured gentleman?"

"No, it's not that," Jason replied. "I gathered from our talks that you preferred travel abroad to being stuck in a museum."

"I've been known to be in museums from time to time." Giving Jason a wink, he added, "You, however, had other places you went to on a frequent basis."

Jason's eyebrows furrowed. "I did?"

Anna cleared her throat. "My lord, I insist you recall that you're in the presence of a lady." Of all things Jason had learned about her first husband, she had no desire to expose him to his indiscretions.

Lord Mason's lips curled up into a smile that reminded her of a cat that was stalking a mouse. "Anna, I can't recall a time when you've been so…outspoken."

"That only proves you don't know everything about me," she said, mustering the kindest smile she could.

"Apparently not," Lord Mason replied. "I gather there's some other things I don't know as well." His gaze went to Jason, and he scanned him up and down. "There's certainly much to learn about my brother who seems like a different person ever since he lost his memory."

"A better person, I hope," Jason said.

Before he could answer, Lady Templeton came up to him, followed by an older gentleman. "Lord Mason, you're much too fast for us." She giggled and turned to Anna and Jason. "What a pleasure it is to make your acquaintance again." She turned to the older gentleman and motioned to Jason. "Father, this is the gentleman who performed that fantastic feat while riding a horse."

"Yes, he is," Lord Mason added. "My brother jumped off of it while it was still running so he could swing up on a tree branch. The whole thing really was quite marvelous. I've never known him to do something like it. I invited him to one of my dinner parties so he could regale us with how he did it, but due to his second wedding to his wife, he wished to spend more time alone with her, keeping her all to himself."

"A second wedding?" Lady Templeton glanced at Anna. "I don't recall hearing about it."

"We ran off to Gretna Green," Anna explained. "We wished for a private affair."

"Private indeed," she replied with a chuckle.

"Yes, usually one wedding is enough," Lord Mason added and then looked in Anna's direction. "That is if you marry the same person. However, if it was someone else…"

Anna's polite smile froze on her face as she glanced at Lady Templeton and her father. Would they suspect the truth now? Would they wonder if Jason was someone other than her first husband?

"Our situation is unique," Jason began, directing his gaze to Lady Templeton's father. "I became ill, and in a state of confusion, I left my bedchamber and fell down the stairs. The fall resulted in a loss of memory. I insisted Her Grace marry me again so I could have a memory of our wedding. Granted, it wasn't the same, but I'm still delighted that I can recall her promising herself to me for the rest of her life." He turned his gaze to Anna and smiled in that charming way of his that made her knees grow weak.

"That's very romantic," Lady Templeton's father said.

"Yes, it was," Anna softly replied, thinking it was so like Jason to make it clear that he cared for her, even in front of others.

"It isn't often a person comes across a love match," Lady Templeton said, "especially when money's involved."

"Yes," Lord Mason agreed. "And both my brother and his wife came into the marriage with a good amount of it."

Anna sensed a double meaning in his words. If she guessed right, he was suggesting that his brother gave her money when she married him, and she gave Jason money when he married her. She clasped her hands together and squeezed them to calm her nerves. The last thing she needed was to give him an indication that he was right. At this point, he was only suspicious and digging to see if she'd give herself away. Fortunately, Jason couldn't fall for it. She'd never been more relieved she and Appleton hadn't told Jason their secret.

"I take it since you two are in London that you're accepting invitations?" Lady Templeton's father asked Jason.

Jason glanced at Anna who gave a slight nod, hoping Lord Mason wouldn't pick up on it since Jason was seeking her input on the matter. She understood why Jason sought her opinion. He knew how she felt about being near Lord Mason and wished to spare her any discomfort. But she also knew it would look suspicious to everyone else if they didn't accept an invitation.

"Yes, we are," Jason told her father.

"Excellent. My daughter and I are hosting a ball in five days, and we'd be honored if you attended."

"We'd be delighted to attend, thank you."

Lord Mason grinned. "You made the right choice, dear brother. No one in all of British India hosts more elegant balls. I dare say, no one in London has matched his genius either, but all of London will know that soon enough."

Her father laughed. "My lord, you flatter me."

"But not beyond what you deserve," Lord Mason replied.

Anna took a deep breath and released it. She couldn't recall the last time she watched Lord Mason trip all over himself to impress someone, and it was making her sick to her stomach. If she didn't sense that Lady Templeton was as horrible as he was, she'd extend her sympathies to the lady.

"Well, my wife and I were about to enjoy the museum," Jason said and took Anna by the elbow. "I don't remember London, and we thought this would be a good place to start."

"Oh?" Lord Mason asked. "Are you remembering pieces of your past?"

"No, it's not like that. I only mean that I have a lot to learn about London," Jason replied. "I apologize for the confusion."

"Seeing as how I haven't been to the museum yet, I have much to learn as well," Lady Templeton's father said. "Why don't we all go in there together?"

"What a wonderful idea!" Lord Mason turned to his brother. "It'll give me a chance to tell you all the wicked things the people in those portraits did."

"Lord Mason, you are a dangerous gentleman for my daughter to be around," her father said with a twinkle in his eye.

"I promise to only speak to my brother when she isn't in

hearing distance," Lord Mason replied.

Her father chuckled and motioned for Anna and his daughter to enter the museum first. With a sigh, Anna realized she'd be spending most of the afternoon with Lady Templeton. Forcing another smile, she joined his daughter and spent a very uncomfortable afternoon at the museum.

Chapter Eighteen

Four days later, Jason decided to go to White's and see if anything there would seem familiar to him. He told Anna his plan during breakfast, and though he couldn't be sure, he thought she wasn't pleased. Mindful of the servants, he held off on asking her why. After breakfast, he went to his bedchamber where his valet helped him change his clothes. Knowing Anna would also be changing clothes, he waited until her lady's maid left her bedchamber before knocking on her door.

"Come in," she called out.

Accepting her invitation, he slipped into her room and shut the door behind him. She glanced up from where she studied her reflection in the vanity mirror and smiled. He couldn't be sure, but there seemed to be a hesitation in it.

"Would you rather I not go to White's?" he asked, stepping toward her.

She took a deep breath and sighed. "You should go to White's. You need to talk to other gentlemen without your wife lingering about like a shadow."

Finding the way she chose to word that statement amusing, he approached her, turned her to face him, and wrapped his arms around her waist. He gave her a kiss and noted the pleasant way she relaxed against him. "You don't linger about me like a shadow."

"Maybe not like a shadow, but you have to agree I haven't let you out of my sight ever since we came to London."

"I take that as a compliment. You hate being apart from me," he joked with a grin.

She chuckled. "Yes, I do enjoy being with you very much."

"That's good to hear. I enjoy being with you, too." He gently squeezed her and added, "If you'd rather do something else, I'd be happy to oblige."

After a moment of silence, she shook her head. "No. You need to go to White's. Gentlemen should go to gentlemen's clubs. It's why they're called gentlemen's clubs. A husband needs to be with other gentlemen from time to time just like ladies need to be with other ladies." She patted his chest and smiled at him. "You need to go. Have a good time. Make sure you miss me, and be happy when you see me again."

"I can do that."

"Good." She kissed his cheek. "Don't be too long."

"No, I won't. I figure I'll be there for an hour or two. But," he added, "I don't think that's any way for a lady in love to kiss her husband. It should be more like this."

He lowered his head and kissed her, brushing his tongue along her bottom lip until she parted her mouth for him. When she did, he deepened the kiss and pulled her more tightly against him. She sighed in contentment and wrapped her arms around his neck. They remained in each other's arms for a good minute before he reluctantly pulled away from her.

"Now that's how you kiss the gentleman you're in love with," he whispered.

She grinned and gave him a playful nudge in the side. "Go before I change my mind and insist you spend the day with me."

"When I return, I'll be all yours, and you can do whatever

you want to with me."

She giggled. "I wouldn't mind taking a stroll in Hyde Park."

"We'll do that."

With a wink, he headed for the stairs and left the townhouse to go to White's. He wasn't sure what to expect when he got there, but as he entered the establishment, someone called out to him. Surprised, he turned and saw Lord Basemore.

"It's good to see you, old friend," Lord Basemore said as he patted him on the back. "I dare say that I didn't think your wife was going to let you come here. She's been terribly possessive of you ever since you recovered from your illness, but I don't think you can blame her. You almost died, after all."

"I don't mind spending all the time I do with her," Jason replied. "Between you and me, I don't deserve her."

"We all have our faults, but I admit that you're more likable than you used to be."

"Am I?"

"I never voiced a complaint, of course, but I always thought you were a bit rough around the edges. It's nice to see you as you are now."

Considering the changes Anna liked in him, he wasn't surprised to hear Lord Basemore express the same sentiment. "Forgive me for not remembering, but are we on a first name basis?"

"We were, but that's because we're cousins."

"We weren't friends?"

"Not like you and Ian are."

It took Jason a moment to remember that Ian was Lord Hedwrett. "I have a lot to learn. What is your first name?"

"Luke." He motioned to one of the chairs. "Are you up for a game of chess?"

Jason indicated his consent, and he followed Luke to the chessboard. Once they sat down, Jason glanced around the room and saw a few other men playing chess. The cheers from the other room caught his attention. "What's going on in there?"

"Oh, that's where you can play cards." Luke glanced toward the room. "Would you rather do that?"

Jason shrugged. "No, I don't think so."

"You might enjoy it more than chess. At least, you used to."

"Maybe I'll try it another time," Jason replied and turned his attention from the other room where another round of applause erupted. "That must be some game in there."

"It usually is when Lord Edon's playing. I don't know how he does it, but he wins almost every hand he plays. He was born with a gift. It used to irritate you to no end because you knew he never cheated. You tried many times to figure out his secret and finally realized he had none. It was just pure, dumb luck, you'd say."

"It bothered me that Lord Edon would win? Then I wasn't his friend?"

"I'm not sure if Lord Edon has any friends. He knows a lot of people, but he doesn't seem to have any close relationships. He doesn't even have a mistress. From what I hear, he visits prostitutes or visits ladies once and that's it. I think it's because he doesn't want to develop any emotional ties to anyone. But to each his own, right? Whatever Lord Edon does, it's not any concern to us."

"Perhaps." Jason paused before adding, "Was I the same way?"

"No. You had friends and mistresses."

"Mistresses?" He didn't recall Anna mentioning that.

"You had five over the course of ten years, if I remember right. There would come a time when you'd tire of them and move on. You always said ladies were to be enjoyed until they wore out their use."

Jason sighed. He should have expected as much based on

his other undesirable attributes in the past.

"It's not uncommon to have a mistress."

"Maybe not," he replied, but he already decided he wouldn't take another one. He couldn't imagine being with someone else the way he was with Anna. "Would it be a strange thing if I admitted that I like who I am now better than who I used to be?"

Luke smiled and shook his head. "To be honest, I didn't care much for who you used to be either."

Jason leaned forward and lowered his voice. "What do you make of Mason?"

He grimaced. "I know he's your brother and my cousin, but I care for him even less than I used to care for you."

"If you don't like him, why did you go to his dinner party?"

Luke laughed. "You really don't remember how things were. Mason isn't a gentleman you refuse. If he invites you to his dinner party, you attend because if you don't, he has a way of making life difficult for you."

"Difficult how?"

"It's hard to explain. When you were upset, it was obvious. You'd come right out and say it. With Mason, he pretends to be your friend until he decides to do something about it, and when he does, you rarely see it coming."

"Has he made life difficult for me in the past?"

"No," Luke replied. "He didn't do anything to you. You would have made his life worse because you had all the money, and Mason wasn't about to let the money go."

"Doesn't Mason have his own money?"

"Not after he lost it to Lord Edon two years ago. You lost some money to him as well, but you had plenty left over and Mason didn't."

"Mason's indebted to me?"

"I suppose you could say that," Luke said. "You have the

steward pay him a stipend every month."

Jason recalled the ledger and remembered seeing Mason's name. "I thought it was standard for me to pay Mason something since I have the title."

"No. Mason has his own wealth. Or rather, he did. Without you there to boost him up, he'd be poor."

"Do you think that's something he might resent?"

"Resent? I don't know how that could be since he's the one who lost his money to Lord Edon after you warned him to stop gambling. He ought to be grateful. If Mason was my brother, I wouldn't give him anything, but then, I don't care for him. You ready to play chess?"

Jason nodded, but his mind was still on what Luke had just told him. He rubbed his chin. Something was wrong. Mason did resent him, and this might be the reason why. But what would Mason do if he resented someone enough? Get him on a horse, knowing full well that he was scared of riding it, and then head for the trees? Jason didn't like the way his thoughts were going, but the more he recalled that day and how fast he had to go to keep up with Mason, he had to wonder if Mason was hoping he'd fall.

"Jason?" Luke asked.

Forcing his mind off of Mason, he turned to the chessboard. "Anna explained how to play the game, but I'm afraid I don't remember all the rules. Will you refresh my memory?"

"Certainly."

Jason listened attentively as Luke gave him the rules. By the way Luke talked, Jason gathered that Luke loved this game. He probably played it any chance he got. But as Jason followed the instructions, he didn't think he cared much for the game. He understood it had to do with strategy, but for some reason, it didn't hold his attention as well as he expected.

Halfway through the game, he turned his gaze to Luke who was studying the board, carefully plotting his next move.

Clearing his throat, Jason asked, "I used to enjoy this game, didn't I?"

"Yes, but you enjoyed it much more if you could win," Luke replied with a mischievous grin. "Should I do a better job of losing?"

"No. You should do your best." He shifted in the chair and sighed. "I don't know what's wrong with me. I don't seem to like many of the things I used to. I don't care for horses or gambling, and now I discover I don't care if I win or lose this game of chess."

Luke sat back in his seat and chuckled. "Well, in that case, there's no real challenge for me, is there? You'll lose just to end the game."

"I'm sorry."

"There's nothing to be sorry about. Chess doesn't interest every gentleman."

"It seems that few things interest me."

"What are you interested in?"

Jason clasped his hands in front of him and thought over his cousin's question. "I enjoyed dancing with Anna at the ball last night, I like listening to her play music on the piano, I have fun watching the balloon launch and walking through Hyde Park…"

"All of these are things you do with Anna?"

"Yes, I think so. But I didn't spend much time with her before, did I?"

Luke shook his head. "You said a wife was meant to give you an heir. Other than that, you had other ways to amuse yourself."

"That being the case, I can't say losing my memory was a bad thing."

"The only thing we had in common before was chess. As much as I love the game, I'd rather spend time with you as you are now than play chess with the person you once were. We don't have to play chess while we're here. We can drink some brandy and have a conversation. We can play cards, and we don't have to play for money. We can even catch up on current events if you wish."

"Current events?"

"Sure. Napoleon's now in exile on Elba. A lot of gentlemen here are glad to see that the usurper got what he deserved. Of course, there's also the trouble we're having with America. It seems it's always one thing or another. Plenty to keep you occupied if you wish to learn more."

"Did those things interest me before?" Jason asked.

"As long as you had your entertainment, you didn't care what was going on," Luke replied.

With a chuckle, he said, "You'll likely find this amusing, but I think I enjoyed playing on Anna's piano. At the time, I tested it out because it was an excuse to sit close to her, but I wouldn't mind doing it again."

"Gentlemen have been known to play pianos."

"But it wasn't something I liked before?"

"No. You liked music enough, but I can't recall you taking an interest in playing a musical piece."

Jason rubbed his eyes and leaned back in his chair. "I don't understand how I can be so drastically different from before. If I didn't know any better, I'd say I was a completely different person."

"Are you happy?" Luke asked.

"Yes."

"Then what's the problem?"

Jason laughed and tapped the arms of his chair. "There isn't one, is there?"

"Not that I can see." Luke stood up and gestured to the other room. "Why don't I introduce you to the other gentlemen here so you can put some names with some faces?"

Jason nodded and stood up. Feeling better, he followed

Luke to the other room.

***

When Jason returned to the townhouse, he asked the footman to get the steward. "Tell him to meet me in the library," he added before the footman headed down the hallway.

As he passed the drawing room, he heard the familiar sound of Anna playing on her piano. He smiled and went to the doorway, careful to remain out of sight. She never seemed to be able to play an entire piece when she knew he was nearby, so to hear her, he learned to stay hidden. She was playing a slow but happy tune. He'd come to learn that she had a tendency to play songs that mirrored her mood at the moment. So right now, she was in a good mood, though a bit thoughtful.

He sighed. As much as he was enjoying London, he missed how carefree she'd been at their country home. He had no idea why she worried so much over whether or not he'd find a way to fit in with the friends they had here. Everyone they came across was more than understanding about his loss of memory. Perhaps in time, she would come to realize that, too, and then she could stop worrying.

He caught sight of the steward who was heading for the library and decided he would see Anna after he talked to the steward. Once he reached the library, he had the steward shut the door and sit across from him.

"I'd like to see the ledger again," Jason said and pulled his chair up to his desk.

The steward placed it in front of him. "I trust you'll find everything is in order, Your Grace."

Jason nodded but didn't say anything as he opened it. He ran through the list of expenses. "Good. I see you and the other servants are getting paid what you should."

"Yes, Your Grace, and we're thankful for that."

"I don't blame you. It's a wonder you all didn't quit." Jason continued to study the expenses. "Are you budgeting for Lord Mason's monthly allotment?"

"I am, Your Grace. Should I stop?"

With a sigh, he rubbed the back of his neck. "I don't remember why I had to begin his allotment. Where is it listed?"

"They're under *M.A.*, Your Grace."

"*M.A.*?"

"Monthly Allotment. I didn't know what else to call it."

Finding the initials, Jason scanned the previous months and compared them to what Mason had received for that month. "That's odd."

"What's odd, Your Grace?"

"Well, I notice that the amounts differ from month to month up until my fall down the stairs. Then it's been the same every month."

The steward nodded. "You used to vary the amount depending on your…mood…at the time."

"Mood?" Jason asked, finding that an odd way of putting it.

"You used to tell me what to pay your brother, and when you were in a good mood, he received more than if you were in a bad mood. Forgive me, Your Grace, but I don't know any more than that. It wasn't my place to question you. I simply followed your instructions."

"Of course." Jason couldn't have expected the steward to do anything more or less than that. "Is the amount he gets now sufficient for his needs?"

"It's more than enough, but whether your brother's content with it is another matter."

"He's not content with what he receives?"

"He has come to me about getting more. I had to tell him no."

"Did you give him more than you reported in the past?"

Jason asked, sensing there was more to the story than the steward wanted to tell him.

He slowly exhaled. "I have, but only in the past. I haven't budged from the allowed expense since you got well."

Jason's gaze returned to the steward's tense expression. He drummed his fingers on the desk as he debated the best way to proceed with his questions. "Does Lord Mason come by often to ask for more money?"

"He has a tendency to spend more than he has."

"I'll take that as a yes." He shut the ledger. "Isn't there any way he can get an income that doesn't involve my finances?"

"The easiest way would be if he married into money."

"And the other way?" Jason asked.

He shifted in his chair and cleared his throat. "I think we both know the answer to that one, Your Grace."

Right. Mason would have to become the duke. After a tense moment passed between them, he said, "I imagine he was disappointed when I got well." He stood and handed the ledger back to him. "Thank you for being honest with me."

The steward rose to his feet. "Your Grace, far be it from me to advise you on your financial affairs, but if you wanted to stop those monthly allotments, I don't think anyone would fault you for it."

No one but Mason, he thought. Things were already shaky between him and Mason. At the moment, it didn't seem wise to press his luck. "I understand the situation with Lord Mason, and I'll be careful where he's concerned. In the meantime, we'll let the allotment stand as it is. It might be that Lady Templeton will marry him and take him to British India."

"That would be a relief."

Jason wondered if there was something the steward wasn't telling him but decided they'd discussed enough for one day. And perhaps with the way servants talked, the less said, the better. "I have nothing else to ask. You may go now."

The steward bowed and left the room.

Jason sat back down so he could have a few minutes to clear his head. He didn't wish to see Anna when he was facing some dark thoughts. Everything added up. There was no other possibility he could see in the midst of all he'd just learned. Mason had every motive to want him killed. Losing his money to Lord Edon, becoming dependent on him for his income, and wanting more money than he was allotted. It all made sense.

So he hadn't been imagining Mason's ill will toward him. Mason might be pleasant to him on the surface, but underneath, he hated him. But what could he do about it? If he gave Mason more money, would Mason really be content with that or would he want more? He suspected Mason's desire for money outweighed anything else. If he didn't marry Lady Templeton, then Jason might be facing a very formidable opponent.

Jason leaned back in his chair and closed his eyes, his fingers lightly brushing the edges of the chair's arms. Something must happen, and it must happen soon because if Mason tried to make him fall off the horse last time he visited Camden, there was no telling what he'd try in the future.

Chapter Nineteen

The next day, Anna couldn't concentrate as her lady's maid finished tying the ribbon in her hair. Her mind ran over so many things. The balloon launch, Hyde Park, the theatre, Lady Cadwalader's ball... All of it had been wonderful, a dream come true, really. Jason hadn't felt the need to slip out of the townhouse to seek entertainment with another lady.

It relieved her to no end that he hadn't accepted Lady Hausen's offer to take her as a lover. The invitation occurred at Lady Cadwalader's ball, and Anna had just returned from talking to Candace when she caught Lady Hausen speaking with Jason in the corner of the room. She came up behind them as they talked, and even if Lady Hausen wasn't doing anything outright inappropriate, Anna heard her invite him to her townhouse sometime. He'd declined and left in favor of finding someone else to talk to, and while Anna hadn't told him she overheard the conversation, her respect for him increased significantly. In many ways, it seemed as if he'd fallen right out of heaven when she'd needed him the most.

"Your Grace?"

Blinking, Anna turned her attention back to her lady's maid. "I'm sorry. I'm afraid I got distracted. What did you say?"

"I only said I was done and that you look lovely this evening."

Anna turned her attention back to her reflection. "You do a wonderful job. The blue ribbons in my hair complement my dress very well."

"It's more than the hair and dress, Your Grace. You are radiant because you're in love. Nothing makes a lady more beautiful."

Her face grew warm. "Yes. His Grace is more than I could've ever hoped for."

She smiled. "Is there anything else you want me to do?"

Anna shook her head. "No, and thank you."

As Anna left her bedchamber, Jason stepped out of his room. She was ready to call out to him when his valet emerged from the room and handed him a pocket watch.

"Would you like to take this?" his valet asked.

"Yes, I suppose it's good to know what time it is," Jason replied.

Especially when you're eager to leave some place, Anna thought, ever in dread of Lady Templeton's ball. She couldn't think of anything that was worse, except if it was Lord Mason's dinner party. Knowing it was too late to feign an illness and cursing herself for not thinking of it sooner, she squared her shoulders back and headed for Jason.

He turned and smiled. "Anna, you're a breathtaking sight tonight."

"Thank you, Your Grace," she replied.

"I know you're not looking forward to this ball, so I thought I'd keep a close eye on the time. We should agree on a time to leave."

"When the first couple guests start leaving, we will, too. That way we'll blend in with everyone else."

"Hmm…" He glanced at the pocket watch and shrugged. "Then I suppose I don't need it."

"I wouldn't take it. If you do, you'll end up looking at it all night, and when you do that, time passes much slower."

"I suppose you're right. All right. I'll leave it here."

He handed it back to the valet and turned to her, offering her his arm. "Are you ready?"

"I suppose so." She accepted his arm and went down the stairs.

"Anna?"

"What?"

"Mason once asked me how I could have fallen down the stairs and not broken my neck. I can see how a fall doesn't necessarily mean a broken neck, but I have wondered why I don't have a fear of staircases. I mean, even now I don't like horses, and I've spent considerable time with mine. I don't understand why since I didn't fall off a horse."

Anna debated what to say. Something probably happened with a horse, but she had no idea what that something was. "Jason, all I know is that I never saw you fall off a horse. It's possible that it happened."

He patted her hand and smiled. "It's one of those great mysteries. Whatever the reason, I'm alive and here with you now, and that's all that matters."

Relieved he wasn't going to press her about the stairs, she nodded. "Yes, it is all that matters. I'm just glad you're here with me."

They reached the bottom of the steps and he kissed her. "I am, too."

The footman opened the front door, and they went to their carriage. On the way there, she held Jason's hand and prayed that the night would pass without any problems. She closed her eyes and wondered if Lord Mason would always be a thorn in her side. She wanted to have nothing to do with him. She didn't suppose she'd be fortunate enough for him to marry Lady Templeton and shove off to British India with her and her father. It would take care of everything if he did. Then she could rest assured that her lie would never be exposed. So far, no one else seemed to suspect the truth. They understood that Jason had amnesia and accepted the new changes in him without any questions. It was just Lord Mason who posed the threat. And she had no idea how that would be resolved.

When they arrived at the ball, she scanned the large room, hoping one of their friends might be there. Beside her, Jason touched her arm. She turned to him. "What is it?"

"Candace is here."

Her gaze followed his and she relaxed. Good. The ball would be more bearable with her friend there. At the moment, Candace was dancing.

"Splendid! I'm glad you could make it," Lady Templeton called out.

The two turned in time to see Lady Templeton and Lord Mason curtsy and bow. Anna and Jason returned the greeting, and Anna offered the most polite smile she could muster.

"It's a wonderful evening for a ball, isn't it?" Lady Templeton asked.

"Yes, it is," Anna forced out, clasping her hands together. Out of the corner of her eye, she watched as Candace continued to dance.

"It wouldn't have been the same without you, dear brother," Lord Mason told Jason. "In fact, I was wondering if I could have a word with you. You two ladies don't mind if we scurry off to talk, do you?"

"I'd never dream of coming between you and your brother," Lady Templeton replied. "Don't mind us. We can take care of ourselves."

Anna hid her grimace. Just what she wanted to do: spend time with Lady Templeton. Her hands tightened as she glanced Candace's way. The dance was done, but she had no way of going over to her friend as long as Lady Templeton wanted to talk to her.

Lady Templeton led Anna to one of the chairs at the side

of the room and sat next to her. "You and the Duke of Watkins make a good looking couple."

"Thank you." Not knowing what else to say, she added, "So do you and Lord Mason."

"Yes, well, about that, I wanted to ask you something, and to get the information I want, I'm afraid I have to be bold. Would it bother you if I were to be bold?"

Reluctant, Anna shook her head.

"Good. My father fancies Lord Mason for a son-in-law, but with our money, it's important we can be assured he'd be coming into our family with some assets. Now, I'm asking you as a lady who is interested in taking care of her financial affairs, would it behoove me to accept Lord Mason's proposal?"

"Has he proposed?"

"Yes, but I told him I needed to think it over. I know your husband is well off, but is Lord Mason?"

"To be honest, I don't know his financial situation. I don't even know my husband's."

"But surely, you have some idea?"

"I assume because he throws extravagant dinner parties and travels that he manages well."

Lady Templeton sighed in disappointment. "You mean to tell me you don't take a peek at things from time to time or talk to the steward, just to make sure you're secure?"

"No, I don't, but even if I did, it would have no bearing on Lord Mason. His financial affairs don't affect me."

"Perhaps you can talk to your husband. He might know something."

That might have been true with her first husband, but it wouldn't be true with her second. And even if her first husband was alive, she'd never ask him about the finances. "Lady Templeton, I don't know how things are done from where you live, but in London, a lady's place isn't in her husband's financial affairs."

"I understand." Lady Templeton rose to her feet and offered her a strained smile. "Thank you for your time."

Anna nodded, sure that Lady Templeton was glad to get away from her. As she watched her weave her way through the crowd, Anna wondered if she should ask Jason about the financial affairs of the estate. She had assumed that the steward had everything under control and that he'd talk to Jason if anything was amiss. But would Jason know what to do if something was wrong? She knew he wouldn't mind if she asked. He was nothing like her first husband.

"Anna, I'm so glad you're here."

Breaking out of her thoughts, Anna looked up and saw Candace. Relieved, she held her hands out to her friend and clasped them. "I was hoping Lady Templeton and her father would invite you here tonight," Anna said.

Candace sat next to her and squeezed her hands. "Considering how close Mason is to Ian, I think Lady Templeton and her father didn't have much of a choice. But I wondered if you and Jason would come, especially with how tense things have been between them."

"Tense between them? You mean Jason and Lord Mason?"

"I don't understand why you call Lord Mason so formally when he's your brother-in-law."

"It sickens me to think of him as anything more personal."

"But you are now referring to your husband as Jason?"

"He's not the same person he was before he lost his memory."

Candace smiled. "You're happy. Really, truly happy."

Anna's smile widened. "Yes, I am."

"I'm glad, Anna. You've been through so much."

"It's a shame we can't give Ian a memory loss."

"If he'd be anything like Jason, I'd love it, and then…"

Surprised that her friend stopped talking, Anna pressed,

"Then what, Candace?"

Candace blinked back her tears and whispered, "Then I wouldn't have to tell him I'm no longer expecting a child."

"What?"

"It's been two weeks since I lost the baby. I was in pain and had no idea what was happening until I saw the blood."

Anna's grip tightened on Candace's hands. "I'm so sorry."

"I don't know how to tell him. He'll be upset. You know how much he wants a son."

"All titled gentlemen want sons."

"Yes, and I hoped this would be it. I don't know what's worse: losing the baby or knowing he'll be back in my bed to try for another one."

"They're both equally terrible."

Candace wiped her eyes with the edge of her handkerchief. "I don't know how I'm going to tell him. I don't want to tell him at all, but I'm supposed to be showing soon and by then, I can't hide the truth."

"I don't know what to tell you. At least you know it's nothing you did. These things happen."

"I know, but it doesn't make it any easier."

No, Anna supposed it didn't. She gave her friend a hug and whispered, "If you ever feel like you're not safe, you can stay at my home."

Candace pulled away from her and wiped the tears from her eyes again. "Ian's not as bad as Jason was. He never raises a hand against me. The worst he does is ignore me unless it's time to work on an heir."

"As long as you're safe, that's the main thing."

"I am. I just don't know how to tell him."

"Give it a few days, think it through, and tell him. If you need to work out how you're going to tell him, you can tell me how you want to tell him. Then we can work on the thing that sounds best."

Candace nodded. "Thank you, Anna. You're a good friend."

She patted her back and sighed, wishing she could do more to help Candace but knowing there wasn't anything else she could offer her friend. Together, they sat in silence and watched the others dance. And as they did, Anna's thoughts wandered to Jason and what he and his brother were discussing.

***

"You want me to go to the circus?" Jason asked. He stood in the middle of the den, studying the piece of paper Mason had given him with information about the circus.

"It's something you should do at least once," Mason replied as he poured some brandy into his glass. "Do you want a drink?"

Jason shook his head. "No." The last thing he'd ever do was accept a drink from Mason.

With a shrug, Mason returned the decanter to the shelf and sat in a chair. "It's the finest brandy in London. Lady Templeton's father spares no expense. Don't be shy. Sit somewhere. God knows there's enough chairs to choose from."

Jason put the paper on the desk and sat across from him, wondering when he could leave so he could be around other people. As it was, he and Mason were alone, and it wasn't a scenario he particularly cared for. Trying to get as comfortable as he could in the leather chair, he asked, "Do you feel that I don't give you sufficient funds each month?"

Mason's eyes widened. Running his finger along the top of his glass, he said, "I didn't think you remembered that little arrangement we made."

"I don't. I had a conversation with the steward."

"Ah. That explains it."

After a long moment of silence passed between them,

Jason asked, "Are you going to answer my question?"

"We've had this discussion often enough over the past two years. I don't see what good rehashing the whole thing will do."

"Considering I don't recall any of those discussions, it's worth rehashing."

Mason chuckled and took a sip of his drink. "Why? Did you think you pay me too little?"

"I'd like to know why I'm paying you at all. You're a grown gentleman, not a child."

"Because you're generous to a fault?"

"Somehow I doubt that's the reason."

A slight scowl crossed his face before he smiled. "I don't see how it's any of your concern since you're not my real brother. The charade is well done. You look just like him, and you give a marvelous job of pretending you don't remember anything. But you don't fool me, Alastair."

Jason's eyebrows furrowed. "Alastair?" He'd heard that name before, but he couldn't recall where.

"Yes, Alastair. That's your name." Mason swallowed the rest of his brandy and leaned forward so he could look Jason in the eye. "You lived in the circus your entire life, traveling from one town to another."

"You're lying."

He threw his head back and laughed. "My real brother is dead, and I'm being accused of lying. It was a very clever ploy. I don't know how you and Anna did it, but you fooled everyone else. Bravo for a job well done!"

Jason bolted to his feet. "I've heard enough."

"You won't be able to leave the room."

Not to be deterred by the threat, Jason strode over to the door and tried to open it. Gritting his teeth, he turned toward Mason who was on his way back to the decanter to pour himself another glass of brandy.

"I tire of this game. I insist you unlock this door at once."

"Not until we reach an agreement."

"What kind of agreement are you talking about?"

"That's much better." Mason took another sip of his drink and grinned. "I'll keep your secret if you give me half your money."

"What?" Jason snapped, unable to believe his brother would not only lie to him about his past but rob him as well.

"I'm not a fool. Lady Templeton will never marry me if she finds out I don't have any money. Her father is far wealthier than many gentlemen at this ball. I'll live very well off her dowry, but I need to have some money going into the marriage. You understand my problem?" Mason walked over to him, and he stepped back until his back hit the door. "Wouldn't you like to get rid of me? See me go to British India where I won't bother you or Anna? Your secret will stay your secret, and I will be very happy. So everyone wins. Now, we're reasonable gentlemen. Surely, you can agree to this. Give us both a happy ending."

Jason shook his head. "It sounds like a bribe to me."

"Bribe?" Mason scoffed. "I think bribe is much too strong of a word when I should be the duke. I was second in line, you know. If it weren't for you, I'd be living very well right now. But as it is, you stole my inheritance. You and that whore you married owe me."

Jason shoved him away, not caring when Mason fell back against the chair and dropped his glass which shattered into several pieces. He grabbed Mason by his waistcoat and pulled him toward him so that their noses were almost touching. "Anna's not a whore, you deplorable excuse for a gentleman. I don't owe you anything. You should be grateful I give you anything at all. It was your stupidity that got you into this mess."

Mason tried to push back at him, but Jason maintained his hold on the waistcoat. "You're stronger than you look," Mason grunted and struck him as hard as he could across his face. "It's a shame you won't be getting that heir. Anna's as barren as the desert. Sooner or later, you'll die, and I'll get the inheritance. You sold yourself to a whore for nothing."

Jason's blood came to a boil, and he punched his brother. The bone in Mason's nose cracked, and he fell back into a chair, his hand covering his bloody nose. To his surprise, Mason was laughing.

"You didn't know, did you?" Mason asked, laughing harder. "Oh, I don't believe it! The little shrew tricked you. You really believe you're Jason Merrill, the Duke of Watkins. I thought I'd been played for a fool, but you're the biggest fool of all."

Jason clenched his hands at his sides, ignoring the pain in his right hand which had struck Mason. "Stop it!"

Mason rose to his feet and pulled out a handkerchief so he could wipe his nose. "Ask her. Go on and ask her about Alastair and the circus. You want to know why you can swing on a branch? It's because you're an acrobat. You did that for a living." He chuckled. "Ask her, Alastair. I think you'll find her answers quite informative." He reached into his pocket and threw the key at Jason, which bounced off his chest and hit the floor. "Go on! You'll find out the truth, and when you do, we'll discuss dividing my brother's money in half."

Jason hesitated for a moment but grabbed the key off the floor and headed for the door. Mason was still laughing, but he was sure Anna would assure him that Mason was lying to him. He unlocked the door, swung it open, threw the key back at Mason, and hurried down the hallway to the ballroom.

Chapter Twenty

Anna just finished dancing with a gentleman when she saw Jason enter the ballroom. His hair was disheveled, and a bruise was forming on his cheek. She looked behind him, but Lord Mason was nowhere in sight. Her gaze returned to Jason who was searching the room. Something in the way he furrowed his eyebrows bothered her.

She headed for him, and as soon as his eyes met hers, she knew something was wrong between them. When she reached him, she asked, "Jason, are you all right?"

He glanced behind him then scanned the room before looking at her. "I don't know. Can we go home?"

Unsure of how serious this would be, she nodded. "Sure. The coach is waiting outside."

Since he waited for her to make the first move, she turned on her heel and went to Lady Templeton's father so she could thank him for a lovely evening. She was aware that Jason followed her, not saying anything and seeming to be preoccupied with something. She scanned the room again but didn't see Lord Mason anywhere. Whatever was bothering him had to involve Lord Mason. Before Lord Mason talked to him, he'd been in a good mood. And now... She dared a glance in Jason's direction as they left the ballroom. He didn't look happy. She'd gotten so used to him smiling and talking that his somber mood made her uneasy.

She waited until they were in the carriage before she spoke. "Jason, what's wrong?"

Staring out the window, he sighed and set his hand on his knee. "I don't know how to even ask. Lord Mason was lying. I know he was lying. He had to be lying. There's no way you'd lie to me, especially not about something this important."

She didn't like the sound of this. Shifting in the seat next to him, she cleared her throat. "What did Lord Mason say?"

Even as she asked the question, she wanted to take it back. It'd be much easier to tell him that Lord Mason never told the truth about anything, that whatever it was that was bothering him wasn't true. She had a sinking feeling that Lord Mason had successfully figured out what she and Appleton did. He'd been there to visit his brother earlier the day he died. He knew how ill his brother had been. He'd been suspicious all along, and something confirmed his suspicions. She had no idea what that *something* could be, but it was enough for him to go to Jason and confront him.

She clutched her stomach and closed her eyes to settle the swell of nausea that threatened to make her lose her dinner. The moment she feared was here. Or maybe it wasn't. Maybe she was wrong and Lord Mason had cornered Jason about something else. Either way, she needed to resolve it.

Clasping her hands in her lap, she asked, "What do you want to ask me?"

Jason rubbed his eyes. "Not here. We should talk when we're alone."

"The coachman can't hear us."

"I'd still rather be in a place where no one is around."

She released a nervous breath and nodded. "All right. We can do that." Maybe if she obliged him and did things his way, he'd be more receptive to hearing her side of the story. He wasn't an unreasonable gentleman. He might understand.

She swallowed the lump in her throat and forced her attention on her gloved hands so she wouldn't cry. She didn't want to think of what would happen if she lost everything she'd gained since her first husband died. Her stomach rolled again, so she took deep breaths to settle it. The ride to their townhouse was short, but being in the carriage and fearing what was to come made it seem abnormally long.

By the time the coachman pulled to a stop, she jerked up in the seat and waited for the footman to open the door. Ignoring Jason's curious stare, she left as soon as the door opened. She hurried up the steps to the townhouse and entered it, not bothering to wait for the footman to open the door for her. She knew running into the townhouse made things look worse, but she needed a moment to herself so she could gather her composure.

When she entered the drawing room, she sat on the bench in front of the piano and closed her eyes. Maybe it had nothing to do with her first husband. Maybe Lord Mason had talked to him about something else. It was possible. Unlikely perhaps, but possible all the same.

"Your Grace?"

She opened her eyes and looked into Appleton's caring eyes. Her gaze darted to the doorway which was clear. It wouldn't be for long. Jason would be coming into the room soon. She swallowed the lump in her throat and gripped the bench. "I think he knows. I think Lord Mason told him."

Appleton's eyebrows furrowed. "But how could Lord Mason know?"

She shook her head and shrugged. "I don't know." She took a deep breath, trying in vain to calm her racing heart. This was it. Everything was crashing in around her. She knew that's what Lord Mason had told him. Deep down, she just knew it.

They heard Jason approach the drawing room, and Appleton turned to face him. "Your Grace." Appleton bowed.

"Is there anything I can get for you?"

"No," Jason slowly replied. "I'd like to be alone with my wife."

Appleton glanced at her, and she gave him a slight nod. Jason waited until he left before he entered the room and shut the door. She braced herself for whatever would happen and faced him.

"I take it that Appleton knows," Jason softly said.

Unable to make eye contact with him, she asked, "What do you want to ask me?"

"Mason said that I'm not really his brother. He said I'm someone named Alastair and that I used to work in the circus. Is he right?"

Her shoulders slumped. "I don't know if your real name is Alastair or if you worked in the circus, but he's right about you not being his brother." There. She said it. The horrible truth was out in the open, and now she'd have to suffer whatever consequences came from it.

For a long moment, Jason didn't speak. He didn't even move from his spot near the door. She couldn't be sure what he was doing, and she didn't dare look at him to find out. Her gaze remain fixed on the piano keys in front of her, though she remained facing in his direction.

"Why did you lie to me?" Jason asked.

Tears sprang to her eyes. She didn't know what was worse: having to explain it or the gentleness in his voice. "I didn't see any reason why you should know. Appleton searched for anyone who might know you, but no one did. We didn't know who you were. We found you on the forest road, beaten and left for dead."

"What were you and Appleton doing in the forest?"

She sniffed and wiped her eyes. "Burying my husband."

"Your real husband. The one I replaced?"

She nodded.

"So when he became ill, he died?"

"Yes," she whispered. "And Lord Mason was going to come here to take his place. The title would have gone to him, and he's worse than his brother was."

Jason approached her, his steps slow as he crossed the room. Lowering his voice, he asked, "How did you plan to hide your husband's death?"

"Appleton was going to tell everyone that he went on a trip. It wouldn't have been uncommon. He'd traveled in the past. I thought that when people started getting suspicious, Appleton and I could gather enough money to disappear so that by the time everyone realized he was dead, we'd be long gone."

"But then you found me?"

She nodded again and finally looked at him, afraid of what she'd see, but he didn't seem to be condemning her as she'd feared. Instead, there seemed to be a spark of understanding in his eyes. Encouraged, she continued, "You look just like him. We couldn't believe it. Our original plan was to ask you if you'd pretend you were my husband, but then you didn't remember anything or anyone and…" She cleared her throat. "It just seemed easier this way. If you didn't know the truth, then when Lord Mason came around, you wouldn't have to hide anything from him, and you'd be innocent of the lie."

"And you don't know anything about my past? Anything at all?"

"No."

He knelt in front of her and placed his hand on her knee. "I know what life was like for you with your husband, and I know what kind of person Mason is. I can't fault you for doing what you did."

It took her a moment to understand what he was saying, and when she realized he hadn't condemned her, she felt as if a weight had been lifted from her shoulders. "Thank you, Jason." She held his hand. "Thank you."

"Anna, I need to find out who I am."

She blinked and tried to make sense of what he was saying. "What?"

"In the carriage, I remembered a gentleman at Gretna Green who called me Alastair. That was the same name Mason called me tonight. That has to be my real name. I have to find out who I am."

Her hand tightened on his as a flicker of panic came over her. "Why? What's wrong with things as they are now? Someone wanted you dead. You were beaten so badly you would have died if Appleton hadn't found you."

"That's not what I'm concerned about. I need to find out if I had a wife."

"No. You didn't have a wife. No one recognized you. Jason-"

"No one Appleton asked recognized me, Anna. And if someone did but they wanted me dead, do you think they would have said they did?"

"But you don't remember anyone from that life."

"Does that mean I'm supposed to forget my duty to a wife I might have had before Appleton found me? And what if there are children? What kind of gentleman would I be if I didn't do right by them?"

"And what of your duty to me?"

He paused, his gaze going to their hands. With a sigh, he returned his gaze to her, his expression resolute even as pain filled his eyes. "If I was married, then our marriage is null and void. You know that."

"But I love you. I don't want you to go."

"I love you, too, but I need to find out. If I find out there's no wife, I'll return. I don't want to leave you, but I need to. I won't tell anyone what I learned tonight. As for Mason, you have another problem altogether."

He released her hand and stood up. Pacing to the

window, he peered out of it and released his breath.

"He knows everything," Jason continued. "He knows more than you do. I don't know how, but he does. Obviously, he's been investigating things for a while. I'll talk to the servants, tell them I'm going to take a trip. I won't disclose how long I'll be gone, but I'll explain that they must protect you. I don't trust Mason, Anna. He knows more than we do about my past, and he wanted half of your husband's money to keep quiet."

Bolting to her feet, she hurried over to him. "Give him the money, Jason. Lady Templeton will marry him if he has it, and he'll go to British India where he won't be a threat anymore."

"It won't be enough." Jason turned from the window and faced her. "I'm not so gullible as to believe he'll be satisfied with half the money. He'll want it all. You said he was eager for your husband to die."

"To get the title, but Lady Templeton will come with more money."

"And the more he'll receive, the more he'll want. I have a sense about him…" He shook his head. "I can't explain it. You'll have to promise me that you'll be careful. Make sure you have someone you trust with you at all times."

She wrapped her arms around his waist and hugged him, taking small comfort in the steady rhythm of his heartbeat. "Take me with you. If you turn out to have a wife," her throat went dry but she managed to choke out, "I'll say I'm your sister. Then I'll do what I had planned to originally do. I'll leave for another country and be out of Lord Mason's way."

He wrapped his arms around her and kissed the top of her head. "I can't take you with me. It's too dangerous. The people who left me in the forest might find me. I can't have them coming after you, too."

"Then don't go at all! Stay with me."

He gently pulled her away from him. "I can't. I have to know who I am."

"You're the Duke of Watkins! What more is there to know than that?" She burst into a fresh wave of tears. "Let the past be in the past. Whatever is out there can take care of itself. You're the duke. You were in the forest when I needed you. You're meant to be with me."

"If there is no wife and children, then I'll return to you." He kissed her, and even if she didn't want to admit it, the kiss was much too final. "No matter what happens, I love you. I'll love you to my dying day."

She closed her eyes and fought to think of something—anything—that would make him stay. But words eluded her, and before she knew it, he quietly strode out of the drawing room. He closed the door softly behind him, and within the next second, she collapsed on the floor, sobbing uncontrollably until she had no more tears to give.

Chapter Twenty-One

Jason could think of only one person who could start answering his questions, and that was the gentleman he'd run into the last time he was at Gretna Green. Don. If Jason remembered right, Don had referred to himself as the 'fire eater'. He had no idea what that meant, but it was all he had to go on, and he hoped it would be enough to find him.

Time had passed in agonizing slowness since the night he left London, and the coachman he paid seemed to take longer than his regular one. He supposed the time dragged on because Anna wasn't with him. He couldn't help but think of her with every mile that separated them.

Half a month of travel came and went before he reached his destination. He checked into an inn before he went to the front desk where the innkeeper was checking his books.

"May I help you, Your Grace?" the innkeeper asked.

"Yes. I was wondering if you're familiar with a gentleman by the name of Don." He chuckled. "You'll think it strange, but he might go by 'fire eater'."

The innkeeper laughed. "Yes, I know the gentleman. Came here when a circus passed through and never left. Married one of the ladies who lives here. Come." The innkeeper led Jason to the window and pointed to a lane not too far from the inn. "Lives down that way. He's a blacksmith now."

Jason thanked him and left the inn. As he walked down the road, he tried not to think of the day when he'd been coming through here in search of a priest to marry him and Anna, but no matter what he did, she was always on his mind. With a regretful sigh for how happy he'd been the day they married, he forced his attention to the task at hand. He found the blacksmith's shop easy enough and entered through the open door. He recognized Don right away, even though the gentleman had his back to him as he shoed a horse.

"Pardon me," Jason called out. "I was wondering if I might have a word with you?"

Don glanced over his shoulder. "Your Grace, I didn't think anyone came to Gretna Green after they married."

Jason stepped closer to him. "As I recall, you called me by another name last time I was here. It was Alastair."

He finished with the horseshoe and gently placed the hoof down. With a shake of his head, he grinned. "I'm sorry about that. It's just that you look so much like him."

"What if... That is to say, I have good reason to believe I might be him, this Alastair that you speak of."

Don crossed his arms and scanned him up and down. "You're the same height and build, and besides that, you got the same face. But didn't you say you're the Duke of Watkins?"

"I'm not sure. I was hoping you could answer some questions for me."

"Let me get this horse back into the stall. Then we'll talk in my home."

Jason nodded his consent and waited as Don led the horse in his direction. He balked and Don paused, stopping the horse.

"Does the horse frighten you?" Don asked.

"I'm trying to get over my fear of horses."

"You really might be Alastair. Alastair fell off a horse during a routine and nearly got trampled to death."

"I was?" Curious, he followed Don to the stall and waited

as he secured the animal in it. "Did this have anything to do with a circus?"

"As a matter of fact, it did." Don closed the stall door and placed his hands on his hips. "It was a new act. Do you remember it?"

"No. I don't remember anything from my previous life. My first memory is of my new life. I woke up badly injured. I was at an estate being tended to by a lady who said she was my wife."

"Except she wasn't?"

"Not at the time. I came here to find out who I really am. A gentleman, Lord Mason, told me my real name was Alastair and that I used to be in a circus. You're the only one who seems to know anything about me so I came here."

"I remember talking to Lord Mason."

"You do?"

"Yes. He arrived here the same day I talked to you."

Jason rushed to the entrance of the stable and scanned his surroundings. He hadn't considered that Lord Mason might be following him, but now he knew Lord Mason had in the past.

"I assured him you weren't Alastair, but then again, I wouldn't have even if I knew you were but had lost your memory. There's something wrong with him."

He turned back to Don. "Yes, there is. How did he get here? I saw no carriage with his crest on it."

"He was in a carriage without a crest on it."

Jason studied his surroundings one more time. He didn't see anything that would make him suspect Mason was out there, but that didn't mean he wasn't lurking nearby.

"You think he followed you here?" Don asked, also examining the village.

"Anything's possible." And knowing Mason's desire for money, he could very easily be biding his time until he could kill him. He had no proof that Jason wasn't the real duke, which was his greatest obstacle.

Don patted him on the shoulder. "Come and we'll have something to eat."

Jason didn't know what it was about Don that made him trust him, but he did. Without another word, he followed him to his home.

***

Anna sat at her piano and traced the keys. The days without Jason dragged from one to another, and for every day he didn't return or send her a letter, the possibility she might never see him again grew stronger. Where could he have gone? If only she knew what he was doing. Camden wasn't the same without him. *She* wasn't the same without him. Did she make the right choice in returning here? Before he left, she made sure he knew she would leave London, but what if he forgot?

She closed her eyes and fought aside her nausea.

Appleton entered the drawing room and closed the door. "Your Grace, I haven't heard you play anything ever since His Grace left."

She opened her eyes, a tear falling down her cheek. With a sigh, she grabbed her handkerchief and wiped her face. "I'm not in the mood for music."

"He didn't say he'd be gone forever," he softly began, "and when he left, he wasn't upset with you."

"But the longer he's gone, the less likely it is that he'll return."

"We don't know that."

Unwilling to be comforted by his words, she turned from the piano and sighed.

"I realize it's a small consolation, but if he doesn't return, you'll still have the child."

Bowing her head so he couldn't see more tears fall from

her eyes, she knew he was right. In all the years she'd been unable to conceive, it struck her as a bittersweet irony that she should be expecting a child now. But without knowing where Jason was, she had no way of telling him.

The door opened and the footman said, "Lord Mason is here to see you, Your Grace."

Now she knew she was going to be sick! She was ready to tell the footman to send him away when Appleton spoke up.

"I'll send him away, Your Grace," he told her before he left the room.

She gripped the handkerchief in her hands and willed Lord Mason to leave her alone. Jason had sent word to him that he'd be traveling for a while, so he shouldn't be stopping by. But if she counted right, this was the third time he'd been by since Jason left.

The footman quietly stepped out of the room, and she finally looked up. The room was, mercifully, empty, but she could hear Lord Mason arguing with Appleton. She couldn't make out what they were saying, but Lord Mason's voice rose and Appleton's remained calm. Why couldn't Lord Mason leave her alone? Why did he continue to hover about? Was he hoping Jason wouldn't return?

She placed her hand on her stomach and prayed she'd have a boy. If there could be an heir, he'd inherit the title. Even better than that, Jason would return. He couldn't be married to someone else. Appleton assured her of that from the search he did. But what if he didn't ask the right people to find that out?

Footsteps alerted her that Appleton was returning to the drawing room. She took a deep breath and glanced at him. "Is Lord Mason gone?"

"Yes, Your Grace. I told him he mustn't return until he receives an invitation from His Grace."

She nodded, wondering if he'd actually stay away. "What does he want?"

"He says he wishes to make sure you're all right." He

paused for a moment and added, "I suspect there's more to it than that."

"What do you think he wants?"

"I don't know. That's why I think it's best if he's no longer welcome here until His Grace returns. His Grace isn't a fool. He can handle him."

"I agree. I didn't think so in the beginning, but he's proven me wrong."

"He'll return, Your Grace," Appleton said. "In the meantime, I hope you'll remember to eat."

"I hardly have an appetite," she whispered.

"That's to be expected given your condition, but it's still good to eat something."

She smiled. "You're always there to take care of me. I don't know what I'd do without you."

He returned her smile. "It's a pleasure to be your butler, Your Grace. I'll ask Cook to prepare some fruit for you."

"Thank you."

As he left the room, she turned her attention back to the piano and stroked the keys. If Jason did return, she'd play anything he wanted to hear, and if she made a few mistakes, then she'd just keep playing. She hoped she'd get a chance to play for him again.

***

"No, I can't do it," the footman whispered.

Mason stood with his horse and studied the manor Alastair stole from him. This place was his birthright, not Alastair's. The title belonged to him, and Alastair had the nerve to hold onto Jason's name and title even after he was exposed for the fraud he was. Looking back at Jason's footman, he said, "Your hands are already bloody, Fieldman. Don't make it worse."

"What blood?"

"The Duke of Watkins died, and that was all because of you."

Fieldman shook his head and glanced around to make sure no one overheard them. "No, he didn't. The poison didn't have enough time to work, and then Her Grace was tending to him all the time so I couldn't slip the drinks to him."

Mason impatiently waved his hand at him. "No, you fool. The poison did work. But the duchess and butler disposed of his body. Where and how, I don't know, but they did. And somehow they found someone who looked just like my brother to take his place. Now that she's with child, he's conveniently gone to France?"

"Do you have proof that His Grace isn't really His Grace?"

"Of course not. They've been far too careful, and they've been using the butler to keep everyone away from the evidence. Appleton must be removed. Once he is, I can find out what I need and you'll have enough money to live a peaceful and quiet life in the country for the rest of your days."

"I can't do it. Appleton's an honorable gentleman, and even if the duke is someone else, he's someone worth working for. I refuse to poison anyone else."

The footman turned to leave but Mason grabbed his arm. "I'll make you a deal. Either you take care of Appleton or I'll find a way to take care of you."

His eyes grew wide. "My lord…"

"I mean it, Fieldman. Either Appleton dies or you do." Without waiting for a response, Mason got on his horse and rode off the property.

Chapter Twenty-Two

Don opened the door. "Francine, we have a visitor!" They walked through the doorway before he shut the door. "You remember what I said about owing you. She'll be glad to see you."

As soon as a young woman carrying an infant entered the room, she let out a cry of surprise and ran over to hug Jason, making sure she didn't make the baby uncomfortable. "I don't believe it! Is it really you, Alastair?"

"I…it appears so," Jason slowly replied.

She pulled away from him and looked at Don. "It appears so?"

"He lost his memory. How long ago was it that you woke up at that estate?" Don asked him.

"October," Jason replied.

"What happened in October?" Francine asked her husband.

"I'm not sure, but that's what he's here to find out," Don replied. "I think we should get something to eat and drink. We can talk in the kitchen."

Francine nodded and handed the baby to Don. "I'll get some soup ready. Come to the kitchen. I don't want to miss anything."

The gentlemen followed her to the kitchen, and when

Jason sat down, Don held the four-month-old infant to Jason. "Do you want to hold him? We named him after you."

Though Jason wasn't sure what to do with a baby, he took the boy in his arms and set him on his lap. "You named him Alastair?"

"We had to." Don smiled and ruffled the boy's hair. "If it wasn't for you, Francine and I wouldn't be together today."

Shifting to better face Don, Jason studied him. "What happened?"

"You helped me escape from the circus. I told you I used to go by 'fire eater'. That's because I could put the end of a flaming torch in my mouth and extinguish it. I also juggled with fire and taught animals to jump through rings of fire. Well, Francine happened to be attending one of our shows in Nottingham, and we both saw her. You also fancied her, but since Francine wanted to be with me, you graciously bowed out."

"I bowed out? So I'm not married?"

"No, and believe me, I'm very grateful for that since it allowed me to be with Francine."

Francine smiled at Don, and Jason recalled how Anna had smiled at him in the same way. Francine and Don had the kind of love he had with Anna, and he'd never been more grateful that he'd stepped aside so that they could be together. He suspected it had been a hard thing for him to do, given the similar sweetness Francine and Anna shared, but no one could ever be as wonderful as Anna. And now he could return home to Anna! He fought the urge to jump out of his chair and return to Camden. Before he left London, Anna told him she'd be going back there, and he didn't blame her since she took comfort in being in the country.

"You did more than let me be with Don," Francine said, directing Jason's attention to her. "You helped him escape."

Jason chuckled. "Escape?"

"She means it exactly as she said it," Don replied. "The circus leader, Iron Jim, was very possessive of those he managed."

"*Owned*, you mean," she added as she poured tea into their cups.

"As she said, *owned.* We weren't people in our own right. We were his property. We were either born and raised in the circus or found as infants. My parents trained animals, and that's how I came to learn to train animals. The fire was something new I added to the act."

"And something Iron Jim didn't want to lose. It was the highlight of the show."

"So what happened?" Jason asked. "How did I help you escape?"

"We were on our way out of Nottingham when you came up with the clever scheme to hide me in a barrel," Don began. "You had the task of disposing the garbage one night and as you collected it, you brought a barrel into my cage. In my place, we left some leaves and placed them under my blanket so when Iron Jim came by to check on everyone, he assumed I was asleep. You put the barrel and other garbage onto the wagon and took me safely away from the circus. I ran back to Nottingham, and Francine and I came here to get married. Since I was good with horses, I became a blacksmith."

"And we've been happy ever since," Francine replied and placed their cups on the table.

He winked at her and picked up his cup. "That we have." He took a sip and looked at Jason. "It took a lot of courage for you to do that."

Though Jason was honored by their words, he still had other questions. "How did I end up at the circus? Are my parents there?"

"No. You were sold into it when you were two days old. No one expected you to survive. You were sickly, but Iron Jim was sure with the right medicine, you'd survive. You were given to a couple who couldn't have children. The man was an expert horse rider and the woman an expert acrobat. In time, you became an excellent rider and acrobat."

"But I fell off the horse during one routine?"

"It was a new routine, but yes, you fell off and nearly died. It happened shortly before you helped me escape."

Jason picked up his cup to drink, but the baby reached for it so he quickly put it back down before any tea spilled out of it. "Do you know who my real parents are?"

"No. As far as I know, no one knew, although…"

"Although what?" Jason pressed.

Don rubbed his chin in a thoughtful manner. "It's possible Willie-the-juggler might know. He was Iron Jim's right-hand man, so to speak. Anything Iron Jim wanted done, he did it, including acquiring new circus workers. If anyone handled your adoption into the circus, it was him. He's probably in his early sixties by now, if he's still alive. I haven't had anything to do with the circus since you helped me escape, so I don't know if you can find him or not."

Jason thought over his choices. He could go back to Anna, assured that he wasn't married to anyone else, or he could see if that twin brother who disappeared from the Camden estate twenty-seven years ago was him. How else could he explain that he looked exactly like the duke he'd replaced? As tempted as he was to return home, he knew Mason posed enough of a threat to find out if he had the right to the title. If it turned out he was the missing twin, then Mason's argument that he didn't have the right to the title would be null and void. Maybe then Mason would leave him alone, and if he didn't…if he continued to give him problems, then Jason would seek out a legal way to handle it.

Jason turned his attention back to Don. "Do you know where I can find Willie?"

"If he's still alive, he'll be with Iron Jim's Circus. Iron Jim does the same route every year, and right now, he should be in London."

"Thank you."

"It's the least I can do for an old friend." Don patted him on the back and chuckled. "It's been good seeing you again. So you got married when you passed through here last time?"

"Yes, and she's a wonderful lady."

Francine placed the food and utensils in front of them. "Eat up. It doesn't stay hot for long." She took the baby. "I'll put him down for a nap. Don't mind me. I'll be back soon."

Don picked up his spoon and grinned. "It's not exactly the kind of dinner you're used to, seeing as how you're a duke and all, but it's better than how we used to eat in the circus." He dipped his spoon into the soup and added, "Tell me what your life is like now."

As they ate, Jason did as Don asked.

***

Two days later, Anna brought a small forkful of roasted lamb up to her mouth and debated if she had the stomach for it. She knew keeping something in her stomach at all times helped ease the morning sickness, but it was hard to get the first bite in. She took a slow, deep breath and put the fork in her mouth. The cook had done an excellent job of flavoring it so that she had an easier time of swallowing it. For some strange reason, certain types of foods were easier to eat than others. She waited for a long moment before her stomach settled.

Relieved, she poked another piece of the lamb with her fork and glanced at the seat where Jason used to sit. She recalled how much he wanted her to eat dinner with him in his bedchamber when he was still too injured to walk down the stairs. She'd give anything to eat with him in his bedchamber again. Blinking back her tears, she took a deep breath and focused on the baby. She had a new purpose, something to live for. A part of Jason would remain with her, in case he didn't return.

From behind her, a loud thump hit the floor followed by a

flurry of activity from the servants who stood nearby. Surprised, she turned in her chair and gasped when she realized Appleton had collapsed. Bolting out of her chair, she ran over to him.

"What happened?" she asked, shoving past the footman and maid who were kneeling by him.

"Please, Your Grace, don't come close," the footman warned her, holding his hand up to stop her from touching Appleton. "I don't think he's feeling well."

"What's wrong with him?" she demanded, not liking how pale he was.

"I don't know. Move aside, please."

She and the others who were hovering over Appleton backed up, and the footman lifted him in his arms. Appleton groaned, and she moved toward him. "Appleton, what's wrong?"

The footman headed for the door. "Your Grace, I insist you not come near him. He is not well, and you have yourself and the child to think about. I'll take him to his room and let you know how he's doing."

"Send for a doctor," she told him, following him as he left the dining room.

"Yes, I will, right after I make sure he's comfortable," the footman called over his shoulder and hurried down the hallway.

She slowed her steps until they came to a stop. Everything happened so fast. Just that morning, Appleton seemed to be all right. He had reported feeling a little strange around noon but assured her it was nothing to worry about and now… And now he'd collapsed while she ate dinner. Her heart constricted and she pressed her hand over her stomach. What was going to happen to him? Was this a simple illness or was it something serious?

A maid came over to her. "Your Grace?"

Anna stared at the hallway as the footman turned down another hallway, disappearing from sight. She wanted to continue going after him, but she knew there was nothing she could do for

Appleton. The doctor needed to take a look at him and tell her what to do. Tears welled up in her eyes. She probably lost Jason. Was she going to lose Appleton, too? Grabbing her handkerchief, she wiped her eyes. It was amazing she had any more tears remaining considering all she'd been doing was crying ever since Jason left. Was this her punishment for hiding her first husband's death?

"Your Grace?"

Reluctant, she turned her attention to the maid who offered her a sympathetic smile. She knew the maid meant well, but the maid had no idea what was really happening. Except for Appleton, the servants had no idea Jason wasn't the real duke and that he might not return. She sighed and turned back to the dining room. She needed to think of the baby. When the doctor came, she'd talk to him, but for now, she needed to eat the little she could manage.

***

It was close to midnight when the doctor finally arrived. Anna paced the drawing room, unable to sleep until she knew Appleton would be all right.

"It has to be punishment," she whispered and swallowed the lump in her throat. There was no other way to explain it.

She heard a set of footsteps come down the hallway and steadied herself so she could focus on what the doctor would tell her. Whatever he recommended, she'd do it.

Doctor Unger entered the room and placed his leather bag on the table. "Your Grace…please have a seat."

She froze in place, her heart racing with dread. "Is it that bad?"

"Your Grace?" He motioned to the settee.

She closed her eyes for a moment and gathered her strength before she walked over to it. It was bad news. Horrible news. It was the same tone he'd used when her first husband took ill. Back then, she hadn't cared, but now... She opened her eyes, gulped and sat down. I'm being punished, she thought. Appleton, her dear friend, was being taken from her in the same way her first husband had been.

Dr. Unger sat in the chair across from her. "He's sick to his stomach and is having trouble holding solids down. He's also developing a fever. This is the same illness that your husband had. But there's hope. Your husband survived, so there's a good chance your butler will, too. I'll leave the same medicine for you."

He had no idea how wrong he was, and knowing it was the same illness that afflicted her first husband—the same illness that sealed his fate—caused tears to fill her eyes. He handed her a clean handkerchief and waited as she sobbed into it. Her dear friend was doomed.

"There's hope, Your Grace. You must take courage from the fact that your husband survived."

She couldn't respond. All she could do was cry harder. Despite his optimism, she knew better. And that was the bitterness of the whole thing. She couldn't tell him why he was wrong. She couldn't tell him this was her punishment for lying about her first husband's death. For the first time since Appleton saved her from the gazebo the night she tried to end her life, she was alone. Even with a house full of servants, she was utterly and completely alone.

Chapter Twenty-Three

After dinner that evening, Anna slipped into Appleton's room. Despite the footman's protests that she needed to stay away from Appleton in case she caught his illness, she knew better. She'd never caught it from her first husband, and she wouldn't catch it from Appleton.

Though the maid had cleaned the bowl he'd vomited in, she caught the foul smell in the air. But the smell mattered little to her compared to the sad state he was in. She shut the door softly behind her and approached his bed. After all he'd done for her…all he'd saved her from… He didn't deserve this.

He opened his eyes and turned his head in her direction. Forcing a smile, he said, "I was hoping you'd come."

She grabbed a chair and pulled it up to his bed. Grabbing his hand, she pressed her forehead to it and cried. "Appleton…"

With his other hand, he patted her hair. "Your Grace, I've lived a full and happy life. I'm grateful you've been the duchess of this estate and that you found love with His Grace. He'll return. There's no doubt in my mind about that. And when he does, he'll comfort you."

"No! Don't talk like that. You can't leave me. You must hold on. There has to be a way we can get you better. There must be some medicine we haven't tried."

"I have no regrets."

She lifted her head. "Stop talking like that!"

He sighed and looked at her with his caring eyes. "It might not be my time, but if it is, I need you to know I'm all right with the way things ended."

She shook her head and bolted to her feet. "I can't believe you've given up. You need to fight this thing. You have to try."

"I am trying, Your Grace. I just want you to know I only wish the best for you."

Wiping her eyes, she turned her back to him. Would she ever stop crying? It seemed all she could do was cry. Surely, at some point she'd have no more tears. Her gaze fell to the empty pitcher by his bed. Taking a deep breath, she picked it up. "Do you think you can drink anything?"

"I might. Sometimes I can keep liquids down."

"I'll bring more water."

She headed out of the room and placed the pitcher on the kitchen table. Since the kitchen was vacant for the moment, she retrieved a fresh pitcher and filled it with water. When she returned to Appleton's room, she reached for the glass on the bedside table but knocked it over by accident. It shattered on the floor. With a sigh, she left the pitcher on the table and cleaned up the broken glass. Afterwards, she returned to the kitchen and asked the maid for a glass before she returned to Appleton's room.

Fortunately, she was able to pour him a glass of water this time. After she helped him sit up, she gave him the glass. "If you sip it, it might stay down."

He nodded and did as she instructed. He took a few sips and pushed the glass away. "I'm done."

She set the glass back on the table and helped him settle back into bed. "I'll stay with you tonight."

"Your Grace, there's no need for that. You need your rest."

"I can rest as easily here as I can in my bedchamber."

"But you need sleep."

"No." She shook her head. "I haven't slept well since Jason left, and I can't sleep at all now that you're ill."

"You have a child on the way, Your Grace."

With a sigh, she pulled the covers up to his neck. "I know, Appleton. I haven't forgotten. I can't will myself to sleep, but I feel better when I can be here with you to see how you're doing. Do you want me to close the curtains?"

"Yes, but I also want you to rest. The footman and maid have been coming in to help me."

"Then I won't do much more than keep you company, much like you kept me company when I had given up on everything."

She didn't want to say any more about the night she tried to kill herself, and she didn't have to. He understood. She saw it in his eyes.

"You don't want to give up on life, do you?" he softly asked.

"No. I deserve what I'm going through. I shouldn't have hid my first husband's death," she whispered.

"You mustn't feel that way. You did the only thing you could do. It was the best decision you could have made. We both know what Lord Mason would have done to you and to this estate if he'd taken over."

She inwardly shivered. "I don't trust him. Even now, I can't help but think he's up to something, and if I knew what that something was, I might scream." Turning from him, she went to the curtains and pulled them closed, casting the room into darkness, save for a single candle that was lit on his bedside table. She returned to him and sat by his bed. "Is there anything you need?"

"No. I expect it to be a long night."

Probably. She wouldn't expect it to be an easy one. Her gaze went to the cleaned bowl within his reach. It was a stark reminder of how ill he was, and it filled her with dread that he might need it. But there was nothing she could do except stay with him and help him, which was exactly what she'd do.

***

"Your Grace? Your Grace?"

Anna slowly came out of sleep, barely aware that someone was gently shaking her shoulder. She lifted her head, wondering when she'd drifted off. She recalled the clock chiming midnight and watching Appleton as he slept after he finally managed to drink a full glass of water. She straightened in the chair and faced the laundry maid.

"What time is it?" she asked, rubbing the kink out of her neck.

"It's seven in the morning."

She studied Appleton who remained asleep and leaned forward. She couldn't be sure, but he seemed to have gotten some of his color back. "Open the curtains."

The maid hurried to do her bidding.

Anna didn't recall Appleton vomiting at any point in the night, but to be sure, she checked the bowl and saw it was still empty. When she turned her gaze back to his face, she was assured that the color had, indeed, returned to his cheeks.

"Are there any soiled sheets or clothes for me to clean, Your Grace?" the maid asked her.

"No. Everything's clean."

Appleton shifted in the bed, and the maid came up beside Anna to study him. "He looks better this morning," the maid commented and touched his forehead. "His fever is gone."

Encouraged, Anna waited until Appleton opened his eyes to ask, "How are you feeling?"

He swallowed and sat up. She hurried to help him, but he stopped her. "I can do it. I feel better. In fact, I think I'm hungry."

Anna's heart leapt with excitement. Her first husband never had an appetite when he was sick. "You are?"

He nodded, and the maid headed for the door. "I'll ask Cook to make some soup."

Once she left, Anna took another good look at him. "Do you really feel well enough to eat?"

"Yes, but not much."

"That didn't happen with my first husband," she whispered.

"I'm aware of that." He smiled. "It looks like your luck is changing. Perhaps His Grace will arrive today."

She wished that were the case, but for the moment, her concern was for Appleton's improved health. "Is there anything I can do?"

"I wouldn't mind another glass of water, and after that, I'd like for you to get some rest and eat."

"Yes, I'll do that." She reached for the pitcher by his bed and poured him a glass of water. "I'll fill this up and bring more water."

"You might as well have the footman or maid do it."

"I don't mind doing it, Appleton, and to be honest, I'm so relieved you're better that I suddenly have a lot of energy. I need to do something with it."

He sighed. "I really hope you'll get some rest."

"I will. I promise." She held the glass to him, and he took it before she left the room to get him more water.

***

After Anna got some rest, she ate a full meal and went to Appleton's room. She knocked on the door as she entered it, and he looked over at her and smiled.

"I hear you were able to keep the soup down," she said as

she sat beside him.

"I did. I'm about to have more."

The tension left her muscles and she returned his smile. "That's wonderful to hear."

The footman came to the door with a pitcher of water. "Your Grace," he slowly stated and glanced at the pitcher on the bedside table. "I didn't realize you'd be in here. I see Appleton already has enough water."

"Yes, I do. Thank you for thinking of me, Fieldman," Appleton replied.

"There's nothing to thank me for," Fieldman softly stated. Clearing his throat, he added, "I'll send more when you need it." He turned to Anna. "In the meantime, Lord Mason is here to see you, Your Grace."

Her good mood took a nosedive. "Is he?"

"Perhaps I ought to get out of this bed and walk around a bit," Appleton said.

"No," she quickly replied. "You need your rest. I don't want you to have a relapse. Fieldman, send some tea to the drawing room."

The footman nodded. "Of course, Your Grace."

After Fieldman left with his pitcher, she patted Appleton's hand. "I'll keep him in the room with me, so I won't have to be alone with Lord Mason. I hope to be back shortly."

"Tread carefully, Your Grace."

"I will," she assured him before she stood up and strode out of the room.

As she entered the drawing room, Lord Mason rose from a chair and bowed. "Your Grace."

She gave the obligatory curtsy. "What brings you here today, Lord Mason?"

"I came to see if my brother has returned yet."

"No, he hasn't."

"That must be some trip to France."

She shrugged and averted her gaze from his, glad that the footman didn't take long in bringing them their tea. "Thank you, Fieldman," she told him as she motioned for him to pour tea into the cups and sat down. "Have a seat."

Lord Mason glanced at the footman before he sat across from her.

"I notice you've been coming by a lot lately," she told him as she accepted the cup from Fieldman.

Lord Mason took the cup Fieldman offered him. "Yes. That butler of yours was a formidable wall with the way he prevented me from talking to you."

"He meant no disrespect. I haven't felt up to receiving visitors in my condition. He did inform you that I'm expecting a child, didn't he?"

"Yes, he did. I suppose congratulations are in order. I think it's strange my brother would leave you alone as soon as you told him the news. After all the time it's taken you to conceive, you'd think he would be telling everyone the good news."

She forced a sip of tea, sure her sudden wave of nausea had more to do with Lord Mason than with her pregnancy. "He left before he knew."

"Oh, then he'll want to return as soon as he receives your letter."

She took another sip and nodded. She had no way of telling Jason, but Lord Mason didn't have to know that. Noticing that he didn't drink from his cup, she asked, "Is the tea not to your liking?"

He glanced at the cup before turning his gaze to the footman. She sensed the two sent a silent message between each other but had no idea what that message was. The exchange caused her a flicker of unease. Then she recalled returning from Gretna Green with Jason and seeing the two arguing. Whatever the issue was at the moment, Lord Mason seemed content and drank from his cup. She lowered her gaze to the tea in her cup.

Lord Mason's tea came from the same pot as hers did. Did Lord Mason think something was wrong with it?

Losing her appetite for the tea, she placed her cup down. When Lord Mason's eyebrows rose, she said, "I've been having difficulty drinking and eating because of the child."

"Of course."

She shifted in the chair, not sure what to make of the knowing tone in his voice and what she thought was a smirk on his lips. "What matter do you wish to discuss?"

He glanced at the footman again. "I'd rather discuss the matter in private."

The hair on the back of her neck rose on end at the thought of being alone with him. "I'm afraid I can't oblige you on that. With my stomach being as uneasy as it is, I'd like him nearby in case I need something to eat. Can't we discuss the matter with him here?"

Though he didn't seemed pleased, he said, "Yes, we can. I suppose I'm not used to having the help nearby whenever I have conversations in my home."

She shrugged. What could she say to that? Not everyone had an unsavory relative who insisted on stopping by all the time.

"I thought you might like to attend a dinner party I'm having."

She waited for him to continue, but he took another drink from his cup and waited for her to respond. Why should an invitation to a dinner party require them to talk in private? Dismissing the silent question, she shook her head. "I'm sorry. As much as I would love to accept, my nausea comes and goes at unpredictable times. I'm afraid I wouldn't be a good visitor."

"I hadn't considered that."

"Is there anything else?"

"No. I'll be on my way." He set the cup down and stood up. With a bow, he added, "I hope you receive word from my brother soon. I'd like to congratulate him in person on accomplishing what was once thought to be the impossible."

Without another word, he followed the footman out of the room. She released her breath and sat back in the chair. She didn't believe him. He had come by for something else, and if Fieldman hadn't been in the room, she would have found out what it was. But there was no way she was going to risk being alone with him.

She stood up, and out of curiosity, she crept out of the room. She headed down the hallway that led to the front entrance. Just beyond the door, she spied Lord Mason and the footman talking in low tones, far enough from the door so she couldn't make out what they were saying. Lord Mason looked agitated, and the footman looked apprehensive. Her eyebrows furrowed. What could possibly be going on between them?

"Your Grace?"

She jumped and whirled around. Pressing her hand to her heart, she laughed when she realized it was one of the maids.

"I didn't mean to startle you, Your Grace," she replied with a smile.

"You were so quiet. I didn't hear you." Relaxing, she continued, "What is it?"

"Appleton wanted you to know he ate some oatmeal and was able to keep it down. He thought you might find the good news encouraging."

"Yes, I do. Thank you."

Deciding to leave the matter between Lord Mason and the footman alone, at least for the moment, she hurried to Appleton's room so she could see how much better he was doing.

Chapter Twenty-Four

Anna slept well that night. Even if she missed the warmth of Jason's arms, she took comfort in knowing Appleton was on the mend. The doctor was encouraged as well and figured he got the right medicine to speed his recovery. He said it was the last medicine he'd tried with her first husband before he recovered. Though she accepted the possibility that getting the medicine immediately after getting sick worked, she wondered if there was more to it than that. What did cause Appleton's illness and why was it so much like what her husband went through before he died?

When she woke up, her first thought was to check on Appleton to make sure he was still feeling better. She didn't even bother eating breakfast. With any luck, he felt well enough to get out of bed today. But as soon as she saw the maid carrying a bowl full of vomit out of his room, her countenance fell.

"Is Appleton," she gulped, "worse?"

The maid stopped and gave her a solemn nod. "I'm sorry, Your Grace. I don't know what happened. Fieldman was so attentive to him through the evening and last night."

As the maid passed her to go down the hallway, Anna clenched her hands together and held her breath. Fieldman tended to him and he was worse? She recalled the times she'd seen Lord Mason talking to him. Fieldman had also tended to her first husband during his illness.

Her mouth set in a grim line, she entered Appleton's room and saw that he was weak in his bed, his face pale and a grimace on his face. He opened his eyes and turned his head in her direction. She tried to smile, but it wouldn't come. There was no way this could be a coincidence. When she'd given him water and oversaw his meals, he got better. Fieldman oversaw these things and he got worse?

"Is it true that Fieldman gave you food and water when you got sick the first time and then this time?" she asked, hoping he didn't detect the bitter edge in her voice.

He thought for a moment and nodded. "Besides the two maids who've been cleaning up after me, Fieldman's been the only one here. Well, besides you."

Just as she suspected. "You are to only eat and drink food and water I bring to you," she said.

His eyebrows furrowed. "Your Grace?"

"I don't have time to explain. I need to talk to Fieldman."

Without waiting for his reply, she stormed out of the room. She hurried down the hall and searched for the footman. With each step she took, she grew angrier and angrier. How could the footman do this to her and Appleton? He was hired shortly after she married her first husband, and in that time, she had no reason to distrust him. She didn't know what hook Lord Mason used to make him do his dirty work, but she had no doubt Lord Mason was behind it.

She found Fieldman leaving the kitchen with another pitcher to give to Appleton. This only served to shoot another spark of rage through her. He could knowingly poison someone after seeing the misery he was putting him through? Taking a deep breath, she stopped in front of him and made eye contact with him. "You are relieved of duty. I demand you give me the pitcher at once, pack your things, and leave. And don't think about coming back. If you so much as set foot on my husband's property, I'll have you shot. Is that understood?"

His jaw dropped and his face turned white. "Your Grace?"

"Did you have trouble understanding my instructions?"

A long moment passed between them until he broke eye contact and handed her the pitcher. "No, Your Grace. I'll leave at once."

Good. She gripped the pitcher in her hand and remained still as he headed for his room. She examined the water in it. It looked harmless. No one would suspect something so common could be used for foul play. She had the sudden urge to go over to Lord Mason's estate and make him drink the contents of the pitcher, see what he thought about being so sick that all he could do was lie in bed and vomit. But what good would it do? Whatever he wanted, he'd find another way to get it. And that was the crux of the whole matter. What was it Lord Mason wanted? Was it her first husband's title? But how did that involve Appleton?

Did Fieldman know? But why would Lord Mason confide in him? He was a footman, not a confidant. No. Lord Mason might bribe him or threaten him, but he wouldn't divulge the reason why he wanted her first husband and Appleton dead. It couldn't be her. Lord Mason wanted to be with Lady Templeton.

Realizing she wasn't going to figure it out—and might not ever figure it out, she took the pitcher outside and smashed it on the ground, watching as it shattered into twenty pieces. If only she could be rid of Lord Mason as easily as she was rid of that pitcher.

She returned to the house and went to the footman's room. Even if he didn't know everything, perhaps he'd know something she might be able to piece together. But when she reached his room, all her hopes disintegrated. The footman had hung himself.

***

When Jason arrived in London, he thought it looked different from the last time he was here—when he was with Anna. It seemed more impersonal, distant, cold. But then everything seemed that way without her. She'd given him a place to belong, a place he could call home in the world. And he'd never been so aware of it until he left her to find out the truth about his past. Soon enough, he'd return to her, and when he did, he'd never leave her again.

But before he could go home and spend the rest of his life with her, he needed to go to the circus and find out if Willie-the-juggler was still there. He prayed Willie was there. By the time he made it to the circus, it had already begun. He paid for his ticket and found a seat in the crowded amphitheater.

As he watched the acrobats swing on the ropes high above the crowd, he waited for something—some spark—to assure him that he'd once been an acrobat, but he felt no hidden memory trying to come to the surface. He sighed in disappointment. It really was as if the past had never happened, except for his fear of horses, but he had no memory of falling off a horse.

Two horses came into the ring, and two acrobats swung down the lower bars and jumped onto the horses. Jason crossed his arms and studied the acrobats as they stood up on the horses and performed their routines. Did he really do all of that at one time? It seemed as if it should have been someone else who did all of those things, but as he watched one of the acrobats grab a low bar and swing up it then swing onto a higher bar, he realized he'd done the same maneuver that day when he and Mason rode their horses. So he had done this routine before.

Another acrobat descended onto the horse and took over. The whole process was done with ease. He couldn't help but be inspired by it as he watched the performers continue their act. The six acrobats had different roles during the routine, but they made the whole thing look like one fluid movement. The fact that there were enough acrobats for the act told him that his role had been expendable, and maybe that meant he had been easy to replace. Maybe that was why no one bothered to look for him when he was dragged out to the forest and left for dead.

As the act came to an end, he forced aside any thoughts of how depressing it was to know how quickly he could be replaced. His life here hadn't mattered. The realization only added to the impersonal feeling he got from being in London. The only place he seemed to matter was with Anna, and maybe that was why he was ultimately led here, to realize that his place was with her. Even if he didn't turn out to be the long-lost twin of Jason Merrill, he was meant to take the title. He'd never given thought to whether or not he believed in coincidences, but perhaps it was time to admit there was a purpose for everything.

He turned his attention back to the circus ring where the acrobats left and Iron Jim returned to the center to announce the next act. His ears perked up at the mention of Willie's name. Though he had gray hair, Willie maintained a bounce in his step as he came to the center. Following him were clowns who made a show of clumsily setting up a table for him and bringing an assortment of balls and fruits to place on the table.

According to Iron Jim, Willie was the best juggler in the entire world. While that might have been an exaggeration to impress the audience, Jason had to admit Willie was skilled at his job. When he was done juggling the items on the table, Iron Jim boasted that Willie could juggle anything and asked the audience what they'd like to see him juggle. One gentleman suggested knives.

Jason didn't think Iron Jim would allow it since it seemed unnecessarily dangerous, but Iron Jim seemed more than happy to prove that Willie could do it. "Ah, a very wise choice. What is your name, sir?" Iron Jim asked.

"Mister Robinson," the gentleman called out.

"Very good, Mister Robinson." Iron Jim turned to one of the clowns. "Bring out the knives!"

The audience grew silent and watched as a clown brought the knives out.

"And just so no one thinks the knives are fake, I'll cut my very own hat," Iron Jim said and proceeded to do as promised.

A drum roll accompanied Willie as he lifted the four knives and juggled them. The impressed gasps didn't go unnoticed by Jason who couldn't take his eyes off of Willie, just as hypnotized by him as the others were.

When Willie was done, the crowd cheered, and Iron Jim held up his hand to silence everyone. "Maybe someone can come up with something a little more challenging. Knives, after all, are too easy, aren't they, Willie?"

"They are, but I love how well they cut fruit," Willie replied.

Willie then picked up two knives and two apples, and while juggling, he cut one apple and ate slices of it, not missing a beat the entire time. When he was done eating both apples, he set the knives down and bowed for the cheering crowd.

"But that's too simple. You need something harder than that," Iron Jim said with a hearty laugh. "Now, who can come up with something harder?"

"Fire!"

Iron Jim clapped his hands together and rubbed them. "Ah, a gentleman who lives a little more dangerously. What is your name, sir?"

"Lord Edon."

"Bring out the fire," Iron Jim called out to the clowns. "I bet Lord Edon doesn't believe Willie can do it, but we don't call Willie 'the juggler who can juggle anything' for no reason. We assure you, my lord, that we don't make the boast in vain."

The clowns lit three torches and brought them to Willie. Willie took the torches one by one and tossed them in the air, quickly establishing a rhythm.

"Are you challenged yet?" Iron Jim asked him.

Willie shook his head. "It's too simple!"

The crowd laughed and cheered while Iron Jim called for another torch. Soon Willie had added another before he juggled other items.

After Willie was done, Jason decided he should talk to him, even though the circus wasn't over. He suspected the best time to get a word in private with Willie was when Iron Jim had the audience to think about. He quickly got up and maneuvered through the people until he reached the ground. He followed Willie until he caught up with him.

"Excuse me? Sir, may I have a word with you?"

Willie turned around, his face turning white before he exhaled and laughed. "Forgive me. For a moment, I thought I saw a ghost. What is your title so I may address you correctly?"

"You might remember me. Does the name Alastair sound familiar?"

"But your clothes…your hair…" He shook his head. "You can't be him."

"So you did know someone by that name?"

Willie glanced around them and grabbed his arm. Jason was ready to protest since his grip was painful, but Willie pushed him into a room and shut the door. Since it was dark, Jason couldn't make out his surroundings, but Willie started whispering, taking his mind off the darkness.

"If this is your idea of a joke, it's not a good one."

Jason frowned. "I'm not joking. I don't remember anything about my past, but I found someone who told me enough to believe you might know an important piece of it."

"Don 'the fire eater'?"

"No," he lied, in a hurry to protect him.

"Of course it was him. There's no one else it could have been, but that doesn't matter to me. You must never come back here, and you must never mention Don. Do you understand?"

"Yes, but I need you to answer something very important for me. You're the only person who knows, which is why I came here."

Willie took a deep breath and released it. "If you try to go to someone with my answer, I'll deny ever talking to you. Understood?"

"Yes. I won't mention you."

"Good. It was hard enough to leave you for dead in that forest."

Not expecting this, Jason pressed, "You left me for dead? Were you also responsible for my injuries?"

"Any you sustained from being dropped off the horse as I rode through the forest to get rid of you, yes, but Iron Jim was the one who did the beating. You let Don get away. It cut into his profits, and if there's one thing Iron Jim doesn't like, it's losing money. We still haven't found a suitable replacement for Don. Now do you understand why being here is dangerous if you insist on calling yourself Alastair?"

"Yes, but is that who I am? Were my parents in the circus?"

He paused. "Is that why you came here? To ask about your real parents?"

"Yes."

"And after I answer you, you'll leave here to never return to this circus?"

"Yes. I promise."

"Very well. The gentleman who brought you here was a duke. The Duke of Watkins. He had a cloak on to protect his identity. He didn't know I recognized him, but he was in the audience with his wife a month before and wanted me to juggle rats. I take it you saw my performance out there?"

"Yes."

"Iron Jim always asks the names of anyone who makes a

suggestion for my juggling routine. It's one of the ways he engages the audience." He loosened his grip, much to Jason's relief. "The duke brought you here because you were a sickly child and the firstborn of twins. He and his wife didn't want a sickly child to end up with the title, so he brought you to me. I worked out the arrangements, but Iron Jim purchased you. Does that answer your question?"

"You're sure it was me?"

"My mind is as sharp today as it was back then. I never forget a name or a face."

Jason nodded, unsure of whether he was relieved or disappointed. He had the birthright to the title, but it was hard knowing his parents hadn't wanted him. Up to this point, it'd been a suspicion. Now he knew the truth. Swallowing the lump in his throat, he focused on Willie. "This conversation never happened," Jason said.

"Good. You do understand."

Willie opened the door and peaked out of it, but before Jason had time to check out the room they were in, Willie whispered, "Stick to the group of gentlemen heading for the exit."

Willie shoved him out the door and shut it behind him. Jason glanced back at the door, figuring whatever was in that room wasn't his concern and hurried to catch up to the gentlemen. He slipped beside them without notice and left the circus.

It'd been a bittersweet experience. On one hand, he'd been granted the answer he most needed, but on the other, he'd learned how expendable he was. His parents hadn't wanted him so they sold him to Iron Jim, and Iron Jim was so furious with him for helping Don escape that he beat him and ordered Willie to take him to a remote forest to dispose of his body. Both times, he knew no one thought he'd survive. Despite the bitter truth of what his life had been, he had the consolation in knowing Anna loved him. She was waiting for him to return, and now that he had the answer he needed, he could. Eager to see her, he quickened his pace. In two days, he'd be home at Camden with Anna, which was exactly where he belonged.

Chapter Twenty-Five

Two nights later, Anna was asleep when she heard someone moving around in Jason's bedchamber. Through the fog of sleep, she stirred, reluctant to leave the dream she had of holding her baby. In the dream, Jason entered the room and sat beside her on the settee, tapping his foot on the floor. It took her a moment to realize someone was walking around in Jason's bedchamber, and as she woke up, she bolted up in her bed in excitement. Jason was back! He returned!

She climbed out of bed and slipped on her robe. She quickly ran the brush through her hair and went to the door connecting their rooms. She flung the door open and hurried into the room when she realized something was wrong. She halted and glanced around the dark room, lit only by the moonlight filtering through one of the windows. She tried to remember if all of the curtains had been closed or not. If she remembered right, they hadn't been open since Jason left.

Someone was in here that shouldn't be, and she knew better than to investigate on her own. She quickly made her way back to her room and softly closed the door. She locked it and went to the cord to alert Appleton that she needed him. A tense moment of silence passed before she heard the sound of someone breathing from the corner of her room. She retrieved a candlestick from her vanity table and turned toward the door that led to the hallway. She swallowed the lump in her throat. The shadowy figure dragged a chair to the door and placed the back of it under the doorknob so no one could enter her room. She glanced at the door connecting her bedchamber with Jason's.

The intruder made a step toward her, and she inched to the door. If he slipped into her bedchamber while she was in Jason's room, that meant Jason's room was the safest place for her to be. She bit her lower lip and studied the shadowy figure. Was he closer than before?

She tightened her grip on the candlestick. If she was going to make her move, she'd have to do it before he lunged for her. She bolted for the door, but he was quicker. He wrapped his arm around her shoulders and drew her to his side. She tried to hit him with the candlestick, but he grabbed it from her and threw it aside. Then he pressed his hand over her mouth. Everything happened so fast she didn't even have the chance to scream for help.

"You shouldn't have gone into that bedchamber, Anna," Lord Mason quietly spoke in her ear. "But since you decided to get involved, maybe you can help me."

Keeping his hold on her, he forced her into Jason's bedchamber and opened another set of curtains, making the room brighter. She struggled against him, but it was no use. He was much too strong for her.

"It's no use trying to get away, Anna. If you cooperate, I'll let you and that bastard you're carrying live. You ought to know by now that I never intended to kill you. I just want the money. Where does Jason keep it?"

She shook her head.

"Oh, excuse me." He removed his hand from her mouth. "Where is it?"

"I don't know."

"Liar!" he hissed.

"But I really don't know. My husband never told me

where he kept the money, and I wasn't allowed in this room."

"Maybe that's true for my brother, but it's not true for that imposter you brought here to take his place." Before she could respond, he chuckled. "I know all about Alastair. I know my brother died. I know you and that butler of yours buried him. Somehow you found Alastair and convinced him to play the part. There's no sense in denying it. I'm not an unreasonable person. All I need is enough money to marry Lady Templeton. Once I get it, I'll go to British India, and I'll never be a problem again."

"I'm telling you the truth. I don't know where the money is."

Grunting, he shut and locked the door connecting her room with Jason's. Then he locked the door leading to the hallway. She gulped. She was trapped. Appleton would be there soon, but he wouldn't be able to get into the room so he could help her. She was alone with him, and that meant she was at his mercy.

"I don't know why everyone insists on making things difficult," he grumbled. "First my brother, then Alastair, and now you. It's all so simple. I need money. I can't marry someone as wealthy as Lady Templeton if I don't bring enough of my own money into the marriage." He walked over to the window and opened it. "So the matter is really simple. Either you give me some money or jewels or something I can use, or you're going to have a terrible fall out the window. Maybe you'll survive it. Maybe you won't. But is it worth risking your life and your child's life to find out?"

She backed away from the window, her heartbeat racing. "I don't know where the money is, but I have diamonds that are worth a good sum. If you let me go back into my bedchamber, I can get them. I also have some money tucked away in my cabinet."

"But will it be enough for what I need?"

He made a move toward her, and she took a step away

from him. She had hoped to get close to the door leading to her bedchamber, but he was closer to it now. She grimaced. He had her blocked.

Someone knocked on her bedchamber door, making her jump. Lord Mason pressed his fingers to his lips and shook his head in a silent warning that she better not say anything. She clenched and unclenched her hands.

"Your Grace?" Appleton called out from her bedchamber door. "Do you need help?"

She finally decided to answer, and opened her mouth when Lord Mason pulled out a pistol and aimed it at her. She closed her mouth. She couldn't deny he'd thought through everything.

"I don't want to get blood on my hands," Lord Mason whispered, "but you're forcing my hand. You think I want to live off the pathetic monthly allotment my brother allowed me for the rest of my life? I want to be free of his strings, strings that even now haunt me since Alastair refused to help me."

"I'll help you," she whispered, clutching her robe and praying he wasn't quick with the trigger. "Tell me where you think the money is."

This time Appleton knocked on Jason's bedchamber door. She jerked and nearly cried aloud, but the pistol made her stop.

"Your Grace?" Appleton called out, knocking again. "Can you get to the door?"

Lord Mason motioned to the small room off to the side of the bedchamber. Without a word, she hurried to the room. She took a deep breath and rubbed her sweaty palms on her robe. This couldn't be happening. It was a nightmare. She was still in bed, safely under her blanket and fast asleep. Soon she'd wake up and breathe a sigh of relief. She cleared her throat and turned to face him.

"My brother kept important items in here," Lord Mason told her in a low voice as he gestured to the desk. "If money isn't in here, there should be information on where I can find it. Or there might even be some valuables in here. Whatever is in here, I know there's something I can use."

"Why don't you open the drawers?"

"I did, but there's a box in the top one that requires a key."

"You think I know where the key is?"

He clicked the gun. "You might not have been close to my brother, but I saw the way you were with Alastair. You and Alastair were close enough where he would have told you anything."

"But I never looked at the contents in this desk."

"I'm starting to lose my patience, Anna."

Her gaze went to his gun then to the thin line on his lips and hard glint in his eyes. As much as she tried to keep calm, her hands shook and tears filled her eyes. "I didn't even know there was a box in one of these drawers." She motioned to the drawers. "Which one is it?"

"Good try, but I don't believe you."

She pulled a drawer open and saw a pile of papers.

"The next one over."

She opened it. By the light of the moon, she saw the box he was talking about. Though she knew there was a very slim chance it would open, she tried it anyway. The lock held firm. She searched the drawer for a key but didn't find it.

"Either you get the key or I'll take care of you. Whether that means shoving you out the window or using the pistol, you decide."

"All right, all right. Um… If a key was that important to your brother, he would have kept it in the bedchamber, right? He'd want it close by in case he needed it."

He waved the pistol to the door, so she hurried out of the room. As long as she was looking for the key, he might hold off on hurting her. She scanned the bedchamber and tried to figure out where her first husband might have put the key. Her gaze went to the cabinet. That was as good a place to search as any.

"Uh…one time, your brother mentioned the cabinet. I-I can't remember exactly what he said about it, but it seemed…actually, I heard it reported that…he wouldn't let anyone—not anyone at all—near it. Th-that being the case, the key must be here."

She knew she was tripping over her words, but she had to say something. Where was Appleton? What was taking him so long? She opened the cabinet and searched it. Her hands shook as she fumbled around for the key.

A harsh bang resonated from her bedchamber door, and Appleton yelled for her to tell them if she was there. *Them?* Who else had Appleton retrieved to help him?

"Anna," Lord Mason snapped, jutting the pistol into her side.

She shrieked and jumped away from it.

He covered her mouth with his hand and pointed the pistol at her head. "Not a smart move, Anna," he growled and dragged her over to the open window.

She tried to scream and struggled to get away from him, but he succeeded in pulling her to the window where a blast of cool air hit her face. Appleton called out her name as he pounded on Jason's bedchamber door.

"Tell him to go away," Lord Mason ordered.

He lifted his hand from her mouth, and she gasped for air.

"Do it," he hissed, jabbing the pistol to the side of her head. "Tell him to go away."

"Go—" Her voice cracked so she inhaled and tried again. "Go away!"

"Good." When Appleton pounded the door hard enough that it cracked, Lord Mason added, "Tell him to stop at once."

"S-stop!" she forced out. "I'm…I'm fine. Stop hitting the door."

He let go of her but kept the gun pointed at her. "Go to the door, open it, and tell him you're fine."

She glanced at the gun and gave a slow nod, praying he wouldn't hurt her if she complied. He was desperate, that much was certain, but he didn't want to jeopardize his future with Lady Templeton so maybe if she gave him what he wanted, he'd leave and never come back. Maybe this was going to be the end of it. Her eyes met his, searching for the assurance she needed. He stood by the window, so she couldn't make out his expression. All she could make out was his silhouette. But then a hand rose up from behind him and clasped onto the windowsill. Scared, she let out a terrified scream.

The silhouette of a gentleman rose behind him and grabbed him. Lord Mason fired a shot into the air. Something in her snapped, and she ran to the bedchamber door as the two gentlemen struggled at the window.

Before she could unlock it, Appleton and the gardener broke down the door. Lord Mason and the other gentleman fell to the floor. Through the moonlight, it took her a moment to realize Jason had attacked Lord Mason. Another shot fired into the air, and everyone ducked. Jason struggled to get the gun away from Lord Mason, but Lord Mason tripped on Jason's foot and fell out the window.

For a moment, everyone stood still, shocked. Then all at once, they headed for the window. Appleton was the first one to join Jason at the window, followed by the gardener and Anna. They peered down at the ground where Lord Mason was on the ground, his neck and legs twisted at an angle that could only mean he was dead. As awful as it was to know he wasn't alive, she couldn't deny the relief she felt at knowing he was no longer going to be a threat to anyone.

She closed her eyes and covered her face with her hands. Was she a horrible person for being glad another gentleman was dead? First her husband and now Lord Mason…

Someone wrapped her in a protective hug, and his arms were so wonderfully familiar to her that she didn't need to look at him to know he was Jason. He'd returned home to her.

"Appleton told me you were in trouble," Jason whispered, rubbing her back in comforting, circular motions. "Since the doors up here were locked and I saw the ladder leading up to the window, I decided to climb up here."

She took a moment to settle her nerves before looking at Appleton who was still peering down at Lord Mason. He shook his head. "The only place he's going is in the ground."

"I'll get his body," the gardener said and hurried out of the room.

"What did he want?" Jason asked, pulling away from her so he could see her face. "Did he hurt you?"

"No, he didn't hurt me," she quickly assured him, still shaking. "He wanted money. He thought there was something in the desk in that room he could use." She gestured to the small room. "He wanted a key so he could open the box."

Appleton went to the desk and lit the candlestick while Jason let go of her and went to the cabinet. Curious, she followed Jason and watched as he retrieved a key from the bottom shelf. So she was right. The key had been in there. She joined Jason as he strode into the small room and placed the box on top of the desk.

"There isn't money in here," Jason began as he unlocked it, "but it does contain something important. It wouldn't have done Mason any good, but it proves I have the right to the title."

Surprised, Anna glanced at Appleton whose eyebrows rose in interest. Turning back to Jason, she asked, "The right to the title?"

He opened the box and dug out a couple of papers. "Your first husband had a twin brother, an older twin brother. But the twin was sickly, and they didn't expect him to survive so the parents and doctor decided to quietly get rid of the twin and claim there was only one child born at the time." He handed her the papers so she could read through them. "That sickly twin was me. I had to confirm it with someone at the circus, but he remembered me and he was the one who left me in the forest the night you found me."

She shot Appleton a worried look.

"Do we need to be concerned about this person?" Appleton asked.

"No," Jason softly replied. "As long as Iron Jim believes I'm dead, there's nothing to worry about."

Her gaze went back to the papers and she read through them.

"So what does this mean?" Appleton pressed.

"It means that Alastair is no longer alive and Jason never died. The only person who figured out I'm not Jason just fell out the window. I see no reason why anyone else should know."

She set the papers back in the box and looked at Jason. "So there was no wife or children?"

"No," Jason softly replied and smiled. "Thankfully, there wasn't."

"I'll see to it that the proper funeral arrangements are made for Lord Mason," Appleton said before he left the room.

Relieved, she collapsed against Jason who wrapped her in a protective hug. Finally, her heartbeat was slowing down and she had stopped shaking. The stress of the past month slipped away. She closed her eyes and relaxed. It was over. Now they could leave the past behind and move on to the future without the secrets and shadows hovering nearby.

"I love you, Anna," he whispered and kissed the top of her head. "I can't imagine my life with anyone but you."

"I love you, too. And it's not just you and me anymore."

"What?"

Noting the confusion in his voice, she smiled. "Shortly after you left, I discovered that I'm expecting a child."

He slipped his finger under her chin and lifted it so he could make eye contact with her. His lips curled up into a grin. "When I set my mind to it, I can get things done."

With a chuckle, she asked, "When you set your mind to it? You think you can just will something like a child and make it happen?"

He playfully shrugged. "If memory serves, it's imperative that a duke has an heir. But we should be diligent. Even if this child is a boy, we should aim for another boy or two or three or so… I don't think there can be too many. You never know what will happen."

"You're planning on having many children?"

"Well, we're bound to have a girl or two. With any luck, they'll be as pretty as their mother." He tapped her nose before kissing it. "And if we don't have a lot of children, trying will be a very enjoyable process."

She laughed and hugged him. "You won't hear me complain."

He cupped her face in his hands and kissed her, his lips lingering on hers until she felt weak in the knees. And the best thing about it was that this was the first of many kisses to come.

***

A year later

Anna placed her cup on the tray and turned to Candace who was seated next to her on the settee in the drawing room of Anna's London townhouse. "Would it be wrong for me to congratulate you?"

Candace took a sip of her tea and shook her head. "No. I realize on the outside I need to wear my mourning clothes and act the part of the bereaved widow, but there's no denying my relief in knowing I'm no longer chained to Ian."

Anna recalled her relief when her first husband died and nodded. "I understand." And truly she did understand, much more than Candace would ever know. "What happened to Ian's title?"

"It went to his cousin who is a much nicer sort than he was."

"And you will live very well off the money left to you."

"Yes."

Anna studied her friend and saw the happiness on her face. She thought perhaps it might be wonderful if Candace could find someone as wonderful as Jason, but she knew mentioning that right now wouldn't be appropriate. Candace needed time to be her own lady without the constraints of a husband. She was still young at twenty. There was time for her to remarry later.

Jason came into the drawing room with their five-month-old son, and Anna stood up.

"Wasn't he taking a nap?" she asked.

"I heard him playing in his room so I decided to bring him down here," he replied.

Smiling, Anna glanced at Candace who rose to her feet. "I don't know why we have a nursemaid when he does so much with Caleb."

"There's going to be a balloon launch, and I don't want Caleb to miss it," Jason replied. "Besides, he'll like all the colors."

Anna went over to them and took Caleb in her arms. She adjusted the hat over his golden hair. "He's too young to remember a balloon launch."

"That doesn't matter. What matters is that we get to spend the day together."

"I think it's a lovely idea," Candace said and touched Anna's arm. "I'll come by for a visit in a few days."

"I look forward to it," Anna told her.

Candace said good-bye to Jason and followed the footman out of the drawing room.

"This poor little boy has no time to rest," Anna playfully admonished Jason. "Ever since we've been to London, you've been taking us all over the place."

"Well, there's a lot to do and see. Besides, I don't take him everywhere. He stays here when we go to the theatre or the balls, and tonight we'll attend another ball. He's growing up so fast. I have to enjoy the time while it lasts, especially since I can look back and remember it." He grinned at the boy and shook his hand. "Maybe when you have a brother or sister, I won't be so demanding of your time, Caleb."

Her heart warmed. "It's wonderful that you want to spend so much time with him, Jason. Really, it is."

He kissed her. "And when we come back, you can play one of your songs for him."

"You mean I can play a song for you?"

"He happens to like the same songs I do. What can I say except that he has excellent taste in music?"

She laughed and kissed him. "I love you, Jason. All right. Let's see a balloon launch."

"And maybe we can get something sweet to eat on the way back. I'd like for him to try iced cream. Maybe tomorrow we'll find another sweet for him to try."

"Our son is one fortunate boy to get so much."

"There's an entire world out there to learn about and who better than his parents to teach him?" Jason tickled the boy under his chin, and the boy squirmed against her, laughing. "We're building memories. Good ones."

Tears filled her eyes, but these were tears of joy and that being the case, she didn't mind them. Jason never did recover the memories of his past, and while she suspected it was for the best, she was glad for the memories they were creating together with their son and would share with their other children in the future.

"May I see you out?" Appleton asked, stepping into the drawing room.

"Yes. I think we're ready." Jason glanced at her, and she nodded. "We won't be more than two hours."

She followed Jason, and as they passed through the front door which Appleton held for them, she caught the expression on Appleton's face and knew he couldn't be happier for her.

"Have a good time, Your Grace," he told her.

"I will," she replied, grateful for all he'd done for her. Had it not been for him, she wouldn't be here today. "Thank you."

He bowed and softly shut the door behind them.

Jason patted the small of her back. "Have you ever wondered what it's like to be up in the air in a balloon?"

She laughed. "Of course not."

"No? Really?" They headed down the side of the street, and he pointed to the sky. "Imagine how fun it would be if we were all the way up there, looking down at all the people and houses."

"Being up at that height is exactly why I wouldn't like it. There is a possibility of falling."

"A slim one. But sometimes you have to take risks to truly enjoy life."

"I can enjoy life with my feet on the ground as much as I can up there."

"I highly doubt that."

"It's true."

While they continued their good-natured debate on the way to the balloon launch, Caleb rested his head on Anna's shoulder, and Anna smiled, anticipating the many adventures that were to come…though none would involve her going up in the air in a balloon.

Coming Soon in the Regency Collection:

A Most Unsuitable Earl

Ethan Silverton, the Lord of Edon, has been called many things. Scoundrel, rake, reprobate, unbelievably lucky, deceitful… But he's never been called a husband…until now.

Ethan is very content with his life. He's carefully sculpted it so that everyone thinks he's a notorious rake. For years, he's worked hard to build his reputation to secure his place as the most undesirable bachelor in London. And it's worked. No decent lady will have him.

But one simple error in judgment has just sealed his fate. His intention was to dissuade a horrid mother from matching him up with her equally horrid daughter. Seeing no one but Lady Catherine without a dance partner, he tells a lie. He approaches Lady Catherine as if they are betrothed, and the ploy works. The horrid mother and her daughter abandon their pursuit of him.

Except Ethan's mother figures out his ploy and is so relieved that she's found a way to marry him to a reputable young lady that she tells everyone of their engagement. To his horror, word spreads and it's his duty to see the lie through. This is the worst thing that can happen, and no one but his mother is happy about it. Not Lady Catherine. Not her doting father. Not even Ethan. But his mother is sure it'll all work out…eventually.

25034933R00132

Made in the USA
Lexington, KY
14 August 2013